C000175932

THE FINGERLESS GLOVES

# DOWN, BUT NOT OUT!

GARY TULLEY

Matador
9 Priory Business Park,
Wistow Road, Kibworth Beauchamp,
Leicestershire. LE8 0RX
Tel: 0116 279 2299
Email: books@troubador.co.uk
Web: www.troubador.co.uk/matador
Twitter: @matadorbooks

ISBN 978 1785899 591

British Library Cataloguing in Publication Data.
A catalogue record for this book is available from the British Library.

Printed and bound in the UK by TJ International, Padstow, Cornwall
Typeset in 11pt Aldine401 BT by Troubador Publishing Ltd, Leicester, UK

Matador is an imprint of Troubador Publishing Ltd

*I would like to dedicate this book to my brother, Brian. Thanks for all the tremendous support you have shown me over the years.*

## CHAPTER 1

# BACK FROM THE DEAD

6.30 in the evening following a cold and miserable day in Docklands, albeit the heartbeat of Stonewater. The daylight had long evaporated. In its wake, the chill from the night air began to increase due to the incoming tidal water rising into the harbour basin. From the bowels of the seaward end, the constant boom from a distant warning bell carried on the low-lying fog. Unceasing, it reverberated around the contours of the basin, and in turn complemented the gentle slapping of rising water against the eroding timber and concrete piles. The Docklands area as a whole had become a political graveyard for years. A six-year regeneration programme had ceased to fulfil the economics of progress. Within a few years of the initial development, the basin locale had been allowed to decompose into a ghetto of sleaze, brought on by the dregs of society that chose to inhabit the vicinity.

On a par with the local fraternity, a certain public house, namely the Albatross Arms, had risen from the ashes due to the notoriety instilled by the clientele that frequented the watering hole, reflected in an abbreviated change of name. To all and sundry, including the police, it was reinvented under the heading 'the AA'. The availability of limited rented accommodation within threw a lifeline to one particular punter. For the last couple of months, the luxury of B&B had proved to be vital to his non-negotiable existence. At first glance, one could be forgiven for thinking the obvious. The fully clothed disheveled figure that lay in a semi-comatose state on an unmade bed momentarily began to stir involuntarily, but to no apparent conclusion.

Meanwhile, strains of barely audible human conversation filtered through the floor boards from the bowels of the saloon bar which was directly underneath the rented room, albeit a bolt hole. The voices from below began to intensify as the habitual punters grew in numbers. Briefly the sound caused the figure on the bed to grimace as his fuddled brain made a bad connection to re-enter the real world. With no written guarantees on offer, sleep-lined eyelids flickered open, exposing bloodshot eyes and sightless vision.

Any further attempt at capitalising on his awareness ran a close second to misery as a futile effort to raise his addled head from the pillow came to nothing. Momentarily, his woeful body shuddered as an involuntary convulsion took over his pathetic frame. The cheap watch he was wearing was saying 7.45am, or maybe it was 7.30pm! Who gives a shit anyway? The name of the day itself would even become questionable. Apart from everything else, one overriding fact remained gilt edged. The following seven or eight hours in the world as we know it would have no bearing on his self-imposed misery. Mercifully, his eyes closed, allowing oblivion to close in.

So this was one Paul Rossetti! Self-styled plastic gangster. Once again at his habitual best, a forty-eight-hour bender behind him, again proving negative in casting off the eternal hatred and torment he'd been made to endure. Like a parasite, it had unconditionally seduced his mind, body and soul. 'Time', somebody once remarked, 'is a great healer'. But in Rossetti's case it would be a self-ordained life sentence of his own making. His misshapen body now bore the evidence relating to his past heinous track record. His untimely escape from a pre-meditated blazing inferno and murder scene had cost him dearly. Being forced to go underground had proved to be expensive. Bent doctors and phony libertines subsequently bled him dry, forcing him to surface.

Through his own elected circumstances his six-year exile had now turned full circle. True to form, fate had stepped in, giving him access to pursue his ongoing vendetta back on the manor that had spawned its origins. The town of Stonewater itself owed him nothing from day one. But returns from a recent gambling outlay had paid dividends. This latest money injection had temporarily got him 'out of jail', hence the bender. The following twenty-four hours could be vital to his miserable existence. For survival, strategic decisions, in his case, were a necessity and needed to be addressed, evil or otherwise. Was the world ready for Paul Rossetti? Maybe. Such a small word. Alternatively a shrug of one's shoulders and then easily forgotten. On the other hand, taken seriously the word itself evoked a hundred options. A snap decision or time to digress might well come into play.

In Rossetti's case the sands of time, it appears, were now knocking on the door of fate. Any previous options worth considering from his torrid past had long been defunct. The choice, in his case, had left him holding the proverbial joker in the pack. Possession of the ace for his next deal would be imperative. To call the tune and think like the hunter, keeping a low profile, would become paramount. Putting himself about at this stage could possibly compromise any future game plan he could muster up. Besides the local plods' interest, he needed to be aware that other 'faces' alien to the underworld still possibly carried grievances from way back. But for all that, he did have one saving grace. In terms of contradiction, the injuries sustained from the inferno could prove to be a blessing in disguise (no pun intended). The flames had done their job well. As a result, the facial scars he'd inherited, along with a badly mangled leg, would serve as a new profile.

A bonus indeed! But it only ran a close second to the cancer of hate that tormented him 24/7. Adjacent to his bed a table held the remains of a half-eaten takeaway. A door of opportunity indeed! For a resident house fly. Meanwhile, less than a mile away in the centre of town a key was opening another door. Only this one appeared, as being positive as it opened, as did the owner, known in the town and the boxing world as one Ronnie Callaghan. Or, more to the point, Rossetti's nemesis.

For Ronnie, today started and ended with business as usual at the gymnasium. His commitment to 'the game' was beyond reproach. The actual running and management of the gym was only one aspect of his exclusive life. Paying the bills came by way of the flower stall he ran in the local market. 'Payment' from the gym centred around the stable of fighters that were associated with his no-nonsense method of training. His touch of glory came by way of personal achievement; any monetary spin-offs counted as a bonus. This little world of Ronnie's had been his second home for the past twenty-five years or so. Since retiring from the paid ranks he'd relished every drop of blood, sweat and tears it threw at him.

So there you have it! Two people, both at the opposite ends of the spectrum but at the same time sharing the ultimate affinity. If, at any given time, Ronnie had sat down and analysed the alleged death or disappearance of Rossetti those six years ago he would have readily dismissed any thoughts on the subject. As far as he was concerned, the affair would remain dead and buried. His last and only recollection was that of a face masked in a wall of flame, and just as quickly gone. On rare occasions a mental image would entice him back into the folds of reality, for a split second he would find himself looking down the barrel of a shooter brandished by Rossetti. Then the thought would simply vanish, to be locked away for future programming. But this was now, leaving all their respective emotions over the years to disintegrate. Suffice to say, fate had other ideas. Unbeknownst to both individuals, due to unforeseen circumstances the paltry distance now keeping them apart only amounted to a lousy £5 cab fare.

## CHAPTER 2

# A DAMP REMINDER

Rain is rain in anybody's language. Ronnie Callaghan, on the other hand, held the sole rights to his own exclusive version. And it would take a fool to contest its origin. A show of verbal abuse skywards did little to ease his ongoing short temper as once again the inclement weather forced him to take refuge beneath a canvas canopy to the rear of his stall. Shivering, he manoeuvred his sheepskin jacket together with his elbows and buried his dripping chin in the folds of the lapels. Utter frustration etched his face. Grimacing through half-closed eyes, he surveyed the market through the unceasing deluge. Never one to hold, he ranted his feelings to the rest of the world. "Piss potting rain!" A fair evaluation under the circumstances. Apart from rearranging his sheepskin, checking his watch had been the only distraction he'd afforded himself in the last hour, as reflected in the weight of his money pouch. A further self-opinionated description of his 'maker', and the rain still persisted.

The writing had been on the wall right from the moment he'd woken up that morning. Any sensible person would have given the market a swerve, but Ronnie being Ronnie there was no way he was going to come out of it a winner. To add to his frustration, a sleepless night due to a stomach upset had been aggravation enough coupled with the incessant beat of the rain on his bedroom window. Putting the two together gave a new meaning to the word 'charming' in his language. Glancing at his money pouch, a swift calculation as to his 'wedge' forced him into a final decision. Fortunately for him, his regular punters had managed to get him out of trouble. At the very least, his stock outlay had been covered. Patience had finally run its course. Glancing across at an adjacent stallholder, he concurred in no uncertain terms: "That does it for me, Siddie, I'm bloody well out of 'ere." It wasn't as if he needed to justify his get-out clause. "Flowers! Flowers!" He exclaimed, "they don't sell in the rain, they only bleedin' grow!" At least he got something right. Any other form of sympathy never showed in the equation.

Siddie had other ideas. "So what happened to the chosen few already? I must be out of favour." He motioned toward his three-tier fruit and veg display, shoulders raised in his indomitable manner, giving way to his creed. Meticulous as ever, the display resembled a Van Gogh in anybody's terms. Sadly, that's all it was, a vision, and an unsold one at that. "Meshugenah!" he swore in Yiddish. "What do I have to do to make a living?" Problem! How do you convince somebody in his situation that tap water is no less dry than its counterpart falling out of the sky? Siddie would run with the latter and class any shower as being personal. But then it was always going to be about money. Siddie Levy's roots ran deep. The lack of folding money resembled a smack in the mouth. As a kid, his father had marked his card well.

"It's a question of survival, my son. Jewish boys learn, and then they earn!" And so it was written. Unlike Ronnie, there was no "er indoors' to contend with. On a day-to-day basis, his empire commenced and ended with the lovely Rachael. If the takings were up, then it reflected on her wellbeing. On the strength of his pouch now, he could make a book as to how his evening was going to go. Muttering under his breath, Ronnie was in the throes of dismantling his stall prior to heading for the lock-up. Under the circumstances, it didn't seem to take as long as usual. With water running out of every orifice, the canvas awning was secured in no time. Like a magnet, the market café began to draw him in. "Damn good idea," he concurred. "A hot drink, waffle and time to come down."

Pausing before moving off, he interrupted Siddie completing a sale. "I'll be in Toni's for an hour or so, if yer interested. Be lucky." His earlier decision to quit, it seems, had now created an epidemic. Nearby stallholders were on the move. Dave 'the China' and Mick 'the Schmutter' were also in the process of pulling out. "You could have sold yer plates with washing up liquid thrown in, they're bleedin' wet enough!" joked Ronnie. Dave 'the China' wasn't impressed.

"Yer a right hand short of a knockout!" he shouted back. Ronnie only grinned and allowed himself to chuckle. He'd heard it all before and put it down to expenses.

Pulling the peak of his six-wedge cap down lower, he headed for the café. It was an unlikely oasis in terms of clientele, but then the proprietor wasn't your normal run-of-the-mill ex-Sicilian bandit either. Even the Mafia couldn't get the rights to his cappuccino! And still it rained. Once inside, Toni greeted him wearing a grin like a Cheshire cat, and pointed to a freshly poured coffee sitting on the bar. He'd spotted Ronnie's movements prior to him entering. Toni was on his case before Ronnie could get his hand out of his pocket.

"No, no, today on the house, my friend. I makka monies, so why I worry, heh?" For a giant of a man, he had the approach of a lamb, and continued, "Please to drink up, your favourite, eh?" Ronnie wasn't about to hold a debate on that score.

"Toni, yer a bleedin' diamond, I owe yer." Picking his drink up, he made a beeline for his favourite table and solace in the mug. Head bowed, gazing into the clouds of his coffee,

Ronnie lost himself. His thoughts drifted aimlessly from the gym to the morning's loss of revenue. For a brief moment, a mental image of Wally Churchill took precedence. A warm smile crossed his face. Closing his eyes he strove to contain the memory of his former friend and ex-champ whose sudden demise eighteen months previous had left Ronnie feeling devastated. At the time, Ronnie stated that the gym would never be the same again. Wally's contribution over the years remained unparalleled. Consequently, his loss became a sad reminder of a diminutive figure, but somebody with the heart of a lion.

"Ronnie!" Somebody somewhere felt tempted to evade his space. "Ronnie!" He quickly became aware of a figure shaking him.

"What planet are you on, my friend?" All thoughts diminished as he looked up.

"Blimey, Siddie, I was fecking miles away. 'Ere, grab a seat, mate." The next thirty minutes was full of light-hearted banter. Deep down, Siddie endeavoured to keep Ronnie in a relaxed frame of mind, his motive being a reluctance to divulge certain information relative to his future. The fact that the information in question came by way of an altercation gave credence to his concern. The sequence of events stemmed from an impromptu confrontation with a punter, whom he now knew to be attached to the local crime division. The problem had been festering on his mind for over a week now. Inwardly, he cursed himself for not confronting Ronnie at the time the altercation occurred. Time and time again, he recalled the delicate conversation he'd been part of. He only had to inform Ronnie for peace of mind. *Walking on eggshells would have been a whole easier*, he told himself. The fact that the third party involved just happened to be the Old Bill created the problem in the first place. Looking at it from another angle, just supposing Ronnie already knew about the altercation and was biding his time before going public with it? No! The connection between Rossetti, Ronnie and Siddie was cemented in time. Siddie dismissed the idea out of hand. There was no way Ronnie would have knowingly kept schtum on the matter. Working on that assumption, the Old Bill must have known that Siddie would have forwarded any information, full stop! It just didn't add up. For a start, Ronnie was the key player, followed by the co-star Rossetti. And Siddie? He was only sitting in the stalls looking on. Sinister undertones began to cloud his reasoning. "Supposing the Old Bill had an ulterior motive for handing him the information in the first place?" His face paled, knowing the consequences that could erupt.

"Motive?! What's all that about?" Ronnie had picked up on Siddie's meandering. "Blimey! You look worried to death, mate. I'd better get you home." Siddie gave him a withering glance. For the time being he was off the hook but his demeanour was in the shit, right up to his neck and beyond. Going home right now wasn't even an option. Facing Rachael in favour of Ronnie didn't appeal to him. Facing the situation head on had far better consequences.

Co-stallholder Dave 'the China' had marked Siddie's card initially, in no uncertain terms, by tipping him the wink. "I wasn't totally sure at first, I thought the guy could have been Weights and Measures snooping around. Acting creepy like, know what I mean? Although he didn't fool me. I thought to myself, 'If he ain't Old Bill then the Pope's Jewish'! Take it from me, the guy was definitely on your case, so just watch yer back. He's been watching yours for the last half hour. As it happens, that's the third time this week I've seen him hovering. For what it's worth, mate, it's the flash-looking guy standing over there wearing the grey whistle and trilby hat."

Looking across, Siddie had no problem in picking the guy out.

Even from fifty yards or so, there was no mistaking the arrogance in his body language as he approached Siddie's stall. At that particular moment, Ronnie was in the lock-up replenishing his stock. *Good timing on the stranger's part, he's definitely Old Bill. I reckon he must have spotted Ronnie leaving his stall before approaching me!* he speculated. Now, standing face to face with the man only endorsed Siddie's earlier impression as being the right one. He decided to let the stranger do the talking on the pretext that Ronnie might make an appearance.

"Siddie Levy, I believe? Nice setup you've got yerself here, good little earner I should imagine?" He lost no time in establishing his intended mark and continued: "By the way, my name's Dawson… DS that is." In making his point, he produced a warrant card as back-up. Siddie had already written the script when he replied, "You could have saved yer breath, you were under orders the minute you entered the market!" Dawson squirmed; he'd been wrong-footed, causing his inflated ego to hang in the balance. Siddie, meanwhile, wasn't about to let him off the hook that easily and prepared to reel him in.

"So don't tell me yer doing me for selling bent bananas?" Dawson's face was a picture and a lousy one at that. Sheer frustration and a sickly grin blanketed his face as Siddie continued: "Okay, so it ain't the fruit. I guess the veg must be iffy, in which case I'll be needing a caution."

Demoralised as he was, Dawson dug deep. There was one trump card left to play; he just needed the right moment to produce it. A sardonic smile crossed his face as he went for the jugular. "Rossetti!" One name, not just any old name, this one just happened to be exclusive. For a few seconds there was a stunned silence. It looked like game, set and match for Dawson as he allowed the verbal poison to spew out of his mouth. The impact it had on Siddie was clear cut, his Jewish blood running cold. It didn't get any better as Dawson twisted the knife even deeper.

"Obviously the name means something to you?" Forced to grunt, Siddie bowed to the man's perception. "Up till now, we've had two explicit sightings of the man in the last month. Both of which were in the Docklands area."

"Says who?" Siddie retaliated. "The schmuck has been dead for six years already." Dawson appeared far from convinced.

"There's no evidence available to support that theory, so we're keeping an open mind. As for me, unlike your fruit, I'm fresh on the manor, so I won't be buying this time around." With that, he sauntered off wearing a smug look.

"Schnorrer!" Siddie vented his feelings in Yiddish. It fell on deaf ears. The whole episode was now over and done with. *Shit! Where the hell were yer, Ronnie? Just when I needed yer.* He only succeeded in adding grief on grief. The reference aimed at his stock alone seemed bad enough. *The putz! Where does he get off? My fruit is kosher. Damn! Ronnie ain't going to like this one bit*, he thought. Alternative clichés flooded his mind. *Could the whole thing have been a wind-up, or even a means to carry favour?* As of now, he found himself facing an awkward situation. Relating the episode to Ronnie ran a close second to a ticking time bomb. Siddie, for the time being, stood alone on this one, and he knew it.

"Blimey, mate! I don't believe it. Have a butchers out the window, I reckon it's stopped raining at last." Ronnie's spontaneous intervention caused Siddie to come back down to earth with a bump. Fortunately for him, the rain had got him out of jail, albeit temporarily. "Err, thanks for the offer of a lift, mate. I'll hang around for a bit, might snatch a few quid."

"Yeah, whatever. Be lucky. By the way, I'm in the gym tonight in case you happen to phone me." They went their separate ways, two very exclusive people linked together by a key of destiny. It would take just one man to turn it, and in so doing open the floodgates of fate. The onus was now on Siddie Levy to do the right thing. He bade Ronnie goodbye and set off toward his pitch. Whatever time remained of the working day would seem like an eternity. But then he had a lot to think about.

Making a case for the defence would have taken a good man; all things considered it had been a shit day. The rain had also taken its toll on the Docklands quarter that day.

None more so than the basin area. In the event, one man stood alone. The landlord of the AA public house, situated at the bottom of Wharf Street, would argue the case that it had never stopped. But he was talking about small, circular pieces of metal commonly known as monetary tokens. And when they rained down, you prayed to God they wouldn't stop! The situation had now become a two-horse race. One Arm Bandit versus One Arm Bandit. As one delivered, so the other was fed. For the last hour or so, Rossetti had found himself on a roll. Lady Luck had been on hand and chosen to stick around. "Lucky bastard" bounced off every wall in the bar. It went clean over his head, as arm after arm crashed down, systematically spewing out the tokens.

"Beats me how he bloody does it," one envious observer remarked bitterly. It was not as if there were any rules attached. And certainly no skill required although gut instinct had its part to play. Reliance on that particular trait had been a way of life to a loser like Rossetti. In comparison, a saline drip wouldn't have stood a chance! The odds were stacked well in his favour as he exploited a no-risk policy. Sequence bars screamed out at him as they crazily spun round, stopping in the interim, allowing the Bandit to rain even more tokens. The ever-increasing pile of tokens he'd amassed was testimony to his inbuilt ability to do his homework. Two weeks of intimidating surveillance had now reaped dividends. With nowhere to go, and ample time on his hands, the bar had doubled up as his front room. The only companion party to his lucrative interest was his eternal glass of Scotch. At least it couldn't answer back.

Without question, the two Bandits now ruled his otherwise miserable existence. The fact remains he'd seen the groundwork through, now it was payback time. Two jackpots in one day was a one-off situation but then we are talking Paul Rossetti here. The landlord took his time paying out. It would appear that a small percentage was only lent so to speak. "There yer go, Rossi, I can't make it any more than that! Oh, by the way, I've taken a nifty out to cover the house rules."

"Rules?! What bleedin' rules?!"

"I'll put it another way: rent! And this just about squares it up." Flourishing the note in front of him was like waving a red rag at a bull. Someone should have told Rossetti that a win came with a price tag. In his case a forgotten-about roof over his addled head.

The damaged skin tissue to one side of his face reddened as his heart began to race. His breathing became erratic as he attempted to control a fuse that was shorter than his memory. According to his standards, any form of logic started and ended at the bottom of a glass. The thought of being drawn into a slanging match didn't appeal to the landlord. Fortunately, a punter at the end of the bar needed serving; sighing with relief he walked away. Rossetti found himself picking up the pieces and reflecting on his mugging. Never con a conner! That was the rule of thumb in his fantasy world; he of all people should have known better.

Since his untimely return from exile to Stonewater, his response to a nagging situation figured highly in the brief moments of sanity his body would allow him at any one time. Time and time again, it had come back to haunt him. On the rare occasion he'd managed a breakthrough invariably the pile of random letters would attempt to manifest itself as a name. Just as it started to become clear, the name would disintegrate, only to repeat the illusion once more. For want of change, the letters would break the routine, screaming out their conclusion. His twisted and tormented mind would run rampant in his quest for an answer. Could it be past or present? The present, he considered, could be ruled out: *It's not as if I've been putting myself about on my return*. In any event, all things considered, the world as we know it was not quite prepared for the infamous and elusive Paul Rossetti just yet!

## CHAPTER 3

# REVELATIONS

Forty-eight hours later, and another day in the life of plastic gangster, Paul Rossetti. His glass was almost empty by now, although for once he felt in control as the cancerous image from his past returned to plague him. His sixth sense seemed to override the situation; this particular sequence felt ordained to be different. Beads of sweat formed on his brow and a surge of realisation raced through his body as a nearby discarded newspaper caught his eye. It appeared to mock and intimidate the need for any conclusions on offer. Undeterred, he grabbed the paper. A certain article had taken over his senses. The heading ran deep into the heart of his illusion as one particular name became glaringly apparent. No more screams or delusions to contest, he'd made a breakthrough. His eyes had now become transfixed by the press cutting, as his rejuvenated brain took in the headline:

DRUGS BUST LED BY DS DAWSON

He hadn't been aware that he was reading out loud. "Same again, Rossi?" The barman had picked up on his verbal charade by completely misreading the situation. He could have saved his breath; his request fell on deaf ears. Rossetti by now had become rapt as he mentally devoured the contents of the cutting. The facts themselves were irrelevant, but the reference to Dawson's rank and track record since his arrival at Stonewater was firmly etched in his mind. There was no mistaking the evidence linking the two from his tawdry past. Rossetti felt gobsmacked and was slow to take in his sudden turn in fortune, deciding instead to milk the moment.

Over and over again, the words spilt from his mouth. "DS Dawson, West End Central!" He stopped short as the full impact of their past relationship turned full circle. A mocking laugh followed as the beneficial monetary consequences loomed large in his thoughts.

"You've lost the bloody plot, Rossi," the barman shouted across in sympathy. His remark fell way short as it was met with yet another laugh. But this particular one had a gilt-edged ring to it. Luck comes in various forms and designs. Today, for reasons unknown, the Lady had chosen Rossetti. The die had been cast and the stage now set. As a result, one person's shady background would now touch the lives of four people over the months to follow. Ronnie Callaghan had yet to meet him! The damning evidence surrounding Dawson's past stemmed from another life prior to taking up residence in Stonewater. His dubious past, through circumstances of his own making, had now caught up with him. The seeds of deception were sown from acceptance of his very first bung. The monkey lining his pocket never felt better. It was all too easy to look the other way. Bigger targets became a way of life, as did the clients he repeatedly ripped off in pursuit of personal greed. Purely by chance, Rossetti entered into the equation via a club raid up West. For Dawson, it resulted in a bust too far in his lucrative reign of egotism. Mouthing off would cost him dearly in the days to come.

Situated in Soho, the club in question had proved to be a win in more ways than one. Being employed as a gopher opened up the doors of opportunity for Rossetti. He could now revel in the sleaze that came with the territory. Drugs, prostitution and the token booze were accepted commodities.

As a bonus, he could now rub shoulders with those faces within the underworld that festered in the twilight hours. By chance, his dream folded overnight; a misshapen loser would never be acceptable in the circles he'd hungered for. Being as isolated as he was gave him the cover that people would pay good money for. Forced into the dregs of lowlife, he soon became productive in more ways than one.

The faces he now associated with were chancers by day and piss artists by night. Sharing a liquid lunch in a backstreet dive with Lenny 'the Snout' in tow, one time, would indirectly turn his life around. From obscurity to division one was a giant step! Fortunately a lifeline had been thrown his way. But could he handle the crown of respect his body craved? Rossetti was no fool when dealing with his own kind; plying a local snout had yielded a welcome return.

"Rossi, do yerself a favour, listen up."

"Yeah, yeah, what can you tell me that I don't already know?"

"Information off the street, and it's kosher!"

"Uhm, sounds promising, on or off the manor?"

"Right 'ere on yer bloody doorstep, mate. I'm talking about a bust!"

"I'm interested, Lenny. So when and where is it going down?"

"It's happening at the office club next Friday night, give or take, 2pm." Rossetti wrestled to control his body language. The SP he'd been party to was priceless in itself. Naming the club was the icing on the cake, seeing as though he'd worked there in the past. By now, the Snout's brain had engaged first gear. What he further divulged became a revelation in terms.

"That bastard Dawson is fronting it! He's gonna do the business."

"So why tell me, Lenny?"

"I don't rate the guy, he's an asshole, know what I mean? And that ain't all, it's supposed to be a covert operation. I can tell, yer know, it ain't even on the Old Bill's books!" At last, the tide had begun to turn in Rossetti's favour. Dawson's reputation as a ranked DS ended six foot from the precinct of West End Central. It had become common knowledge that his underworld activities extended to personal gain. The two had never met on a professional footing, and Rossetti fully intended keeping it that way. Or at least for the next few days. Working on the assumption that Lenny 'the Snout' had got it right, an idea began to materialise. Okay, so his reasoning would be based on nerve. Hell! Existing on his shattered nerves had been an occupational hazard for years! Outlining his game plan consumed the rest of the evening. He realised that the odds in his favour were flawed, but the prize, should he get a result, included the head of a bent cop. Propped up by personal blackmail.

Lenny, it seems, had come up trumps. The bust occurred, as did the timing related to it. Dawson's henchman forcefully cleared the club of punters. Within minutes a 'convenient' bag of cocaine was discovered in the toilets as the manager protested his ignorance. "We can talk about it in your office," suggested Dawson. The man was under orders and he knew it. Rossetti had also read the script right. Losing no time, he made for the office in a different direction. Once inside, he set his mobile on voice recorder, and placed it in a convenient position, at the same time ensuring it was well secluded. With seconds to spare, Dawson and his 'victim' appeared. Rossetti now found himself in an awkward position. "What's that crippled piece of shit doing? Get him out of 'ere!" Rossetti slunk off; for once in his miserable life he felt happy to oblige. His covert mobile had three minutes' recording time left to run if his plan was to succeed. Raised voices from within the office gave him fresh hope.

"I'll do him up like a fucking kipper!" he convinced himself. "I'll bleed the bastard dry, you see if I don't," he ranted. Just then, two faces approached; one pointed to the office as Dawson emerged. He wore the face of a lottery winner, but Rossetti was wearing the crown. Retrieving his mobile later was all too easy. On examination, the contents were as explicit as they were audible. A small outlay allowed him to transfer the audio file to a disc. He did, of course, ensure that he had a back-up copy himself – for personal reasons, the original being a present for Dawson no less. There was, of course, an additional rider attached: a specific amount of money to be paid into a bogus bank account when it suited Rossetti. Failure to do so wasn't even an option.

Dawson, by default, had inadvertently dug himself a hole he couldn't get out of. From then on, Rossetti was in his face and living the dream. The only way out for Dawson would be a change of scene. Purely by chance, a posting to Stonewater on the coast had bailed him out. Suffice to say, he accepted it without fuss. Two months later, oblivious to Dawson's unplanned exit from hell, Rossetti was left floundering as to what might have been. His well of ambition showed signs of drying up. It would appear there was a recession in the black market business. His six-year exile in London had run its course. With this in mind, a return to Stonewater appeared to be on the cards. The idea of pursuing Dawson's whereabouts didn't hold water; for all he knew he could be working on planet Mars!

Fortunately, the only aspect that hadn't dried up was his memory. It constantly reminded him that a belated date with Ronnie Callaghan needed reviewing. Within a few hours of deciding his abysmal future, he'd departed from London owing money everywhere, and headed for Stonewater. He would never have known at the time that in the following fortnight a chain of spontaneous events would be about to unfold due to an ill-fated sighting of him by a local plod. Identity, although crucial, had never been in doubt. The constable who had fingered him had been familiar with the case from way back. "It's the face, guv, you don't easily forget a face like that!" The thought of Rossetti sharing the manor with him could kickstart his downfall. Little did Dawson know that the local rag had now given Rossetti the kiss of life once again. And so, as a result, it had become a two-horse race focusing on revenge. Or was it? Dawson had been well informed that Rossetti was desperate; under the circumstances he needed to act fast whilst keeping a low profile at the same time.

The Callaghan-Rossetti link now figured highly in his strategy. By using the right approach through a third party, namely Siddie Levy, Callaghan would unwittingly find himself coerced as a pawn of convenience in bringing Rossetti down permanently, paving the way to a successful conclusion. One man's conscience would hang in the balance on the strength of his altercation. Unfortunately, Siddie Levy found himself destined to serve as a go-between, thus setting the wheels of fate in motion. So we are now talking a four-horse race with unlimited hurdles to cross. The odds of survival were on a downward spiral the moment Siddie Levy made a belated decision to resurrect Paul Rossetti.

"Believe me, Ronnie, if there was an easier way of telling you then I sure as hell don't know it. The way that schmuck Dawson laid it on me, I knew I needed time out to think. In the event, I owe yer that much, knowing that eventually I would have had to tell you what happened." Siddie, like it or not, was in a no-win situation; relating his recent altercation concerning Dawson was proving untenable.

"Christ's sake, Siddie, I can't believe you've known about this for a poxy week." Ronnie was at a loss, struggling to take in Siddie's bombshell. "Rossetti! Dawson! Who's next? Bleedin'

Terry Winters?! This has to be some sort of a wind-up. I mean, c'mon, I'm in the market four or five days a week, why approach you? No, it doesn't make sense to me." Convincing Ronnie wasn't going to be easy.

"Trust me, the guy came across as being kosher. Like it or not, you seriously need to take it in."

"Serious? The guy's been brown bread for the last six years and now yer telling me he's running loose in Docklands? So where's he been all this bleedin' time, in a poxy health farm?" Siddie shrugged his shoulders in a defeatist manner.

"Maybe I shouldn't have told you in the first place and kept me mouth shut!"

"Nah, yer did the right thing, mate. Keeping schtum wouldn't have proved anything. I'd rather you heard it from me, than somebody else."

"So now it's out in the open, where do we go from 'ere?"

"Your guess is as good as mine, mate. Tell yer what, I'll make a phone call, get it sorted. This Dawson guy could be anybody as far as we know."

"No bloody way!" Siddie exclaimed emphatically. "He's kosher alright, his ID told me that!"

"If you say so, mate. Although the more I think about it, the more iffy it seems to get. It's almost as if this Dawson geezer wants us to do his dirty work for him. Know what I mean?" Logical reasoning required consideration. Siddie's face was clouded, as were his thoughts. Could Ronnie be clutching at straws? Who's to say he wasn't right? And it needed to be said.

"Silly I know, but…" he faltered.

"Yeah, go on, I'm listening."

"What if Dawson and Rossetti were somehow linked?" Ronnie shook his head vigorously; he wasn't buying it.

"No chance! A bleedin' dog wouldn't stand for Rossetti, the geezer's an island."

"Well, it was worth a thought, but I take yer point." Siddie appeared to be disillusioned by his frugal attempt to shed light on the situation. Their conversation was going nowhere fast, as cracks began to appear in his body language.

"Ah, let's just forget it ever happened, there's far too much shit flying about."

"I ain't gonna argue with that, mate. I'll keep an open mind on the matter. In the meantime, nothing changes and life goes on." Ronnie had made the point, end of story, although he did have this vacant look on his face.

"Are you okay? You look miles away," said Siddie; the last time he'd seen that look on Ronnie's face happened to be on the night that Slatteries' 'died'.

"Ronnie!" This time louder; still there was no response. "I said are you okay? You look as though you've seen a ghost." At last, Ronnie got the message. Glancing up, he replied in a defiant manner: "If I had done, mate, we wouldn't be having this conversation, would we?!", which amounted to one aspect of his reasoning. But overall, their singular conclusions were flawed. Only time itself would become accountable.

## CHAPTER 4

# YOUNG BLOOD

Saturday came and went. For Ronnie it fringed on eternity. The overriding fact that he would be back in the gym the next day gave him an escape route from the nagging doubts he'd harboured concerning the Dawson affair. *Almost there*, he told himself. Tightening the shackle on the top rope, he sighed with relief. *There, that should keep 'em quiet for five minutes*. Standing inside the ring gave him the opportunity to take stock of the surroundings. Momentarily, he challenged his meticulous system of preparation. *Could I have missed anything?* he asked himself. From the very start, it was a selfish request with no subsidy attached. God only knows, he'd used the same routine a thousand times!

Checking his watch reminded him that the gym would come alive in twenty minutes. His contentment was at a peak; this was his personal domain and he revelled in its entirety from the wall timer to the resin on the ring canvas. Nodding graciously, he allowed himself a brief moment of self-satisfaction. The last twelve months had gone well for him. 'Big' Tommy Russell, the resident manager and would-be promoter, could rest easy in the knowledge that his stable of fighters were a force to be reckoned with due to 'yours truly' as an acclaimed trainer, aided and abetted by ex-middleweight Dave Molloy. After his dismissal from the paid ranks he willingly took over the mantle of chief whip, vacated due to the sad demise of Wally Churchill. It went without saying that Ronnie felt pleased to have him around at that time.

Other faces sprang to mind as he digressed. Last but not least was, of course, Mickey Gibbons. Unfortunately, the damage he sustained via the Paul Rossetti scenario some six years ago gave vent to a catalogue of problems. It was one fight that Gibbons would never win. A year after the Terry Winters affair, the BBBC called the last round on his career, forcing him to retire. Somebody once remarked, 'You can take the boxing out of the man, but you can't take the man out of boxing'. In Gibbons' case, the gym became his second home and he remained a staunch friend to Ronnie.

Unlike the vast majority of training sessions, this particular morning was draped in nostalgia. Tommy Russell's latest signing to the paid ranks revolved around a young kid with great potential under the name of Danny Simmons. Ronnie, if called upon, could recall their very first introduction some six and a half years ago. At that particular time, Simmons was a fresh-faced twelve-year-old. Standing on a dustbin peering through a window wasn't for him! That particular day belonged to him as he forced open the door to the gym. An altercation based around his determined character ensued, leaving Ronnie to confront him. It terminated in honours even as eventually young Simmons fled back out of the gym head held high. He had then, and still retained, the overpowering degree of self-confidence required to make his mark in life.

"Hi Ronnie! You got a minute?" The unmistakable tone of Russell broke his chain of thought. Now fully aware of his presence, Ronnie glanced across as his larger-than-life form swept through the gym door. His distinctive body language was a giveaway. *Looks like he's got some sort of a business deal on his mind, if I didn't know any better*, Ronnie mused. Pointing toward the office, Russell exclaimed, "We need to talk now!" His manner was short and direct. Nothing new there then!

"Bleedin' fight managers, I've had 'em for breakfast!" Word for word, his request had already been pre-empt due to Ronnie's sixth sense. "Yeah, yeah, be right with yer." He was still wearing a grin when he confronted Russell minutes later.

"You look like the cat who's got the cream," uttered Tommy.

"I wouldn't argue on that score, mate. Put it down to young Simmons, I guess. The kid's a breath of fresh air. Reminds me of a young Mickey Gibbons, know what I mean?"

"Absolutely! You have to say his pedigree is a bit special. I'm lucky I've got an option on him. Saying that, it's down to you to do the business, mate."

"That's the least of my worries, Tommy. The kid's a natural born talent, although I don't want to push him too hard at this stage. He needs to realise that punching for money is a whole new ball game. Mind you, he ain't nobody's fool. It won't take him long to adjust to a new regime."

Tommy nodded in a positive manner. "I'm sure you're right, mate. Which is just as well…"

"You've got him an outing," Ronnie interjected.

"Yeah, as it happens. We're looking at seven or eight weeks' time, although nothing has been finalised as yet. Let's see how his training pans out."

"D'ye know where the venue is likely to be?"

"Southend Leisure Centre most probably. The usual novice rules apply, opening six rounder on the under card."

"Good call, who's promoting it, by the way?"

"Your old pal Charlie Cochrane as it happens. We had quite a chat. Turns out he's been a bit iffy lately. Nice to see him back and doing what he's good at!"

"Amen to that! The guy's a bleedin' icon within the game.

Not only that, he's good to work with, he ain't gonna mug yer off."

"As you say, never in doubt. I can trust Charlie to get us a good match at this stage of his career. It'll be a test to bring out his potential." Ronnie confirmed Russell's logic. "We've had this conversation before, more than once. If anyone can get Simmons a result on the night, it'll be me!" Tommy smiled.

"That's what I like about you, Ronnie. You've got the bollocks to say what yer mean. I'll leave it all to you. Keep me posted on weekly progress updates, right?" With the small talk out of the way, the stage was set for business as usual. Ronnie spotted Dave Molloy exiting the shower room and beckoned him over.

"Well, it all starts 'ere today for the kid. You know the SP. Ease him in gently."

"Sure, no problem," replied Molloy and concluded, "Onwards and upwards, mate."

"Please God!" echoed Ronnie, and made his way toward the ring. Elsewhere, Danny Simmons wasn't the only one left facing a challenge. The recent Dawson revelation had put a fresh slant on his spiraling future. Mentally, Rossetti found himself coping with an ego surge as a recrimination period started to formulate in his head. It had been six long years since he'd blown Terry Winters away. The memory, plus the feeling he derived from the five rounds of vengeance ripping into flesh and blood were now only classed as being lent, although the hunger for personal retribution still remained a priority. Fate, it seems, had arrived, ready on hand to awaken that once-dormant seed of power which came in the form of a cancer he could nurture at leisure. The larger it grew, the more intense his yearning for revenge could manifest itself. Almost as if the evil that ran in his veins told him that, like a phoenix, he would rise from the ashes. Or, in the real world, a miraculous escape from the inferno that was Slatteries' gym in Docklands. A glimmer of hope lay in his cards, and better still he retained the bank! The odds in his favour were now doubled. As the underdog he held a full house. More than enough you would argue; haven't people murdered for less? In Rossetti's case, a royal flush now offered him the redemption he craved.

Two characters now emerged from the sequence of cards he held in his favour, namely Callaghan and Dawson. All he had to do now was to call the trumps in the order of the insanity his addled brain had reasonable access to. They say that madness has no boundaries; it would take somebody special to wage a one-man double vendetta. In that case, look no further than Paul Rossetti! His only problem, should one occur, would be one of priority: Callaghan or Dawson? The act of topping his glass up in the past wouldn't have constituted a debate, when based on the termination of two people's lives. His embittered thoughts clashed in turmoil, while his sodden brain wrestled for a conclusion.

Deep down, something prompted him that Dawson was in the frame. He stopped to take stock; a sinister smile crossed his face as he nodded approvingly. *I must be stupid! The answer was staring me in the face, and I couldn't see it. It has to be Dawson. He'll be easier to get at!* By now he'd more than convinced himself. *Besides, I've still got the original tape on him. I can use that as fodder.* Having completed its work, the Scotch was entitled to an opinion. His face reverted to a triumphant leer before breaking into a heinous laugh. "It won't be long, Dawson," he ranted. "Yer as good as dead, d'ye hear me?" You could be led to believe that there was a ring of truth in his delirium. What he didn't know, should it have surfaced, was that Dawson had become aware of his presence in Docklands.

But just to add to the confusion the two proposed targets were complete strangers to one another. Not that it would have affected any game plan Rossetti could bring to bear. On the contrary, he felt in full control by making it his business, ensuring that the two would meet up. Preferably wearing body bags in a downtown morgue! An image of the scene featured highly in his senses. Without warning, his face contorted into a mask of insecurity followed by a sense of utter failure which suddenly blanked out the image. An ice-cold wave of fear and nausea swept over his trembling body like a tsunami. Convulsions followed, lifting and dropping his insignificant body at their leisure. He felt powerless to utter a sound as a rope of despair around his scrawny neck tightened, choking his very existence in the process. The self-induced seizure took its time to climax; there are no rules that govern the actions of the subconscious.

Question! Had his audacious quest for revenge lulled his brain into a fool's paradise? Or could the inevitable happen? Blinded by revenge he'd overlooked the consequences. Namely, that both paths led headlong into forming one conclusion: the opening of Pandora's Box. If so, would he be man enough to see it through? Only time itself would tell us the answer to that as his sweat-ridden body slumped backwards in a heap on top of his bed.

The odious smell from the previous night's Scotch became a wake-up call, albeit midday. Suffice to say, his breakfast call had missed its sell-by date, leaving him with the all-too-familiar option. Hold it right there! You don't kick a guy when he's down; today could well be a special day. From the minute he'd forced his eyes open his persona had felt an awareness. From the depths of his private hell an angel of mercy, it seems, had sponsored his lust for revenge. In a reversal of fate, his subconscious had turned full circle, and by doing so had ignited a keen sense of normality in his person. He'd done nothing to warrant a reprieve, desperate as he was to lay ghosts. On the contrary, he could now think straight on a personal level.

As with most situations, money comes into play. To achieve is to speculate. In his case, it wouldn't have taken a stewards' enquiry to emphasise the point in question. Six years ago he'd lifted his game. Without prompting, heroin took a back seat to the thrill generated by a snubnosed .38 Cobra revolver taking over where fear had left off. God! It had felt so good just holding it. He likened it to a woman's body as he caressed the trigger, waiting for the inevitable climax that followed.

"Fuck the world, I need to get off!" No, Rossetti, it's your goddamn choice, but yes! You will require a shooter to see it through. "Sedgeman, Sedgeman, yeah, it's all coming back to me now, that was his name. He was always good for a hardware deal. I need to make some enquiries. Hopefully the geezer is still on the manor."

A wash and a shave later found him lurking in a dingy downtown poolroom, the dingy in-house lighting causing him to curse as he checked his timing. No, if anything he was on the early side of things. To make matters worse, cigarette smoke hung from the ceiling in layers, causing him to wretch as it hit the back of his throat. He was still coughing when an alien figure emerged from behind a curtain of haze. "Rossetti?" His body stiffened as the stranger confronted him. "Is that you, Rossi?" Seemingly satisfied he continued. "Poxy light, can't see a thing 'ere, let's move over to the bar. How the fuck do they play snooker in 'ere?" he added.

"Yeah, you got that right, I wouldn't want a pony on the black ball, would yer?" Feeling uneasy, he'd decided to make small talk. His observation fell way short as Maltese Pete ushered him closer to a nearby overhead strip light. He'd come this far; there would be no turning back now. Rossetti knew from way back the importance of their meet. His heart began to race as the middleman seemed content to eyeball him for a few seconds. Finally, he broke silence.

"So, business. You want to do some business, right?!"

"That's what I'm 'ere for." Rossetti endeavoured to raise his game; he could have saved his breath, Maltese wasn't impressed.

"On the phone you spoke with Sedgeman in mind, right?"

"Yeah, I think you get the picture. I need to get tooled up, know what I mean?"

At this point Maltese appeared to be in no rush to pursue any negotiable deal.

"Tell yer what, you get the drinks in and we'll talk about it." Rossetti felt on edge and it showed in his makeup. Maltese had one foot in his gut and it was getting to him in more ways than one.

*The man's bleedin' colder than the ice in my Scotch,* he told himself and shivered slightly. Although the two were in no way connected, Rossetti recalled his track record from way back. *To my knowledge the guy's done more time than a fucking carriage clock! And half of that was spent in solitary.* Obviously the years had taken their toll; he'd become a spent force in comparison. But you didn't fuck with the man if you had a love of fresh air. Downing his drink, Maltese got straight to the heart of the matter.

"I can tell yer nah, Sedgeman's out the equation, in fact he's brown bread!"

"Yer kidding me!" Rossetti could feel his expectations slipping away. It wasn't meant to be like this.

"The stupid bastard blew himself away nearly eighteen months nah."

"What! Like suicide?"

"Nah, while he was repairing a sawn-off shotgun with a bottle of vodka for company."

"No shit!"

"Bit of a poxy mess by all accounts. It took the Old Bill

nearly three days to get his fucking head off the ceiling, know what I mean?"

"Selfish bastard, so where do we go from 'ere then?" Desperation had set in.

"Nothing changes, we can still do a deal. Personally, I came out of it alright."

"How come?" Rossetti asked nervously.

"I owed him a monkey at the time on a specialist tool he was working on. Saying that, it was far too hot to offload onto the street." Rossetti cringed. The prospect of any deal on offer going belly up wasn't a scenario he relished. *The man's a fucking animal*, he convinced himself. Momentarily his chain of thought shattered as Maltese continued.

"So what are yer looking for exactly toolwise?" He was now pressing for a deal of some kind.

"Hmm, short range, snubnose and no ID. Oh, and a full clip, of course." A sickly smile crossed Maltese's face before replying.

"Short range, eh, must be somebody yer know well. Not that it's any of my business, yer understand. Mind you, could take some time sorting one out, there ain't a lot of call for a Cobra at the moment." Rossetti's face caved in; he found himself in the last chance saloon. Obtaining a shooter was paramount to his plans. Fortunately, Maltese threw him a lifeline as he continued.

"Most of my clients tend to keep their victims at a distance, that way it doesn't get personal, but you," he sniggered, "you obviously like to get a fuck out of it, right?" He now found himself stewing in a situation of his own making; Rossetti was out of his league and it showed. Maltese could be seen as old school; the smell of fear came with experience. But then he did carry this exclusive aura of persuasion to a great height. Body and brain alike were squirming as Maltese primed him for the kill. In the end it all came down to money. Or in Rossetti's case, the lack of it.

The ante began rising faster than his blood pressure as a settlement figure was put on offer. It became a case of 'pay up and look good'. Rossetti was now like a puppet on a string as Maltese slowly pulled the strings to drag him in. "We're talking a lot of dough 'ere. I've got overheads to consider, people to keep sweet, know what I mean?" At this stage he was well into Rossetti's face as he stated the final payoff. "I'm gonna require a carpet up front and a further £400 once I've delivered. One other thing, keep yer nose clean. If yer get a tug from the Old Bill and I get involved, yer a dead man walking, you understand?" Maltese had laid it out on the line for him and followed it up with an open palm in respect of a down payment. *Another bleedin' sucker!* he told himself.

Truth is, he'd taken an instant dislike to Rossetti from the word go. So join the fan club of one! Then it became money over time; it felt so good in his hand; checking it made it feel even better. Rossetti felt slaughtered as he looked on. He'd just handed over £300 in cold blood to a manic gun dealer who could well be in Spain the following day. "Yer looking as if you've got a problem, Rossi? You gotta learn to trust people," Maltese explained. "Just leave it with me, I know where to find yer when I'm ready. In the meantime, you'd better get yerself a day job, you still owe me £400, okay? By the way, we never had this conversation, right?!" With that, he turned on his heel and disappeared into the gloom. Once again Rossetti had been hung out to dry as his craving for respect disintegrated around him. Feeling isolated, he retrieved his glass from the bar; even that was empty. Out of luck and almost potless wasn't a recipe for ambition. He slunk out of the poolroom to be met by a wall of daylight. For a second, he felt completely disorientated, a far cry from the twilight zone he'd become accustomed to, isolated and threatened as he was in a world that screamed out normality. His alleged career could now be found at a crossroads; alternatives were on a walkabout inside his brain. One appeared to be more prominent than its counterparts. *Maybe an injection of manpower is worth considering*, he told himself.

His insecure mind reached back in time some six years ago. A mental image of Ricky Peters and the Traveller came through. Moneywise, he'd never been short of a wedge. Okay, it was never going to last forever, but working as a firm had produced results. And who knows what the final outcome could have been by taking Terry Winters' reign of self-supremacy out of the equation. But that was then and this was now. At least it gave him time to digress. Question and answer time came into play as he focused on Maltese Pete's actions. Like a magnet, the man's uncanny perception of fear came to the fore, his ability to dictate and control a situation simply by aura. A persona to crave for indeed. Secretly he envied the charisma, albeit hostile, surrounding the man.

*The guy's a spent force in retrospect and yet I let him fucking walk all over me. He had me for poxy breakfast. I gotta learn by it!* he reasoned. *Let people know where I'm coming from, yeah, that's the answer*. Fifteen minutes later his cab pulled up outside the AA. Easing himself out of the car, he shoved what money he had into the cabbie's open hand.

"Oy, yer £2 light, guv," the driver responded sarcastically. If ever there came a time for him to prove a point, then it had to be now.

"Not as short as the three fucking roads you added to the journey, you asshole, nah piss off!" Now that wasn't hard, was it Rossi? For a minute Rossetti lingered for a while deep in thought as he watched the cab disappear into the distance. A look of satisfaction crossed his face. Maltese had been a long overdue wake-up call. Now would be the time to take stock, reassess the Dawson scenario. The sudden urge to rush into a vendetta from choice needed serious planning. Time seemed unimportant at this stage. *I still have the tape*, he reminded himself. *Maybe an outing will stir things up, at least he'll know I'm on his case. From now on I'll be the one doing the pushing!*

"Usual, Rossi?" prompted the barman as Rossetti entered the bar.

"You can shove it! I got things to do," came his reply. The look on the barman's face was priceless as he watched Rossetti hobble up the stairs to his room. Lowering the intended empty glass he turned to his colleague: "I think you'd better phone for an ambulance, I reckon the guy's flipped at last!"

## CHAPTER 5

# ILLICIT CONVERSATION

"You going to get that or do I have to?" The request came across as an order rather than a suggestion. Meanwhile the phone continued to ring. "Now, Hollins!"

"Damn! I never will get this blasted report finished in time." Leaving off, he swung his chair round and lunged at the phone. "Stonewater CID, DC Hollins speaking, how can I help?" Nodding positively he glanced across at his boss.

"Yeah, no problem, hold the line, I'll put you through. You can take that on two, Sarge."

"Who the hell is it?"

"I don't know, it's an outside line, they didn't say." Pecking order came into play as the connection was made.

"DS Dawson speaking, what can I do for yer?" He visibly stiffened at the enquiry. "Give us a second." Lowering the receiver he cupped the mouthpiece with his hand before continuing. "Hollins!" he yelled. "Lose yerself for ten minutes, get yerself a cup of tea or something. Oh, and shut the door behind yer." Tutting, the young DC bowed out of the room wearing a look of disdain. An impatient Dawson ensured he was gone before committing himself to the caller.

"Ernie? Yeah, sorry about that, can't be too bloody careful, know what I mean? So what's occurring?"

"Not a lot, Harry, you know how it works, same shit different day," came back the reply.

"Right now I'd welcome the shit!" Dawson fired back.

"Blimey, that bad eh? You make West End Central sound like a bloody holiday camp."

"Don't knock it, mate, you're on a winner up West. This Stonewater dump is something else. If you can imagine hell with fucking seawater that gives yer half an idea."

"I hear what yer say but you're bound to be pissed off after Central, c'mon."

"The thing is, Ernie, it doesn't end at that. There happens to be a lot more to it."

"Meaning what exactly?" Frowning heavily Dawson paused before answering, allowing his brain to fast forward.

"Just for the record, where are you speaking from, Ernie?" The latter sensing a situation put him at ease.

"You can relax, Harry. If yer worried about a tap, don't be! Right now, I happen to be in a private club up West. You were saying?"

"Oh, yeah. Truth is, it ain't fucking happening down here."

"Give yerself time, Harry boy. It's not that big a manor, you'll soon find a clue."

"Don't get me wrong, Ernie. I'm into a few victims already. But I've also inherited a crock of shit to go with it. And it ain't healthy!"

"I see, ain't like you to get any grief though. What's the SP, a bad payer?"

"Huh, I wish it was that bloody easy, if only."

"So try me."

"Nah listen up, this is going to take some swallowing. Rossetti! Remember him? Rossetti, the little shit, is running loose on my fucking manor in Stonewater. How's that grab yer?"

"Rossetti?! You're having a laugh, Harry, that nonce couldn't afford a coach trip round a telephone box! He must have blagged the fare to get to Stonewater."

"Trust me, mate, the SP is kosher. My man tells me he's been sighted a couple of times. I've got no reason not to believe him. My problem here though is one of involvement. By that I mean a certain tape Rossetti might have in his possession. I'm stymied whichever way yer look at it."

"Yer jumping the gun, Harry. What makes you think he knows yer working on the manor?"

"I don't, in a word! I can only keep schtum and hope the bleeder doesn't know. I mean, how could he know? There's just no poxy way."

"Yeah, it makes sense. Saying that, you can't ignore it. If you need to, then get a third party involved, flush him out on the quiet, let them do the bloody business. You've got a fucking great pond on yer doorstep, it can't be that hard!"

"Yeah, yeah, I realise where yer coming from, mate."

"Good, not only that, you mentioned a tape, right?"

"Wish I hadn't, but yeah."

"Christ, sounds like it could be a bomb waiting to go off."

"Only if I let it. Trust me, Ernie, I'm dealing with it as we speak, but from a different angle."

"Go on."

"I've got information that says Rossetti had a nasty run in with a local guy a few years ago. An ex-pro fighter by all accounts, and it all kicked off in Docklands. I made a point of delving which gave me an idea. Apparently, Rossetti nearly mullered the guy. His name happens to be Ronnie Callaghan. He still runs a gym in the town. For what it's worth, he'd have Rossetti's head on a fucking plate given the chance."

"So what's yer angle?"

"I've managed to feed a staunch pal of his with certain information regarding his presence back on the manor. On the strength of that, I'll sit back and, please God, Callaghan will do the business for me."

"You wouldn't want to make a book on it, Harry, but I like yer style."

"I don't have a choice, mate. Listen, I'd better go, I can hear somebody coming, probably my DC. Yeah, be in touch, like I say, bye, mate." Slowly, Dawson replaced the receiver. For a minute, he found himself up West. Okay, so their conversation was illicit, and cheap with it, on the patch he'd been forced to relinquish. Bread and butter comes to mind. But this was Stonewater! He'd broken the rules; it was now a case of 'pay the piper', namely Paul Rossetti.

Through sheer greed he'd inherited a monkey on his back, leaving him with an overwhelming urge to offload it. That would be his first mistake, his second being a show of arrogance in believing that Rossetti could be oblivious as to his whereabouts. Fate, it seems, had once again intervened by carving out a succession of personality intrigues. All destined to share a collision course, fraught with mayhem and murder in the coming weeks.

CHAPTER 6

# THE CHINA TOWN EXPERIENCE

Rossetti was pushing his luck as usual, so nothing new there then. He'd developed that particular aspect from way back as a means of survival. The urge to cash in on his personality could now be found wanting and blinded by egotism. What the hell was he thinking of? Highly dangerous and called Canal Street, the heartbeat of Docklands. He should have known better. At night it became a magnet for crime, drugs and prostitution. For this reason, alone, it needed to be heavily policed. As a result of their 24/7 activity it became known as Plod Alley by the local crime fraternity. From Rossetti's standpoint keeping a low profile was paramount. A chance sighting or the odd loose word could put paid to his lacklustre independence. The AA, it seems, had now run its course in terms of scalability. Faces and places were the all-important injection that he craved right now. It meant securing a vital foothold in the world of sleaze.

The sanctity of a nearby shop doorway offered a welcome reprise from the bustle of the night people. As yet, he found himself excluded from their way of life; he studied them from a distance and likened them to ants on a mission. *My turn will come, and when it does, the world will recognise and respect Paul Rossetti!* he convinced himself. Putting the resident smell of car fumes and commercial business to one side, the air never tasted sweeter as he took in the whole package. It caused an upsurge in his blood, allowing an adrenaline rush to seduce his body. The buzz it injected instantly captured his imagination as a feeling of déjà vu crept back into his system. *I'm back!* he reminded himself.

Back, as in body, maybe. But as yet, the ladder to his lust for success could well have been drifting in space somewhere. Closing his eyes, he inhaled deeply, gulping down the ambience carried on the night air. Even three lines of heroin would have had no effect as his enlightened brain took off on a roller coaster of nostalgia. His eyes flashed as he shook his head, intent on telling the world. "Yes! I'm fucking back!" he cried out loud.

Nearby, a semi-drunk figure faltered in his stride and looked across at him through bleary eyes. For a couple of seconds the two eyeballed each other. Finally, the drunk broke the deadlock.

"Back?!" he retorted. "Back to what, front?!" A confrontation appeared to be imminent as Rossetti rose to the invasion of his private space.

"Why don't yer get off my case, you asshole!"

"Case?! Would that be, as in suit or head?" came back the reply. Rossetti found there can only be one thing worse than an educated drunk, and that's two of them, and he was forced to check himself. It was clear that he was on a hiding to nothing; the aggressor just happened to be both of them! Without realising it, their verbal altercation had caught the attention of Joe Public; in no time a small crowd had started to gather. "Shit! I don't need this crap, I'm out of 'ere." Spotting a gap in the crowd, the drunk became history and Rossetti managed to get clear. For once his line of thought remained positive. Minutes later, he exited Canal Street in favour of the back doubles – out of sight and out of mind, and possibly the clutches of the Old Bill.

Assured of his safety, he pulled over to regain his breath while he located his bearings. Glancing upward, a sign affixed to the side of a building caught his eye. Like a magnet it began to draw him in, at the same coercing his brain to adjust to a period in time. The sign itself related to direction and simply implied that the centre of China Town lay a few blocks away. The distance was relevant, but the locality became a reference to an era from his past. He clung to the welcome shadow of a doorway, as a force of memory unfolded within his subconscious. This particular vicinity would have been familiar territory some six years ago. He now recalled his role, set in a crime-ridden reign of terror and notoriety within the precinct of the area. On looking back, the forced exile that coincided with it was now irrelevant to his newfound makeover.

"Yeah, I'm fucking back!" he ranted, although this time there was a certain ring of smugness attached as he continued to rant inwardly. *Yes, you can tell the world that Paul Rossetti is definitely back!* True to form, it only took an audience of one to share his doctorate of fantasy. Moving on, old haunts and faces came to mind as he furtively made his way toward China Town.

Figuratively, he'd moved on in one sense. But what he'd failed to consider in his self-induced absence was so had Stonewater. Time indeed had brought about changes. Sophistication and a new order were now in play. The days of 'pay up and look good' had long ceased to be a means to an end. Social security now prevailed at the top end of survival. Keeping to the shadows where possible, he entered the outer region of China Town. Stopping short, he sighed with relief, and not before expressing his reason. "Thank fuck for that, it's still there," he muttered. His clinical observation centred around an enclosed narrow walkway adjoining a warehouse. Due to its ease of access over the years, it became known as the

Beijing Passage. Purely out of habit, he threw a last-minute look over his shoulder and entered.

On reaching the far end, the sudden change in atmosphere met him head on as a blend of Oriental culture and cuisine wafted on the cool night air like a plague; it seemed to swarm all over his being. Momentarily, his composure hovered between normality one minute and his own private world of celluloid fantasies the next. "Shit! Ain't the manor I used to know!" he exclaimed out loud, and continued, "Dunno what Ricky Peters and the Traveller would make of it nah. Poxy place is looking more like the bloody Smoke than ever." Stopping short, he found himself having to rub his eyes. Brightly coloured shop fronts and billboards combined with overhead strobe lighting were continually throwing out iridescent shadows of various colours, causing him to blink.

As his sight adjusted, one restaurant in particular caught his interest. Crossing the street, it seemed to draw him in ever closer. Slowly, recognition set in as the eating house loomed large through the low-budget overhead lighting. Once again, a further blast from his past had returned to mock his festering memory. "Hell!" he exclaimed. "Couldn't forget this gaff in a hurry." Taking a step backward, he checked out the frontage once again. He shook his head in disbelief. "I can't believe they still call it the Mandarin Palace." For the time being, he opted to linger awhile, purely to savour the outcome of a past milestone on his illegitimate path to self-destruction.

*I remember that bleedin' night like it happened yesterday*, he recalled. *When I think back now, we did the business in style, no fucking messing!* The emphasis being on the operative word 'we' as opposed to 'I'. In retrospect, his present line of thought related to a 'firm' operation, when teamed up with past gang members Ricky Peters and the Traveller. At that time, it formed a personal induction into the world of sleaze, the aspect in this particular case being one of protection money. That night, a certain sum of money became a takeaway as opposed to rice and noodles, including a few broken ribs. As Rossetti's maiden public engagement coordinating an organised racket, the night in question had proved fruitful in more ways than one.

On a personal level, a cancer of trepidation had been surgically removed with the aid of a baseball bat sponsored by 'Strike it Rich Ltd', and so his CV in crime had now spawned. On reflection, his initial hit within the rackets had been measured in blood and sheer terror, verified when questioned by the restaurant owner at that time as he relived the sequence of events. Instinctively, Rossetti's subconscious jolted a further step back as more facts became available. "Loy... Loy... Yeah! That was his fucking name, Johnny bleedin' Loy." He recalled the manager's horror after a request for 'services rendered' was refused. The Traveller offered to play a game of ping pong with him, the difference being that he was going to be the ball and the plate glass window destined to become the net. Needless to say, the money in question ran short of a dispute.

*The asshole couldn't wait to pay up once the Traveller had put the frighteners on him*, he mused, and went on, *I wonder where the silly bleeder is now? He's probably working as a Samaritan in Hong Kong. He certainly had a fucking death wish that night!* Blinded by a tirade of sarcasm, he now found his own self-preservation wanting. Any further thoughts on the outcome became redundant when an obnoxious passerby, hell bent on a mission to nothing, careered into him, forcing Rossetti to collapse into the gutter. "What the fuck?!" The altercation ended as quickly as it started. "Look where yer bleedin' going, asshole!" he shouted. His verbal retaliation fell on deaf ears. His aggressor was long gone.

With recrimination past its sell-by date, he became alerted by the sound of a wailing police patrol car siren carried on the night air. Rossetti could be excused for thinking that it doubled up as background music in a show of support for the sick egotism related to his initiation. Sadly for him, his mode of thought dropped to ground zero as the wailing increased in intensity. He sat bolt upright, and shot a rapid glance in the direction it appeared to be coming from. The twin headlights in the distance told him nothing that he didn't already know. "Shit! I'm out of 'ere!" seemed appropriate enough, although stating the obvious was too easy. Unfortunately, the situation in his case contained a hidden agenda, or worse.

For the time being, he wasn't about to go anywhere. By a quirk of fate, due to his fall the shoe on his gimpy leg had somehow got itself wedged in the grating of a surface-water drain in the gutter. Instantly, a cold wave of panic came into play as the patrol car drew ever closer. Two stark reasons stood out as far as his wellbeing was concerned: simply, life and death, but not necessarily in that order. The 'life' aspect could result in implication in an outstanding murder. And the second...? Who gives a shit anyway? He had it coming to him, poor bastard!

By now, he found himself hallucinating on fear alone as his futile efforts to free the offending shoe ran from maybe to zilch. As a token gesture, the sombre overhead street lighting appeared to mock his progress, as did the rest of the world at large, taunting him into becoming a whimpering wreck. Joe Public were also ignoring his pleas for help as they went about their business. At least one spectator had made the effort to turn up for his show: the Grim Reaper, it seems, had bought all the tickets! Rossetti was staring certain death in the face.

By now, his his blood pressure was at breaking point, and his pathetic frame oozing sweat, as the car appeared only yards away at this point. The headlights looked as large as dustbin lids in his three-dimensional vision of life prior to death. In spite of his predicament, the complexity of the brain, as we know it, allowed him a split-second reprieve as a feeling of déjà vu took over his being. A particular wheel in time had crept up on his miserable life and, in the process, had now turned full circle. His subconscious ran riot as an image depicting his nemesis Ronnie Callaghan foisted itself like a leech onto his moment of truth. The image in turn moved on to reveal Callaghan cowering in a similar gutter some years ago. Thanks to the untimely threat alluding to a red Mercedes under the orders of himself, that moment had now materialised into one of stark reality as the role of fate reversed its commitment to one of pleasure. All forms of sensibility ebbed away now, leaving in its wake a heaving shell of hysteria.

He began screaming out loud, although he wasn't even aware of the fact as the stench from burning tyres filled his mouth and nostrils. As an added extra, the acrid odour from petrol fumes added to the moment as the car came to a shuddering halt a few feet away from where he lay traumatised. Once again, Rossetti had cheated the Devil incarnate. Winning the lottery was a non-runner in comparison. Even he wouldn't have traded places for such a prize, knowing that the world would have been short of one less asshole! In no time at all, a small crowd had gathered at the scene. One figure in particular stood out as he wrenched Rossetti's shoe free and ably helped him to his feet. The door to the squad car opened, and the officer emerged looking somewhat shaken himself as he approached them.

Rossetti's unknown benefactor immediately turned to confront the officer on the pretext of hopefully gaining favour. There could be no mistaking the air of confidence that went with the patter. "It's okay, officer, there's been no harm done, and he's with me." The officer tutted before replying, "You can tell him from me, when he's sorted himself out, that he's one lucky person. I would never have seen him if you hadn't waved me down like you did." The stranger shrugged his shoulders in a nonchalant manner, and continued, "Least I could do for a mate, you know how it is. Besides, it's not every day you get your foot caught in a grille, is it?"

"Well, er, yeah, I hear what you say. When he finally comes round, you can remind him how lucky he was by acting the way that you did."

"I'm sure he'll appreciate it, officer. I guess in a way you could say he put his foot in it, so to speak!"

"In more ways than one, sir! Well, like you say, no damage done. I'll leave you to it."

"No problem, I think the situation calls for a stiff drink."

"It certainly would put the colour back in his cheeks, sir."

"Wouldn't do me any harm either come to that. Right, we'll be on our way, c'mon, Johnnie, let's get you home. Thanks again, officer. Be lucky." Propping up Rossetti as best he could, they went on their way and headed for the centre of China Town. The officer watched them leave. A cynical thought entered his head. Five or so minutes previously, he'd been pursuing a possible crime while doing 70 mph, and in the same breath an unexpected incident occurs.

*I can't help thinking that I missed something there*, he told himself. *Strange now I come to think about it. The victim never spoke a word. From start to finish it was all about his mate.* Any more thoughts on the matter were instantly sidelined as HQ demanded an update on his call-out. The patrolman's hunch, it appeared, didn't want to go away that easily. Two hundred yards or so down the road the incident came back to haunt him. A gut instinct took over and reflected in his uncertainty. *I just get this feeling that somehow I got conned back there!* The shadow of doubt remained with him for the rest of his shift; come to think of it, he didn't get much sleep either that night.

Meanwhile, Rossetti could be found struggling to regain his senses. As yet, doors needed to be opened, allowing him to enter the world of the living. His life, or rather existence, had dramatically gone from A to Z in as many minutes. At this juncture in time, he now found himself in the middle and leaning toward the starting line. His subconscious suddenly jolted into action. "Johnnie? Who the fuck is Johnnie?!" The stranger tightened his grip on him, replying, "Keep yer voice down, I'll explain later. We need to find a pub, trust me." On the back of that statement, Rossetti would have kept schtum for a week. Head bowed, he allowed his keeper to take the lead. In no time at all, he felt himself ushered through the doors of a dimly lit bar. "Ah, this gaff will have to do. Out of sight and out of mind, eh?" Rossetti wasn't about to argue on that score. Besides, he was a fully paid-up member of the Licensed Victuallers Association; he couldn't give a shit! As bars go, he got the impression this particular one had gone and made a bad comeback in the process. The sort of place you'd take your toupé in case you were recognised.

"Christ! Hope my Scotch is wetter than the fucking floor?!" muttered Rossetti, and continued, "I've heard of spit and sawdust before, but this gaff is all spit!" Any further thoughts on the subject were dismantled as the stranger placed their drinks on the table.

"There yer go, get that down yer throat." Grimacing as he did so, Rossetti duly obliged. At least it went toward resurrecting what brain he could muster. Still shaken from the incident, it did little to rearrange his personality disorder. As per usual, he was about as sociable as a cobra with a hernia.

"Just who the fuck are yer?!" he demanded. The stranger replied low key, "That ain't important at the moment, just get yer head sorted, then we can talk." He obviously didn't know Rossetti well enough to know that his brain still required ongoing surgery. Downing his glass, Rossetti placed it on the table. Slowly, he fixed the stranger's attention through half-closed eyes, pausing before speaking.

"Why me?!" 'Ungrateful bastard' wouldn't have been out of place, considering the circumstances. Leaning back in his seat, the stranger smiled in an engaging manner. Raising his arms to emphasise his point, he replied, "Why not you?!" and threw the question back at him. Touché it seems, and Rossetti to serve.

*Smart arse, but cool with it,* he concluded inwardly.

"I'll tell yer why not! It's just that I've got this thing about faces, and yours keeps telling me something. Assuming I'm right, that bit of grief with the Old Bill earlier on could have been a bit nasty. Know what I mean? Good job I happened to be on yer case. Saying that, I've got half an idea I know you from way back."

Rossetti didn't appear to be swayed by his omission, and instead decided to be evasive. "Know me?! I doubt it, unless of course yer owe me money." His reply stank of sarcasm, and fell way short of gaining any ground.

Seemingly unperturbed, the stranger continued in the same vein.

"Maybe that's the reason why I'm asking."

"Save yer breath, you've got me mixed up with some other face."

"Probably. Look, relax, I ain't the Old Bill. Like I said, it's all about faces with me. By the way, the name's Donk, Frankie Donk, that is," and he proffered an outstretched hand. Rossetti declined his offer with a wave, and replied, "What sort of a name is that, for fuck's sake!" Still the stranger appeared unmoved by Rossetti's aloofness.

"Name? Oh, it's Dutch as it happens, but people who know me in the business call me Frankie 'the Rinse'." For a brief second, a flicker of recognition crossed Rossetti's face, and just as swiftly died a death.

"Yeah right, and I'm Thomas the fucking Tank Engine. So what d'ye do for a living?"

"At the moment ducking and diving. Basically, I used to work in the laundry business."

"What, shirts and stuff?"

"No!" He smiled in a cryptic manner. "No, on the contrary, I used to launder money as an occupation. Hence the monika."

"You said used to?"

"So I did!"

"What happened, the well dry up?"

"That, and a few clients dying on me."

"No shit, anyone I know?" he asked brusquely.

"Wouldn't have thought so, although at the time Docklands was a no go zone."

"Almost immediately, Rossetti felt intrigued by the reference to Docklands, in turn, placing their conversation on a different slant. *Maybe the geezer's kosher after all*, he told himself, and decided to delve.

"Gimme a name?" he fired. The stranger took his time answering and practically spelt it out.

"The Butcher!"

"I don't know any bleedin' butchers!"

"Okay, so let's try Tito 'the Butcher' Santini! Mean anything to yer?" Instantly, Rossetti took a sharp intake of breath in a lousy attempt to cover up the obvious.

"Shit! That name's a blast from the past, and yeah, I knew him alright, or at least I did before he got himself mullered."

"Now that's interesting… go on." It would appear that the two had now got something in common, at last.

"As I was saying, Tito and me, we traded together just after he split from Terry Winters' firm. You probably know, Tito made his wedge by running the Latin Quarter rackets."

"Absolutely, small world. Right, all I gotta do now is to try and figure you out. I get the distinct impression you've been away on a government 'holiday'."

"That noticeable, eh? But no! I'm too bleedin' fly for that, mate. Although I'm looking at a twelve stretch if the Old Bill had their way. But in one sense yer right, I have been away. I was forced to leg it off the manor and finished up in the Smoke." The Rinse nodded and intervened before Rossetti could finish.

"That would be five or six years ago, I believe?"

"Yeah, that's when the rackets went down the karzy, when Tito and myself were giving it large on the scene. I used to run around with Ricky Peters and the Traveller. Anyway, cut a long story short, when that hitman Buffy Manilla mullered Tito, I had grief of my own to sort out."

"Namely, Terry Winters, if my hunch is right?" the Rinse concluded. Before continuing, Rossetti checked himself. It had just occurred to him that he'd been mouthing off on an ego confession. The Rinse could have written a book on his 'previous'. *Oh what the hell!* he told himself. *I've come this far.* Deliberating wasn't an option as once again he took up the story.

"You got him in one! That bastard had it coming to him, I done him up like a kipper! After I finished with him, the only thing left was six teeth, and two of them were gold!" The Rinse laughed outwardly in response to his latest revelation.

"You'd have to say he caught a right bloody cold then, didn't he? Not much of an investment was it? But then he ain't looking for a pension now is he?" Again he laughed solidly, before continuing, "So what brings you back on to the manor then? Business or pleasure?"

"That's the easy one, mate, a fucking headache by the name of Callaghan, and a bent copper. The pleasure," he added, "will come later!"

"Uhm, Callaghan, the name rings a bell. Doesn't he run a gym in town?"

"You got him in one, sunshine." The Rinse nodded assuredly before responding.

"Now it all makes sense! You gotta be Paul Rossetti? No disrespect, mate, but yer boat had me going for a while. Tell yer what, I'll grab a bottle and we can have a session, talk about the old times, know what I mean?" Rossetti had come a long way since departing the AA that evening. There was no way he could have envisaged the present outcome as it stood. Thirty minutes ago he was a prime candidate for a pauper grave. Now here he was, spilling his guts to a complete stranger… or not?

*This is the bollocks*, he told himself. *Might even do myself a bit of good 'ere.* He hadn't felt this good in years. A sniff of mutual respect hung in the air as a vision of a ladder appeared. This time around, he noticed that he'd managed to gain a foothold. More than ever, he felt determined that nobody, or anything for that matter, would topple him as before. This, according to him, was his time! The desire to succeed had somehow never looked sweeter as his degenerate mind became addled with vengeance.

"Right! Where we were?" Momentarily, the Rinse broke his chain of reasoning by placing fresh glasses and a bottle of Scotch down on the table.

"Don't fuck about, mate, do yer?" Rossetti came straight to the point and proceeded to fill their glasses.

"So who shall we drink to then?" The Rinse raised his glass to get a reaction. Rossetti appeared unmoved; even his face remained blank and emotionless. Etiquette, or so he imagined, was the name of a racehorse! Or given a second chance, it could have stretched to the next drink maybe? In the event, the Rinse put it all in perspective.

"You ain't got no class, Rossi. If I can call yer that? So I'll say it for yer: here's to crime, long may it reign." His effort overall remained futile; Rossetti had already downed his Scotch and was in the process of pouring another. When he finished, he calmly replaced the bottle on the table. Glancing up, he gazed directly at the Rinse; at the same time a quizzical look came across his face. Raising his glass reverently, he said, "To absent friends!"

"Say what?"

"Like I said, absent bleedin' friends."

"Blimey, Rossi, you picked that one out the hat. Take back what I said previously. By the way, anyone in particular?" The reply, when it came, was vehement and to the point.

"That asshole Terry Winters fits the frame, he's more than fucking absent!"

"Amen to that!" the Rinse concurred. "You don't know it, but you did me a right favour in taking him out. The bastard took me for a nice few quid when I was laundering."

"No kidding, what's the SP?"

"Well, I'd arranged to pick up this particular wedge one night. In all, it came to about £80,000 in used notes as I recall. He'd asked me to 'lose' it for him as a favour. I'd done a few deals with the guy previously, so I thought, why not? Why should this one be any different? Anyway, my end was sorted. I had a syndicate on call ready and waiting, the usual bollocks. Within minutes of handing the wedge over, I'd paid the man his balance on the deal, up front. He was in a fucking good mood that night. The guy kept laughing to himself and I couldn't figure out why. Twenty-four hours and a contract later, I found myself forced to go underground."

"The lousy bastard! What an asshole, doing yer own up. Blimey, he really tucked you up."

"You ain't kidding! I bet he was still laughing when the syndicate screened the wedge. Every other note turned out to be counterfeit!"

"There yer go, win some, lose some! It's all about getting by… survival. I often wonder what Ricky Peters is up to. Guarantee it's all quality with him."

"Bleedin' good money getter, the guy. The best in the business," the Rinse chuckled.

"So would I if I had a gorilla for a pet!"

"Yer obviously talking about the Traveller, right?"

"Absolutely! Incidentally, how did yer get on with Ricky?"

"Sweet as a nut, apart from money, that is."

"But you said…"

"… Yeah, I know what I said, thing is, the guy is granite hard when it comes to divvy-up time. He's so tight, he only breathes in!"

"I've got a contact number for him somewhere. I need to dig it out, could lead to something interesting. By the way, where yer putting yer feet up these days?"

"Over at the AA at Docklands basin, I got a room I rent. D'ye know it?"

"I should do! It was the bollocks when it was called the Rat and Trap. I did more deals in there than a croupier on a good night."

"Yeah, but that was a six stretch ago, what are yer up to nah. Yer can't look back."

"You got that right. I'm kicking a few ideas about at the moment. But yeah, yer right, no point in looking back."

"You never did say?"

"What, exactly?"

"China Town… business?"

"Possibly."

"Can't believe you bailed me out tonight, the Old Bill would be well pissed off if they knew the strength."

"Well, they ain't ever gonna know, are they? So I guess that makes you and me even, Rossi, everything considered." Once again the bottle was offered, if only for distraction.

"Nah, keep going, large for me, mate." The Rinse, at this stage, was adamantly clear in his choice, and totally addicted to the proposition he was about to lay on Rossetti. His persona automatically reverted into 'business' mode. Short, sharp and direct. "How would yer like to earn yerself £5,000? For a few hours' work! Cash of course." Rossetti's breath was now having to play catch-up with his lungs as the offer hit him between the eyes. Finally, he pulled himself together.

"Christ almighty, Rinse, that's serious dough."

"To you maybe, but then you don't strike me as being exactly minted. Know what I mean?"

"So yer caught me on a bad day. It ain't always gonna be like this, I promise yer. Get meself sorted and I'll be moving up." Booze was one thing, attitude another! Drunk or sober, the Rinse embraced attitude. His burden, albeit a request, appeared heavy and he needed to offload.

"How d'ye feel about blowing somebody away, Rossi?" Simple enough question to an online hitman. Okay, the wedge would be negotiable, as was Rossetti's state of mind. At this point, no response appeared to be forthcoming. Momentarily, he found himself caught up in a personality crisis, whilst waiting for his brain to engage. "I said I ain't always…!" The message finally got through as the impact of the statement honed in on his fuddled brain. "Are you for fucking real, mate? I mean, is that an opinion? Or an offer?!" The severity of the agenda reflected in the tone of his voice as the Rinse replied, "I can assure you, Rossi, my offer is gilt edged. As for yer fucking opinion, I don't need it. Yer track record tells me all I need to know. If there's a problem, I'm…" Rossetti cut him short.

"Hold up, pal, things are getting a bit heavy, moving too fast. No! Course it ain't a problem, we just need to talk about it a bit more." Reaching inside his jacket pocket, the Rinse gestured with his free hand.

"Relax, Rossi, just testing the water. Here, take my calling card, you can reach me 24/7 if need be. In the meantime, here's a nifty, yer look as if a bleedin' good meal wouldn't go amiss. Enjoy the rest of the bottle, and when yer sober give us a call. Oh, one other thing, keep yer nose clean. Be lucky." Rising from his seat, he turned on his heel and exited the door and out into the real world before Rossetti could pursue any further line of enquiry. For a brief moment, a sudden feeling of isolation reached out and grabbed him. Clutching hold of the calling card as a means of stability ran second to juggling with a red-hot poker. The card could be his passport to success and salvation. Shuddering, he could almost feel it falling from his sweaty palms and through his fingers. A wave of panic swept over him like a tsunami, causing him to verbally hallucinate. *God! Can't lose it… mustn't lose it… shit! It's crumpled.* Fortunately for him, his brain, insignificant as it was, kicked his ranting into touch when firing back.

"What is your fucking problem, Rossi?!" No brownie points for the Scotch then? Inwardly, the same voice was a sympathetic saviour helping him back to a form of normality. Well, at least in his world. Attempting to extract the card from his hand felt more like diffusing a time bomb. Laying it on the table, he began to iron it using the flat end of his glass. Had he blown it again? At least he had the price of a decent meal… maybe. *Where the hell did I put that bleedin' nifty?* Thankfully, his subconscious, as usual, was on hand long enough for him to get his head into gear. Gingerly, he placed the card into his top pocket, swiftly followed by the £50 note which happened to be glaring back at him from the table.

Draining the remnants of his glass, he staggered to the bar and ordered a cab. Fifteen minutes later found him back in his room at the AA. He wouldn't have remembered dropping off, or getting undressed come to think of it. So there you have it! Another day in the life of plastic gangster, one Paul Rossetti. Given the option, the vast majority of would-be felons would have willingly settled for the sanctity of three mother-in-laws in lieu!

CHAPTER 7

# TO CALL OR NOT TO CALL

"Double up on those jabs, Danny. Remember, points make winners!" Standing on the ring apron, Ronnie was heavily engrossed in percentages allied to young Danny Simmons' training programme. Any other day, the task would have fallen to yours truly to have physically pushed Simmons around. Unfortunately, a wrist injury sustained at the market had curtailed his input to one of verbal activity. As part of the stable, it fell on the heavy shoulders of Dave Molloy to wear the mantle for the time being. It was now nearing the end of week one, given up to an intensive fitness and method regime prior to Simmons' eagerly awaited debut and into the paid ranks. For his part, Ronnie had no qualms as to the kid's outcome. The knowledge he'd accrued stemmed from a lifetime's experience on both sides of the ropes.

Getting the balance right in preparation was paramount. The well-worn adage 'Shame he left it all behind in the gym' was deemed a recipe for disaster. The secret lay in the knowledge that your 'boy' had reached that ultimate peak as opposed to a premature conclusion. Then, and only then, would it be the given moment to savour the blood, sweat and tears invested in readiness for the big night. Nobody could be more relieved at Ronnie's decision than Dave Molloy. Simmons' last two rounds of the session had proved to be a role reversal as he relentlessly drove his mentor backward. Combinations honed in from every angle, and when the situation arose his choice of counter punching left a lot to be desired.

The admiration for Simmons' skill clearly showed in Ronnie's outlook. Satisfaction was etched into his rugged face. Right now, his interest focused on what remained of the final round. "Last ten… step it up, Danny… hang in there… good man." For a man reputed to be short of temper, he didn't hold back when giving out praise. "You excelled yerself tonight, son, yer beginning to think like a pro, which is a big step forward. Not only that, I've noticed yer getting selective in yer body shots as well. Keep thinking upstairs and downstairs, and work to make that opening. Remember, Danny, behind every good fighter there lies a mature brain, that's how champions are made! Oh, and one other thing. Dave was in there pushing you around tonight for your benefit, the difference being that he doesn't hit back! So when yer back pedalling from a guy who's gonna take yer frigging head off, think 'brain' and remind yerself, 'How the hell can I turn this around?' Because, three bloody minutes seems like a ruddy lifetime when yer getting hurt, okay? Right, yer better get on with yer groundwork, then grab a shower. Incidentally, I'll say it again, I'm more than impressed the way yer shaping up."

"Thanks, boss, I won't let you down on the night," Simmons replied.

"Don't do it for me, Danny, do it for yerself, you're the one taking the leather, not me." Towelling him down, Molloy echoed Ronnie's previous observations.

"Listen, and take in everything he tells yer, kid. For what it's worth, he straightened me out when I needed it, and yeah, like Ronnie said, you were useful in there tonight." Simmons accepted the compliment with the respect that went with it, and ploughed his remaining energies into his groundwork. A few minutes later, Big Tommy Russell appeared through the door to the gym. Cursing under his breath, he acknowledged Russell's intentions and made his way over to the office.

"Grab a seat, Ronnie, and you can talk me through it." His eagerness for information was plainly evident. *The man's not his usual bubbly self*, Ronnie mused. On this occasion, a hint of expectancy hung in the air as he made himself comfortable. Continuing where he'd left off, Russell opened up.

"I'll be frank with yer, mate, I've had a shit day!" Ronnie wasn't impressed. His watch was saying 11.15 and he had a home to go to. Diplomatic as ever, he decided to humour him.

"Nice to know yer only human after all, Tommy. Don't tell me, let me guess, you've done yer bollocks at Kempton Park and the rent on the gym is due?!" Any reaction went clean over his head.

"Right now, I'd settle for half of that as it goes, mate. I'm just living in hope that Simmons is producing."

"Yeah, well stand on me, that's one bet you can put yer bleedin' house on. Yer can't lose, the kid's gonna be a sound investment. At this moment in time, you have to say that his progress is at the top end of good, and that's in every department."

"Thanks, mate, I feel a whole lot better knowing that and I appreciate yer input."

"Before I forget..."

"Yeah?"

"Any news regarding Simmons' opponent yet?" Typically, Ronnie was in front of the game by pushing for answers. Russell was adamant when replying.

"I thought we'd both agreed to hold back on that part of the deal?"

"Yeah, we did at the time, but at least a name opens up options." Sensing his impatience, Russell felt obliged to appease him.

"If it makes yer feel any better, I'll contact Charlie Cochrane and get back to yer with the SP, okay?"

"Suits me, Tommy, I don't do phones, I'm all allergic to mobiles."

"In other words, I do my job and you do yours?" Russell caved in and ceded to his logic without question. He knew Ronnie better than he knew himself at times. His passion for results was beyond reproach. "Oh blimey, I nearly forgot. I'm off the manor for a few days, but I will still contact you in the event!" With everything taken into consideration, the session, as a whole, showed signs of positiveness. On a more personal level, Ronnie could argue that Simmons had exceeded the levels of progression expected of him. Turning the key in the door, he once again paused for reflection. His face could have told a story. "If only they could all have been like that," he murmured in a dreamy fashion.

The horn resounding from a nearby stationary taxi briefly interrupted his chain of thought. "Yeah, yeah, I'm just coming, mate," he called out. The passenger door was already open, and he eased himself in next to the driver.

"Yer a lot later than normal, Ronnie," the driver observed. "I'd have a fiver, Tommy Russell had something to do with it! I passed him down the road," Ronnie chuckled.

"You don't miss a trick, do yer? But yeah, yer right on both counts. Basically, if yer looking for a result, then you've got to put the time in, know what I mean?"

Ten minutes later after paying the cabbie off, Ronnie entered his flat. Purely out of habit, he decided to check his landline for any calls monitored in his absence, and proceeded to dial 1571. Frowning heavily, he slowly replaced the receiver. "Strange," he muttered. "Wonder who the hell that could have been?" The call in question had been logged at 21.00, and whoever was responsible had declined to leave their name or number. His dilemma still played on his mind as he sipped a coffee following a long-awaited shower. *Don't get it!* became foremost in his thoughts. *Whoever it was obviously doesn't know me, but has still managed to get my number even though I'm ex-directory.* To anybody else, a trivial matter and part of life. Ronnie, nevertheless, had other ideas. His cocooned way of life had been threatened, and he now found himself short on answers.

What transpired during the next thirty-six hours resulted in an all-or-nothing scenario in which two missed calls and a long overdue positive connection took over Ronnie's life. The original call was still fresh on his mind when the phone sprang into life some twenty-four hours later. As yet, Tommy Russell hadn't decided to make contact regarding certain information via Charlie Cochrane. The mocking dialling tone added an air of expectancy as he snatched at the receiver in anticipation. "Tommy? That you, mate?" A day in waiting finally watered down to a few seconds of longing for a response that was never going to happen, followed by a further stunned silence as the line died a death a few seconds later.

Ronnie's face distorted into a mask of anger as he replaced the receiver. Utter frustration consumed his body as he slumped back into the nearest chair. Speaking through gritted teeth he vented his feelings out loud. "Ex-directory? And I'm getting this shit! Somebody is gonna pay," adding, "that is a guarantee!" It would take some time before his statement could be realised. In the meantime, it was a further eight hours before he finally got a reprieve from his dislodged state of mind. From the moment he picked up the receiver, his attitude remained guarded.

"Ronnie?"

"Who the fuck is this?!" For someone who had waited some sixteen hours for an all-important call, his response left a lot to be desired as Tommy Russell unwillingly took the brunt of his ongoing mood.

"Blimey, mate! You had a break-in or something? Thought I'd got the wrong number for a minute."

"Ah sorry, guess I need to chill out a bit. Be honest with yer, I wasn't sure whether it was you on the end or not."

"Oh, I thought I made it quite clear I'd get back to yer?"

"Yeah yer did, fair play to yer. Put it down to a spot of grief I've had to put up with recently."

"Anything I can do to help? I try to avoid grief whenever I can."

"No not really, Tommy, personal shit, but I'll sort it. Right now I'm more interested to hear what you've got to say."

"Businesswise, I'd like to think we've got a right result. I didn't contact you before, mainly because Charlie needed a medical report on Simmons' opponent. These things take time; you know how it is."

"Sure, tell me about it! At least the SP sounds positive." Any unwanted grief on Ronnie's part was shelved as Charlie sought to put him at ease.

"I managed to pin Charlie down to a venue. Southend Leisure Centre is definitely on the cards, and the opposition is also sorted."

"Getting better all the time, mate. Simmons' opponent, any track record as such?"

"Yeah, two outings to date, won one, lost one, so I figure it's an even deal on the night for Simmons."

"Fine, I can live with that. So, providing we're talking weights, we've got ourselves a fight."

"Gilt edged! As I say, Charlie's on the case so it's all on the night." Russell could have sworn he'd heard a sigh of relief on the other end of the line. At least something constructive had emerged from their conversation. They continued talking shop for another five minutes or so, and he concluded by arranging a further meet the following week for an update on Simmons' progress. The remainder of his evening saw Ronnie in a more settled frame of mind. Russell's belated intervention had given his precarious outlook an injection of belief once more.

Right now, an early night appeared to be the best bet, as the thought of a Monday market and an early rise hovered in the background.

Siddie Levy was under no illusions either; Monday mornings didn't exactly set him alight. Up to now, this particular day was no exception, except to say he'd inherited the brunt of Ronnie's mood swings for the last couple of working hours. His genuine concern for Ronnie finally came to a head. "What is it with you? I don't need this crap already. What's occurring that I should know about?" Backed up into a corner, Ronnie struggled to find the right words. Glancing across at Siddie, he paused before replying, "That obvious, eh?"

"You look seriously pissed off, which makes me pissed off. We need to talk, you got a better idea?" Ronnie checked his watch; a verbal showdown in public was the last thing on his mind.

"Tell yer what, grab a minder and I'll see yer over at Toni's in ten minutes. You get the coffees in and we'll have a waffle." Siddie readily agreed and nodded. Never a gambler, he jumped at the chance. A couple of quid, he considered, would be a good investment if it meant exposing Ronnie's singular attitude. Not only that, business was getting iffy; now seemed to be the right moment. Removing his money pouch, he cast his eye toward a nearby trader, Mick 'the Stitch', a rag trade stallholder. Beckoning him over, Siddie explained his intentions.

"Thanks, Mickey, I owe yer one." He then waved his hand across his fruit and veg setup. "If in doubt, the asparagus is kosher pricewise. Anything else you can do a deal on. I'll be about half an hour, mate." Handing his pouch over, he headed off toward the café with an open mind and a glut of stock that needed shifting. He was well into his coffee by the time Ronnie turned up. So where do we begin?" Siddie enquired hesitantly as Ronnie made himself comfortable.

"One I can live with, two's a fucking joke, know what I mean?" Siddie felt thrown in at the deep end and questioned his irrational outburst.

"Hang on already! You've lost me completely. Are yer saying you've got woman problems?"

"If only!"

"What then?"

"Poxy phone!"

"Meaning?"

"You tell me! Two missed calls one after the other, that can't be bleedin' right."

"Yeah, now I see yer problem, glad we got that one sorted. Strange, yer not listed either, are yer?"

"Exactly! Some asshole has got access to my number, and I need to know why." His voice became more and more heated.

"Calm down, mate, there has to be a rational explanation to all of this. Maybe someone is trying to sell yer something, it does happen."

"Yeah, if that's the case, then why ain't they talking to me then?" Siddie searched for a reply that didn't exist. On the one hand, Ronnie could be a drama queen at times. Nevertheless, a ring of uncertainty remained, which implied certain aspects needed consideration. For the moment he thought keeping an open mind on the matter seemed to fit the bill.

"I really don't know what to say, mate. It all depends on how far you want to run with it. If so, it could entail outside involvement. Know what I mean?"

"What?!" Yer don't mean Old Bill, surely?"

"Well, no, I wouldn't go that strong. Look, let it ride for the time being. If it happens again, then yeah, something needs to be done about it." Deep down, Ronnie wasn't happy one way or the other. His impatience for a conclusion had been blinded by common sense. Finally, he bowed to Siddie's integrity and agreed to disagree. As they headed back toward their respective stalls, it quickly became apparent that the look on Siddie's face screamed apprehension. Any medals he might have won on the day were now skating on thin ice.

Of the two, it was Ronnie who managed to grab a decent sleep later that night, but then he didn't have the grief of owning a stall half full of unsold fruit and veg and a tempestuous wife called Rachael to contend with.

## CHAPTER 8

# MURDER IN MIND

Question! How many times and how loud should you have to knock on a door to gain the occupants' attention? In Paul Rossetti's case, the hard-done-by barman at the AA needed the patience of a fifty-year-old virgin, it seems, when attempting to arouse him in the interest of a belated breakfast. Protocol finally gave way to shouting. "Rossi! You bloody awake?" Stupid question anyway and still no response. "Phone message for yer!" But then, twelve o'clock on a Saturday morning, who was he kidding? Rossetti had only been asleep for a few hours. Since his spontaneous arrival in Stonewater, he'd decided to place a preservation order on his wellbeing. Any so-called socialising had been restricted to closed doors and semi-darkness.

On the flip side, the recent episode linking him to Sergeant Dawson had been a windfall he wasn't about to ignore. The fact that he himself was a wanted face on the manor only intensified his twilight form of life. Slowly, he'd managed to infiltrate the haunts that were exclusive to the breed they imbibed. All options laid bare, the road he had chosen proved to be undoubtedly rocky. Thus far, it had become a never-ending fight for survival. Suffice to say, the scene had developed into a now familiar, but necessary, enhancement to his world of sleaze.

In real terms of contact, faces from his distant past were

getting used to the idea of having him around. That in itself opened up the floodgates of benefit. The notion of 'Here today, gone tomorrow' could now be whittled down to minutes should a certain situation arise. On the strength of a phone call, a safe house could become a reality. Thus far, the AA had served its purpose, although he was well aware that a careless whisper, or worse still, a 'falling out', could well terminate his illicit freedom. In spite of his track record, Rossetti was nobody's fool when a choice came down to the wire. On a personal level, he had nothing to lose and everything to gain in terms of vengeance.

With all options barred, his precarious future now lay in the hands of Dawson and Callaghan if, and when, circumstances surrounding the two became relevant to his wellbeing.

For his part, Dawson was clearly in the frame for an early 'retirement', with or without a pension. Callaghan's demise, on the other hand, needed extreme planning until the timing was perfect. Hell! There was no rush, he'd waited a lifetime, and having bungled the first attempt, there was no way he could afford to fail again. A grave mistake would be tantamount to a death wish. On reflection, his presence in Stonewater, given the facts, was slowly turning in his favour. A steady income via the bookies and playing pool allowed him to keep his head above water. For the immediate future, any plans were placed on ice.

His biggest asset, if and when it ever materialised, would be a shooter. It had now been a couple of weeks since his meet with Maltese Pete. Any contact since had ground to a halt. Acting on advice, plus the SP he already had on the guy, he decided to abort the idea of contacting him regarding the deal they had struck. If he ever needed a reminder, an acquaintance who marked his card was about as delicate as a chocolate fire grate when foisting his opinion. "There's two reasons why yer need to keep off his back! The first, yer get for nothing, he calls it a public warning! Should you default on a payment on the second without an instalment plan, yer wind up with a shattered kneecap! So like I say, give the geezer a swerve, and if there happens to be any folding outstanding, don't make any arrangements for the next day, unless yer like grapes and visitors!"

He'd heard it all before, but under the circumstances that avenue of thought became a no-no. On the plus side, his personal rankings amongst his own had left him feeling self-confident. Or, as one observer put it, "I knew Rossetti when he was an all-time miserable bastard! Now, he's an arrogant miserable bastard!" But at least he was being noticed by the sleaze he latched on to. None more so than Frank 'the Rinse', who'd spent the morning trying to make a connection with him regarding a lucrative deal on offer. Seeing, they say, is believing. But on the odd occasion it all comes down to the subject matter being credible. In this particular case it took a double take from the bemused barman as Rossetti ventured into the bar, otherwise known as his bolt hole.

His trademark limp, although obvious, was different to his usual sub-normal gait. His outgoing persona caused the barman's jaw to drop, squinting, as he did, to justify his uncertainty. *No! Surely not, he must be on crack*. His 'dilemma' crossed the floor and approached the bar. No! The barman hadn't got it wrong. For a self-ordained cripple, nee manic killer, he now carried an uncharacteristic spring in his self-induced deformity.

"Uhm, I see yer finally decided to surface at last then, Rossi? What will it be, the usual?" With punters thin on the ground, the barman elected for conversation to kill time. Waving his hand, Rossetti hesitated before replying.

"Scrub the Scotch and give us a beer, will yer."

"A beer?!"

"You heard the first bleedin' time. You fucking deaf or what?!" he retorted. His remark came across as a challenge rather than a statement. An air of expectancy seemed to engulf his twisted body as he continued: "Oy, yer can forget the bloody pump, I ain't interested, just give us a bottle." The somewhat confused barman duly obliged, and continued a further line of enquiry, leaving Rossetti to swig his first drink of the day.

"So what's occurring, Rossi? Yer looking a lot sharper than usual. If I didn't know any better, I'd have to say yer numbers came good." It turned out a bad move on his part; attempting to patronise Rossetti was a big mistake. On reflection, he would have achieved a whole lot more by teaching fish how to swim. Momentarily, Rossetti toyed with his beer bottle which was now half empty, glaring, as he did, at the barman who by now began to feel ill at ease. Rossetti's cold eyes drilled into the barman's face as the last of his beer slipped down his throat. Slamming the empty bottle down onto the bar top, his icy stare never faltered, finally allowing his mouth to crease into a sneer, climaxing in a verbal outburst.

"Know something?! Yer wanna know something? I'll fucking tell yer, shall I? Yer right on three counts! One, I'm sharp because I'm on the case. Two, you don't bleedin' know me. And yeah, the only numbers I'm interested in are poxy phone numbers, got it?!" The barman's blood ran cold; by mouthing off, he'd inadvertently locked himself into a situation of his own making. This was a side of Rossetti he couldn't relate to; the man was in his face, full stop. His mind raced as he struggled to find a cop out. Thoughts came thick and fast, then it hit him…

*Shit! I knew there was something*, he swiftly reminded himself. *Numbers! Phone! Message!* It all fell into place as a welcome sense of relief honed in. The information to which he'd previously been privy had been sidetracked by Rossetti's blast of egotism. "Christ, yeah, the telephone!" he exploded.

"Phone? You holding something back on me?"

"It's just dawned on me."

"It had better be bleedin' good."

"There was a message, somebody phoned this morning asking to speak to yer. I wasn't 'ere myself, I didn't start my shift until later. I don't..."

Rossetti cut him short before he could finish; he'd heard enough. An upsurge of blood caused his pulse to race in sympathy in the knowledge that a breakthrough could be on the cards. Momentarily, he found himself on the rack, and wanting. God only knows he was desperate for a connection of sorts linked to the real world, albeit fantasy. Belief in his self-ordained lust for revenge had recently emerged from under a stone of fanaticism. The ladder of improbability that was had now become a distinct reality when fuelled by a drink or two. His cold eyes suddenly switched to the house phone resting on the bar top. Like a magnet, it began to draw him in body and soul. Momentarily, the sudden fixation caused by the phone, allowed deep-seated scenarios to emerge, in doing so, causing him to shudder slightly.

Pulling himself together, he quickly turned his attention back to the subdued barman.

"A number! Did they leave a bloody number?!"

"Like I said, I came in at the wrong end, sorry I can't help yer. If it's that important they will get back to yer." Frustration led to a feeling of isolation as Rossetti concurred with the barman's reply. Ordering another bottle, he decided to stay put and see the rest of the evening session through. Living in hope, that the money he'd lashed out on booze might just turn to out be fruitful.

In spite of the half dozen or so bottles he managed to throw down his throat to counter his impatience, he struggled to shake off his negative mood. Glancing at his watch, he noted it was fast approaching eleven o'clock. Any other night, at this time he would have been contemplating the services of a downtown club. *I'll give it ten minutes*, he thought, *then I'm out of 'ere.* Space was beginning to be a priority as the punters lined the walls and ceiling. The booze-filled atmosphere complemented their rowdy banter as the climax to a night's drinking prevailed. Glancing around the bar, Rossetti downed his remaining drink. *Noisy bastards!* he concluded, and made as if to leave.

"Rossi! Yer wanted." Above the hubbub and heaving bodies, he thought he heard echoes of his name. His body stiffened and his lips pursed in a search for recognition.

*Nah, can't be*, he convinced himself. *That does it for me, fuck the pub, I'm off.* His hasty decision was short lived as a hand descended onto his shoulder, forcing him into a no-win situation. He spun round, eyes blazing in anticipation of an altercation. Confronting him was the regular barman, his hands held high in mock defence.

"Take it easy, Rossi, yer too jumpy. I thought you'd gone. I've been trying to get hold of yer." Rossetti didn't appear to be convinced and resorted to a verbal attack. The barman held his ground and replied, "I ain't here for your benefit, Rossi, so get out of my bloody face. If yer interested enough, I came to tell yer, there's a guy on the phone who insists on talking to yer!"

"Yer having a laugh, ain't yer?" and gestured at his ears to make his point. The barman wasn't impressed; he needed to be elsewhere and it showed.

"You're seriously pissing me off now, Rossi, d'ye know that? Tell yer what, there's an extension in the hallway, you can take it on that, and while yer at it, get a bleedin' life!" Rossetti found himself forced to back down. Growling in response, he forced his way through drunken bodies in pursuit of the exit and whatever lay beyond. His brain began to fire up as he lunged at the receiver. "Yeah! Rossi speaking, what's occurring?" he shouted. In contrast, the caller came across as cool and collected in response to Rossetti's tone.

"You took yer time getting 'ere, think yerself bloody lucky I'm still holding. And if you had asked, it's Frankie 'the Rinse' speaking!" Etiquette, it seems, prevails at all levels of society, excluding, of course, the likes of Rossetti whose only claim to a level of sorts started and finished with a humpback bridge. The onus was now on him to appease the Rinse.

"I should have known it was you, Frankie," he gushed. "What can I do for yer?" A pregnant pause ensued before he replied, "I got a situation I need to deal with on a personal level."

"Are we talking Muscle involvement?" ventured Rossetti.

"No! No, it's gone beyond that! This particular bit of grief is heavy." The emphasis on 'heavy' gave a whole new meaning to their conversation. Rossetti's interest now ran a close second to three lines of coke as the Rinse spelt out the situation in no uncertain terms.

"Putting it mildly, myself and a few other faces have inherited a bucketful of unwanted fucking grief! It appears that we've got a public nuisance running loose on the manor." Rossetti could feel himself elevated to a borrowed high. The verbal that spewed out was music to his ears, giving vent to his own singular insidious desire to rid the world of Dawson and Callaghan. Pumped up and full of assumption he replied, "You obviously want me in on the firm, Frankie." His egotistical manner didn't cut any ice with the Rinse, who quickly dispelled any forthcoming notion he held.

"Yer too pushy, Rossi, in fact, you don't even rate a

consideration as things stand, although I won't fuck with yer when I say this is the big one! Meaning it will entail untold planning and the time to carry it out. Having said that, we need to arrange a further meet, that way I'm prepared to give you the full SP. By the way, don't try to contact me, you understand? We haven't had this conversation, so I expect you to keep schtum on this one, got it? I'll get back to yer within the next couple of days. In the meantime, keep yer nose clean and chill out."

Rossetti wasn't afforded any more air space to reply as the line suddenly went dead. Slowly, he replaced the receiver. Gritting his teeth, he inhaled deeply in an effort to regain his composure, which by now had become somewhat disjointed on the strength of their radical conversation. What he couldn't possibly have known was that the last three minutes would ultimately change his life in the days to come. The cards of fate had been dealt once more. For his role, aces figured prominently in his favour. How and when he decided to call them into play rested in a collusion of other players, also feted by destiny and participation. All drawn to his precarious future by an infinite calling, but not necessarily by design.

There was no disguising his born-again attitude as he made his way back to the bar. For a psychopathic killer, he'd now been plucked out of obscurity in the space of a few minutes. Lady Luck could take the rest of the night off as far as he was concerned. The fact that he'd been approached at all spoke volumes.

In his twisted imagination, his less-than-secure future now boded well. The exposure he craved could well pay dividends when respect became an issue. This, in turn, ran hand in hand with money. The worst way, he'd be out and about, a face to be reckoned with, when associating with his own kind. Given the facts, even Rossetti himself would have succumbed to the truth if challenged. The Rinse had thrown him a lifeline of opportunity; the onus would now be on him to deliver. As from now he would find himself walking a tightrope, laced with apprehension until the Rinse made contact again. In the meantime, Dawson would figure highly as an alternative when compiling a game plan to bring about his pre-determined demise. With so much to dwell on, any previous instigated plans with Ronnie Callaghan in mind, were set aside for the foreseeable future.

## CHAPTER 9

# YOUR DEAL!

An invasion into the mind of Rossetti would probably reveal the following update: "It's just that I know where I'm going, I'm the man!" In retrospect, you could almost forgive his blinding arrogance, but then he would continue, "And at the moment, so can you, Callaghan, but then I can change my mind to suit. That poor bastard won't have that luxury in time because I'll be acting for him and my mouthpiece will be a fucking shooter doing all the talking!" So endeth the first lesson, or the Gospel of Vengeance according to Rossetti. For somebody as homicidal as he could be, his imagination appeared to be bigger than his mouth.

Time had been called as he entered the bar, although the afters would shortly follow for a selective few –whoever's face and wedge fitted. Rossetti elected to join them, not for their verbal diarrhoea, but merely as an observer. As from now, he was under orders and a self-employed recluse until the Rinse decided to resurrect him from semi-retirement. Less than forty-eight hours later found him steeped in the throes of apprehension. Even before the barman had opened his mouth to speak, Rossetti firmly believed that at last something was going down. The bar, businesswise, had taken more money in crisp sales than booze, so he couldn't fail to hear the phone bleating when seated at the bar the following morning.

"That'll be for me, Billy, I can guarantee it." The barman

proffered a wry smile before replying, "Blimey, Rossi, bloody Mystic Meg ain't got nothing on you! As it happens, somebody is asking for yer," and added, "Must be nice to be wanted."

"Huh!" he fired back. "That's something you won't have to worry yer bleedin' head about, just give me the poxy phone." Inwardly, the true meaning of the term 'wanted' stuck in his craw. Cursing the barman, he made himself known to the caller. "Yeah! Rossi speaking, can…" He wasn't given the chance to continue as the caller interrupted.

"That's all I need to know. We've never met, so I'll be brief. I represent the Rinse concerning a meet. Now listen very carefully. Once I've hung up you leave the AA and make yer way to the bottom end of Martin Street, opposite the basin sidings. A car will be picking you up shortly. Move, I'm hanging up now!" For a few seconds, Rossetti could only stand there dumb struck as he wrestled with the speed of the information he'd received. Zombie-like, he replaced the receiver. As if in a trance, he made his way through the bar. The barman picked up on his movements as he neared the exit door.

"Rossi! You've still got a drink left in yer glass," he shouted. He should have saved his breath as the door closed behind him. Five minutes later, Rossetti nervously awaited the arrival of an unmarked car as directed. He didn't have long to wait. A sleek limousine silently appeared from the bowels of the Dockside sidings. Purring, it drew up alongside the kerb. Rossetti craned his neck forward but to no avail as the tinted windows gave nothing away as to the occupant's identity. For a brief moment, he felt a sudden stab of fear on the strength of the call. His fears were short lived as the front passenger window slid down, revealing a grim-faced Frankie 'the Rinse'.

"Glad you could make it, Rossi." His welcome was short and to the point. Nodding, he indicated to the rear of the car, the door opened and Rossetti climbed in. For a bid car, his seat offered little in the way of comfort, mainly due to the size of the gorilla he was sharing it with. He likened him to a better-looking version of the Traveller, but then anybody would. The Rinse broke into his thoughts by swinging round to face him.

"Sorry about the security, Rossi, it's essential I'm afraid. As from now, you'll be in the dark so to speak for obvious reasons, yer know the rules." Swiftly, the gorilla produced a neckerchief and promptly blindfolded him. He offered no resistance as the full weight of a heavy arm draped around his shoulder.

"Shit, Frankie!" Rossi exclaimed. "Anybody would think I'm gonna do a runner." The Rinse chuckled.

"On the contrary, Rossi, I think the guy half fancies yer, but a word of warning. Don't fuck with the man unless yer mean to!" Rossetti winced at his audacious suggestion and was at the heart of the implication almost at once.

"Are yer saying that he's…"

"Yeah, yer got it in one! The guy is gay. Rossi meet Donna!"

"Donna?!"

"So I'm led to believe. Apparently he's got a thing about kebabs, you can figure out the rest for yerself!" Rossetti was beginning to get pissed off. And it showed as he squirmed under the weight of the gorilla's arm. Raucous laughter filled the car, adding to his misery.

"Okay! I get the message, so what is this really all about?" He was needled and it showed.

"Easy, Rossi! Nothing personal yer understand, this ain't in the script. Be patient, your time will come soon enough." Rossetti, for better or worse, grunted in reply. Due to the blindfold, he felt totally alienated and to make matters worse, a sudden urge to relieve himself kicked in.

"Can't believe this is fucking happening," he muttered under his breath.

"You got a problem back there, Rossi?" the Rinse enquired.

"Yeah, yer could say that! Look, how bleedin' long?"

"I told yer, be patient, we're almost there now." The journey itself had seemed like an eternity for Rossetti, closed down as he was. But at least he could think straight. Prior to getting into the car he'd made a point of checking his watch. In the event their meet went sour, the distance to the covert location they were heading for could be a problem. That thought was kicked clean out the water as another thought kicked in. *Could be they're just going around in circles for all I know.*

Any other designs on the matter dissolved as the limo finally came to a halt.

"There yer go, Rossi, what did I tell yer? Wasn't so bad, was it?" Nodding profusely, Rossetti grunted something inaudible, sighing with relief as the gorilla removed his arm from around him. In no time at all, the blindfold was forcibly ripped over his head. The sudden exposure caught him unawares as the light of day temporarily blinded him. Blinking to adjust his eyesight, he stretched out his arms and breathed in deeply. Feeling somewhat relieved, he checked his watch. The alleged journey, he noted, had taken less than twenty minutes.

Within seconds, the passenger door to the limo was thrown open, and he made short work of getting out in spite of his gimpy leg. Swiftly glancing around, he attempted to take stock of his surroundings. It soon became clear that he'd arrived at a warehouse of sorts. The acrid odour from disused oil and acid filled his nostrils in spite of the shattered windows on two sides. *Well past its sell-by date!* he convinced himself.

"This way, Rossi." The Rinse motioned towards a flight of steep steps at the end of the derelict building. Accompanied by the gorilla and the driver, they negotiated their way to the top, finally entering what once resembled an office. Once inside, business began to kick in straight away as the Rinse lorded over the meet.

"This is where it all starts, Rossi! Saying that, you're not 'ere because yer the flavour of the month. But what I can tell yer is that there is an offer on the cards which just might be of interest to yer, or not, as the case may be."

"If you think I've got the credentials, Frankie, then I don't have a problem with what you've got in mind. All I'm asking for is the SP."

"Fair comment, Rossi. But on a need to know basis, yer gonna have to bear with me for a minute. I'm bound to tell yer that I represent a consortium on this one, and part of our deal states that my associates remain anonymous. How d'ye feel about that?"

"Providing any part of the wedge on offer doesn't... I'm easy." The Rinse chuckled at his double-edged remark before replying.

"Always the comedian, eh, Rossi? Money will be the least of yer problems providing you accept the contract on offer." At worst, the ice was broken, as any existing tensions between the two disintegrated, allowing the Rinse to continue.

"It would seem that a certain asshole of late has made my colleague's business interests take a dive in profit, big time! All due, to a reign of underhand persuasion."

"Okay, so what's new about that?!" Rossetti asked and shrugged his shoulders.

"Normally, nothing at all! Except to say, that this particular asshole in the frame just happens to be the Old Bill!"

"Fuck's sake, Frankie!" exclaimed Rossetti out loud. "That's one hell of a bucket of shit yer got yerself!"

"Yeah, we don't need reminding! On a personal level, the problem as such doesn't bother me. But if my associates ain't earning, then neither am I, know what I mean? Basically, we've all had a gutful of the nasty little bastard, so the problem needs to be addressed, hence the reason for this conversation."

"Does this asshole happen to have a name?" enquired Rossetti.

"Oh yeah, we fingered him good and proper!" The Rinse came across as adamant. "The piece of shit trades under the name of Dawson." The full impact of his disclosure forced Rossetti to sit bolt upright. His heart rate surged to a new level, rendering him momentarily speechless. He felt consumed by a blanket of coldness that enveloped his body, causing him to shudder. The Rinse readily picked up the obvious change in his body language and questioned his change in demeanour.

"Something I said, Rossi? Or maybe you know more than what I do?" The question was point blank and Rossetti needed to think fast. Any suggestion that his own link to Dawson should become public could well jeopardise his own game plan to hit him, working on the assumption that the contract on offer failed to materialise. The mere thought of other faces knowing his business was far too risky. To bluff his way through at this stage made sense.

"Nah, don't get me wrong, mate, I just can't believe what's going down. The geezer's got more front than Brighton! By the way, what rank does this asshole hold?"

"The bleedin' worst, Rossi, he's an eighteen carat bent cop, with a DS trade plate round his neck. What's that do for yer?" Rossetti tore himself apart for an answer, but safe in the knowledge his cover hadn't been blown. A snap decision on his part briefly got him out of it again.

"It's obvious to me the guy has got himself a bleedin' death wish. He needs putting down, fucking blown away, know what I mean, Frankie?"

"Yer got it in one, Rossi. Just what I expected yer to say." For a moment, Rossetti found himself having to question his own inane decision. Had he inadvertently put words into Frankie's mouth? Two shattered knee caps might have sufficed as a successful outcome to appease the firm, although Dawson would have a case to plead otherwise. Continuing, the Rinse spelt it out in no uncertain terms, glorifying his line of reasoning.

"Yer just the guy to do the business, Rossi, and that's why yer 'ere, so let's talk money!"

On reflection, not only had Rossetti got 'out of jail', but the lottery was staring him in the face at the top end of lucky. Their meet had now done a complete turnaround, and he just happened to be holding all the aces. Not only would he have the pleasure of a hit on Dawson, but also an added bonus in the form of a substantial wedge for carrying it out. In truth, the contract had materialised into something he could only have dreamed about. And as an added rider, the firm were ignorant of his illicit connection where Dawson was concerned.

For the first time in his torrid experience, he now found himself savouring a win-win situation. Smiling discreetly while milking the moment, he accepted Frankie's offer to talk business. "Yeah, let's do that!" was all he said, but with a ring of confidence attached. But then again, he could afford to be confident. The contract on offer was undeniably his for the taking, and he relished the prospect of its contents.

"You've obviously got a figure in mind, Frankie? A hit like this one is surely a one-off and entails suitable consideration. We're talking a lot of dough 'ere. As you so rightly put it, it's, quote, 'heavy'. Then of course you've got the hardware to think about. If I'm supplying the shooter, then the ante needs upping. All things considered, yer need to come up with a kosher figure, making the hit a viable one."

The Rinse's face took on a serious note as he punctuated each word with his finger.

"Don't push yer luck, Rossi, both sides need to be sensible about this. If we can't agree terms, it's possible an offer could be made off the manor. Frankly, it's in your interest to call it right!" Rossetti swallowed hard.

The mere thought of a third party possibly lurking in the background had momentarily stunted his ego trip. Besides which, one particular outsider immediately sprang to mind in the form of professional hitman Buffy Manilla. Lip service became a necessity as he pushed the Rinse for a monetary offer.

"As you say, Frankie, we need to level the ante on both sides. What's the asshole worth to yer, brown bread of course?" Steeling himself in anticipation Rossetti gritted his teeth as the Rinse replied.

"I ain't here to mess with yer, Rossi, you understand? We as a firm are prepared to lay out £20,000. Half on account and the balance on proof of death. There would be certain guarantees of course, where trust is concerned." As usual, Rossetti was reading into the deal all wrong and made sure he was being listened to.

"Guarantees?! Proof? You gotta be winding me up? If I was to say to yer there's a stiff lying in the morgue with two fucking bullets in his head, that's good enough for me! The poor bleeder ain't likely to get up and walk out like nothing's happened!"

"Relax, Rossi! We know yer more than capable of carrying out the hit, our prime concern is that you don't do a runner with the down payment!"

"Simple!" he fired back. "I ain't likely to, for the same reason you'll still owe me the balance, right?"

"Touché, Rossi, the shooter of course will be down to you personally. So I can presume that we've got ourselves a deal at last?" The pair promptly shook hands, and the Rinse handed over the down payment of £10,000 as agreed. "In yer own time, Rossi, but don't leave it too bloody long, the asshole's had a good run as it is. By the way, they're all used notes."

"Nice one, Frankie, rest assured he'll get his alright. I'll mess him up a bit first, know what I mean?" The Rinse nodded as a vague look crossed his face.

"Yeah, whatever, just get a result. You're on yer own now. The next time we get to talk, I need to know that the fucking nuisance is brown bread. Well, that concludes our business, so I'll run yer back to the basin, okay?"

Purely out of habit, Rossetti checked his watch before they departed.

Strangely enough, the return trip only took ten minutes, he noted, forcing him to smile. The fact that he'd been blindfolded again reinforced his theory regarding the location of their meet. *Must think I'm stupid!* he told himself as he made his way up Martin Street via the AA. There's stupid and then there's Rossetti's version. The cash injection he'd inherited would bail him out for the interim, but the knock-on effect of a certain amount of grief went hand in hand with the blood money. Sooner rather than later there would be a price to pay, a slice of which included obtaining a shooter via the exclusive Maltese Pete.

Time would also become a factor when dealing with the hit. As from now, the firm would be on his back and pressing for a result. Blinded by the wedge in his pocket, he'd unwittingly dug a hole larger than his ego could handle at any one time. For the time being, arrogance would suffice, until such time it became necessary to address the reality of his negative chances of survival.

Today was just another phase in the life of one Paul Rossetti.

## CHAPTER 10

# CAUSE FOR SUSPICION

From an outsider's point of view, it would appear that Stonewater Police HQ was no different from any other nick if it comes down to parallels, the backbone, of course, being mainly uniform and the CID. For one young PC in particular, the rigid combination of footwork and administration was accepted as part of the territory, although in his case it proved to be a burden he executed to the letter. Fair to say that PC Reginald Hollins was exclusive amongst others, and destined to go far. So quoted his superiors. True, he was young and ambitious, up the DI's proverbial arse, but never a 'kid a kidder' type of cop. For a freshman he carried a wise head on young shoulders. His immediate work colleagues shunned any form of brinkmanship owed to him, and constantly ribalded his acute dedication to the job.

This particular morning, he cut a lone figure as he pored over a series of statements. As per usual it was left to him to kick-start the day's proceedings. Placing the file he was working on to one side, he glanced at the travel clock situated on his desk. *8.30am*, he mused. *This place will look like Piccadilly Circus in five minutes*. Reaching across, he grabbed another file and buried his head in its contents. A slight headache was beginning to leave its mark as his work rate progressed. The morning, it seems, had the makings of a bad day… again!

The 'problem' in question had become an ongoing

headache he'd been forced to endure, especially when pecking order reared its head. DS Dawson had burst in on the scene a few months previously, carrying a mantel of doubt as to his credibility and alleged integrity. On the plus side, his work rate seemed to pay dividends when it came to results, to which the files that littered his desk bore testament. *It's just this forceful aura he's got about him, especially when he's on somebody's case. I can't get my head round how he manages to do it*, thought Hollins.

As DC Hollins would tell you, "The man is an island, and bloody arrogant with it. He doesn't give nothing away. Putting it mildly, I think DS Dawson is an asshole!" Strange! The well-worn adage, 'A lot of people can't all be wrong' springs to mind. Hollins' on the other hand, adhered to his own brand of thinking. Given the time and the opportunity, he would relish the prospect of bringing Dawson to heel. The wheel of fate, had he been aware, had started to turn for him the minute he'd set foot in Stonewater. Only time itself now had carte blanche as to his destiny. DC Hollins looked up as Dawson strode into the office, engrossed as he was in reading a file. That would count as the first mistake of his day. The second would be to offer up a light-hearted "Morning, Sarge, good day for the race!" A sarcastic "Is it?! And I don't bloody gamble" was a reaction he could have well done without. But then we are talking Dawson here. Right now, the man was only interested in facts.

"Any calls, messages, Hollins?"

"Nothing registered, Sarge, as far as I know, but the guv'nor is carrying out an update and evaluation in room three at nine o'clock this morning. We're expected to attend."

"In that case, get Barnes to stand in for me. I need to organise some bodies for the club and drugs run later on. Which reminds me, yer on overtime tonight!"

"But Sarge, I've got..."

"You can forget it. Unless of course, you want a spell with Traffic." Hollins felt obliged to bite his tongue as he was forced to back off. It was by no means the first and wouldn't be the last time that Dawson had mugged him off. Little did he know at the time that his thoughts could be synonymous with those of a 'dead man walking', echoed of late by none other than Paul Rossetti.

The time was around one o'clock when Hollins finally left the station canteen for a lunch break. He noted that the office appeared to be buzzing as he approached. He couldn't help but pick up on Dawson's figure, framed through glass panelling adjacent to the passageway. For some unknown reason, Hollins stopped short prior to entering and focused his attention Dawson's way as he sat at his desk, chin in hand and looking deep in thought. *I'll bet money he's plotting some poor bastard's downfall*, he convinced himself. Suddenly, what appeared to be a smirk crossed Dawson's face as he removed his hand. Reaching out for a nearby landline, it was noticeable that he dialled a six-figure number, leaving the smirk to grow even wider.

To Hollins' estimation, the dialling tone would only have run for a matter of seconds before he happened to hang up. *What the hell is that asshole up to, I wonder?* He dug deep for a plausible answer, which was lost as Dawson once again repeated the process. The only difference being that this time he hung on longer before deciding to replace the handset. By now, the smirk had morphed into a cynical smile. Hollins did a double take, not that he needed to be convinced as his inner thoughts said it for him. *If that guy is kosher, then I'm…*

"Nothing to do, Hollins?" The DI had spotted him as he attempted to analyse Dawson's reaction.

"Up to me neck in it, guv! Just thinking out loud."

"On your way, son, it all happens in there." And he

pointed toward the office door. Hollins lost no time going in and shooting a positive glance at Dawson, before sitting down at his desk. Burying his head in bookwork was proving negative; the phone scenario wouldn't go away. Attempting to collect his thoughts while preoccupied with a file in one hand and a report in the other was futile. Over and over again, his reckoning came back to haunt him, each time bearing the same unsolicited conclusion. He asked himself the question, 'Why would anybody set out to make two accelerated phone calls, and be happy in the knowledge that a response wasn't forthcoming?'.

His mind delivered 'game, set and match'. As from now, Dawson would be under a one-man surveillance of intrigue as Jobsworth took over. The one outcome he could rely on would prove to be positive later on in the day. At the end of his shift, he could knowingly look back on a shit day, while at the top end of things Dawson would be celebrating owing to a substantial cash injection from the night's club run in Docklands.

## CHAPTER 11

# SIDDIE COMES GOOD

Closing the bathroom door wasn't even an option. The interference wasn't about to go away without a fight. The monotonous overtones from the phone in the lounge continued to test his patience to the edge. "Rachael! Can you get that? I'm in the bathroom." Fresh from the shower, Siddie Levy was in the process of towelling himself down as he made his demands. Downstairs in the kitchen, engrossed as she was in preparing the evening meal, Rachael left off in response to Siddie's plea. Her eyes weighed heavy as she replied to an audience of one.

"Oy Vey, I do this, I do that!" Her rambling ceased as once again Siddie continued to rant from upstairs. "The phone! Pick the bloody phone up, it could be business already!" Tutting, she shrugged her shoulders in her own indomitable manner and headed off towards the lounge.

"What sort of putz does business this time of day anyway?" She finally caved in and made herself heard. "Leave it to me, Siddie, I'm on my way." In the event, Siddie had to have the last word.

"Rachael Levy, you're a klutz!" he shouted, his voice tinged with relief. She smiled and shook her head.

"I should be a klutz, huh!" she remarked. "He's obviously had a good day at the market." She was still smiling as she picked the receiver up and made herself known. Within seconds her face evaporated into one of concern as the caller cut in. The message he conveyed was brief and one that Rachael could quote if challenged. Slowly she replaced the receiver. Already alarm were bells started to ring as she turned to face Siddie, who by now was at the foot of the stairs.

A look of knowing etched his face; he wanted answers. "And?!" Rachael didn't mince her words in reply.

"It's Ronnie, he needs to talk. I'll set another plate, he'll be here in thirty minutes." It became an all-too-familiar pattern the Levys had been accustomed to over the years. On the flip side, a visit would have been to socialise; in contrast, a phone call was at the opposite end of the spectrum. Invariably, it meant that he was in trouble of some kind, if not later than sooner!

"Damn! It doesn't sound good to me. I think we could be in for a long night, Rachael."

"You're that sure?" Siddie checked himself before replying. The facts relating to his recent altercation concerning Dawson were put to one side purely for reasons of his own choosing. For the time being, diplomacy ruled the moment.

"Well, not out of choice, Rachael. Although Ronnie's had his problems of late, that could be his reason for calling." Rachael wasn't prepared to let it drop that easily.

"The market! Maybe he…" Siddie swiftly repelled her line of reasoning.

"Not a chance, I would know that already. I happen to know he took a nice few quid today." He heaved a sigh of relief as Rachael broke off their conversation, and made her way back into the kitchen while he remained speculating as to what might have been. Fair to say his initial instinct about Ronnie couldn't be faulted. There just remained a question as to the level of grief he somehow knew was inevitable, and secondly, how to confront it.

Rachael was on Ronnie's case the moment he came through the door. She brushed away any preformed ideas he'd conceived by ushering him into the dining room. She pointed at the table she'd taken pains to set. "First we eat! Then you talk!" Ronnie felt under orders but nevertheless obliged. Unlike previous spontaneous meetings, the atmosphere became somewhat clouded, mainly due to limited conversation. Finally, it was left to Siddie to break the uneasy silence. Pushing his plate to one side, he glanced hopefully across at Ronnie to gain his full attention. But Ronnie appeared to be on a walkabout on Mars...

He paused before speaking as he considered all the possible scenarios he faced. *You put a man inside of a ring! Give him an order! And that man becomes a fighting machine! A destroyer to order and now this?!* His thoughts reigned for a split second, in which time Ronnie looked up and caught his eye.

"Oh sorry, mate, I was bleedin' miles away." Patting his stomach, he expressed his thanks for the meal in his own exclusive manner.

"I don't know what cloud yer fell off, Rachael, but that was the business!" Rachael raised her arms and looked skywards.

"Schmaltz! I feed the man and I get schmaltz already!" She laughed outwardly and motioned them both toward the lounge. A sense of welcome relief swept over Siddie. There was nothing more to say except to himself. *He's back. Everything is kosher so now we can talk!* Making himself comfortable, Siddie decided to take the initiative from the offset. With a case to answer, he was fully aware that Ronnie's mood lay somewhere between edgy at best and a half-frayed tightrope.

"So where d'ye want to start, my friend?" Siddie had gone for the jugular all options barred, leaving Ronnie backed up in a corner, and the only way out was to give some answers. He was also aware that Ronnie could be at his most dangerous with his back to the ropes. His reply, when it eventually came, was direct in approach and set the mood for further discussion.

"Start? I'd have to say probably where we both left off about a week ago." Siddie scratched his forehead and cast his mind back. At best, he recalled a certain phone scenario, but decided to hedge his bets when replying rather than force an unwanted issue to resurface.

"I'm sorry, mate, yer gonna have to elaborate on that, I'm totally lost here." Looking perplexed, Ronnie nevertheless remained calm, although adamant, when he divulged the facts in hand.

"The poxy grief I had to do with my phone, surely yer remember?" Siddie swallowed hard. *Only too well*, he told himself and concurred in a positive manner.

"Of course! I should forget so soon."

"Good! That's something, at least it's a start." By now, Ronnie was out of his eternal corner and firing as he continued. "Well, you ain't gonna believe this."

"So try me?"

"What if I say I'm back to square one because I'm being targeted again? It can't go on, it seriously needs to be sorted, mate!" The possible implications were now laid bare, leaving Siddie wallowing in no man's land.

"When? How?" he replied guardedly.

"Let's see now, timewise I'd have to say between 1 and 1.30 this morning. Yeah, that's about right."

"Obviously while we working, so how did it come about?"

"Well, that one's down to you."

"Sorry, I don't understand."

"You made a point of making sure I checked my landline, when and where, right? Tonight I got home, I found there were two registered calls all in the space of three or four minutes. The caller has left no name and obviously hung up. Basically, the same outcome as before! I ask yer! What's the bleedin' point of it all? As I said before, if somebody is out there solely with the intention of winding me up, then they're doing a bloody good job at pissing me off!" Ronnie was in the centre of the ring now and mixing it. Siddie knew he had a fight on his hands and the onus was on his stable to deliver. Without question he felt side footed as a mental image of Rossetti kept emerging from within countless layers of possibilities.

The sixty-four-dollar question was had Ronnie visualised the same outcome? He decided to assume the latter and to keep an open mind on any alternatives. "You need to take a step back, my friend. Don't let them think yer worried, you don't need to play the mind games."

"Hang on a minute, you insinuated 'they'!"

"Purely guess work, Ronnie." His misplaced reply was bad timing in terms of speculation, causing him to silently curse under his breath. Ronnie had a point; 'they' could be misconstrued as being a conspiracy. On the flip side of things, even on his own Rossetti would be bad news enough. To quote Ronnie: "If this latest episode is down to him, and it all comes out on top, I swear I'll muller the bastard!" Strong words indeed! Although even an abstainer would have to agree if odds came into play. Which now leaves Dawson as an accomplice of sorts cavorting as a double act.

By his own admission, Dawson had gone to great pains when tracking down and confronting Siddie by exposing Rossetti as a genuine connection between the two. Ronnie appeared to be impatient and considered he wanted more. "So what are yer thinking? That two people are maybe involved?" Siddie chose to remain cautious as he digressed.

"The last time we had this conversation, I recall your theory on a possible link between Dawson and Rossetti."

"Yeah! And I bleedin' well stand by it."

"Okay, now I agree that this Dawson schmuck ain't yer usual run-of-the-mill local plod. All of a sudden, he's arrived on the manor, already putting himself about, and for what reason?"

"I dunno, but he must have a strong motive, he's Old Bill for Christ's sake!"

"Exactly! But only in name, Ronnie. But yeah, a motive for his own benefit. Think about it, I'm sure he's aware of your past track record concerning Rossetti."

"Leaving me where exactly?"

"I'll tell yer where! This is only supposition, mind, but let's assume for a moment he's got something on Rossetti, or the other way around? And you just happen to be slap bang in the middle of it?"

"Right, go on."

"It's feasible he could be using you to carry out his dirty work for him! I'm not sure how he's playing it yet, but whatever way yer paint it, it stinks, mate. The guy's a putz!"

"Point taken, I can see where yer coming from nah, nobody would go to all that grief." He faltered briefly. "Unless, unless they were bent of course!"

"Precisely!"

"So where do we go from 'ere?"

"We don't! You carry on like the calls haven't happened and keep schtum. I suspect that one of us will get a visit pretty soon. More than likely it will be you, mate. Like I say, don't let the asshole think for a minute yer affected by it. Sooner rather than later he'll push his luck. People like him don't reign for long. Besides, he's bound to have various other spin-offs. Probably up to his neck in protection and drugs scams if the truth be known. Stand on me, Ronnie, I could write his bloody future on the back of a postage stamp already."

"Siddie Levy, I owe yer, you've bleedin' done it again!"

"Done?!"

"Got me out of it."

"You seem to be forgetting something, my friend. I'm also involved. Make no mistake, this time around we're in this together. I can't have you running off head strong like yer did all those years ago. Just remember, I'm the one with the chutzpah, you stick to the leather business!"

## CHAPTER 12

# DEATH ON DELIVERY

"Morning, Sarge." Benson stiffened and looked up from examining the duty roster in acknowledgment, then proceeded to rub his bleary eyes. The bland expression of his face made plain his feelings. With less than ten minutes of his shift remaining, he wouldn't have given a damn if the nick was on fire. It had been a long night, all considered. Two assaults, a break in and a suspected rape had seriously undermined his patience. The two token drunks now resident in the cells had in a way proved a welcome relief in the early hours and as such were duly classed as in-house entertainment. All in all, a fairly average night shift for the nick. Benson, on the other hand, wouldn't hesitate to prefix 'night' with the word 'shit'! Now, with minutes left to go, the opportunity arose for him to offload his built-up sentiments.

"Oh, it's you, Hollins. I sincerely hope that your shift has more going for it than mine turned out to be." Hollins was on his case before he'd finished.

"Don't say anymore, I get the idea. No offence, Sarge, but it doesn't work on me. You're forgetting something, I happen to be on Dawson's team. Another month working with him and I'll need to go for counselling!"

"See what you mean, son. How unlucky can you get? If it was raining lager you'd probably have a fork in your hand! As it happens, there is something you can do for me."

"Why not? Go for it."

"Can you make sure that Sergeant Dawson gets this package. The guy who brought it in said it's extremely important and that he would understand the contents, okay?" Nodding briskly, a disconcerted look crossed Hollins' face; his brain was geared up elsewhere.

"The package, did it arrive by courier, Sarge?" He perked up.

"No, nothing to sign for, except to say the messenger was dressed in leathers."

"Presumably he arrived on a motorbike then?"

"Yeah, I guess he did." By now, Benson had lost all interest in their prolonged conversation and it showed in his body language. Moving swiftly, he forcefully pressed the security button, enabling Hollins to gain entry. Clutching the package, Hollins reacted as quickly and headed off toward the canteen. At worst, there were still ten minutes of sanity remaining before all hell was let loose. As for his own personal workload, he could look forward to an early briefing followed by countless files to sift through. The other ninety per cent of his grief had two legs and a big mouth and lorded under the name of Dawson. Having made himself comfortable in the canteen, he gazed deeply into the bowels of his cup of tea. "Oh my God!" he muttered, and sighed, "Any bloody weaker and I'll be able to see the bottom!" Pushing the alleged tea to one side, he got up and left, wearing a disgruntled look. "I just knew it was going to be another shit day!"

Zombie-like, he slowly made his way towards his office, which was situated on the first floor. His body language spoke volumes as he broke the habit of a lifetime by disregarding the lift in favour of the stairs. Clearly his mind appeared to be elsewhere. Dawson's delivery had managed to unsettle him. Wishful thinking and reality were at war as the package continued to burn a hole in the palm of his hand. To anybody of normal persuasion, a bog-standard 9 x 6 jiffy bag wouldn't even rate a secondary glance. It's just that this particular one happened to have Sergeant bloody Dawson scrawled on one side. His passion for the job had now landed him into a situation of his own making. Like a magnet, it began to draw him in. He'd have willingly given up a year's pay just to be a fly on the wall, watching as Dawson exposed the contents.

His reasoning was backed up by a calculated gamble with a recurring conclusion. There was no doubt whatsoever in his mind that Dawson's future lay inside the package. Reverently, he placed it on Dawson's desktop. Any onlooker could be forgiven for thinking it contained a parcel bomb, although Hollins would have agreed, but in a different light. His reaction, when it came, was anti-climactic. Hollins had sought refuge behind a folder as Dawson gingerly picked up the package. For reasons of his own, he'd held back on any would-be information, deciding instead not to make an issue out of it. Seconds later, Dawson swung round to confront Hollins.

"D'ye know anything about this, Hollins?" he grunted. In hindsight, the question became irrelevant the second it was spawned. It went clean over his head. His own logic lay elsewhere. *Everything and anything… but fucking nothing… three bags full, Dawson!* His frustrated mind vented his inner feelings.

"Hollins!" Lowering the folder, a naïve look appeared on his face as if to order.

"Oh sorry, Sarge, I got caught up in this case file." As an actor, he wouldn't have qualified for the back legs of a donkey in a pantomime, although Dawson seemed at ease with his reply. He went on. "I should have mentioned it earlier. Sergeant Benson asked me to forward it on to you."

"Strange," Dawson muttered. "No message or anything?"

"Afraid not, Sarge, that's as far as it goes, you'd best take it up with Benson sometime."

"I don't think that will be necessary, and it's Sergeant, you little shit!"

'Cocky bastard' sprang to mind, but he'd gleaned something from their conversation. It clearly showed that Dawson hadn't been expecting the package, in spite of Benson's omission: quote, "He will know about the contents".

*More than anything I need to find out what's inside the package!* he convinced himself. Two hours later he was no more knowledgeable than before. Hollins glanced up from the files he was poring over and feasted his attention on the package. He'd lost count by now of the number of times the process had occurred. As yet, Dawson had made no effort to open it. Two or three times, his hand had settled on it, only to be withdrawn. It was almost as if he didn't want to know what it contained. Right from the start, since his awareness of it, he'd become unsettled and agitated. Without warning, he suddenly rose from his desk on the backend of a belated decision.

"I'm just gonna make a call, Hollins. I'll probably be gone about ten minutes if anybody needs to know."

"And where would that be, Sarge?" As a gesture, it was a complete throwaway line that might have worked. But Dawson wasn't biting.

"That's my bloody business!" he snapped.

"And while yer at it, get those damn reports ready for Division." Hollins watched him go, before returning to the work in hand. Plucking one out at random, he studied it briefly before surmising on its contents.

"One day, please God, I'll be writing one up on you, Dawson, believe it!" Jobsworth came into play once again as his curiosity intensified. "Why the hell would he want to go outside the office just to make a poxy phone call? There's three phones here as it is! If he isn't bent then I'm the Chief bloody Constable!"

Meanwhile, Dawson appeared desperate to offload.

"That you, Billy? Good. Listen, can we talk? Fine, yeah my end's safe. Saying that, I've got a little problem down here needs sorting."

"How big is little?"

"As big as I allow it to fucking get, Billy. It's unwanted grief in the shape of a package, would yer believe?"

"Sounds to me like yer got yerself a bleedin' fan club, Harry."

"Billy! You ain't listening to me. The last poxy package I had if yer remember was from up West, compliments of that little shit Rossetti. So now yer know where I'm coming from?"

"Meaning you've opened it up?"

"No! Not yet. It arrived this morning, dropped off at the front desk, IC unknown."

"Naughty! So now it's gone public, that ain't healthy, mate."

"Exactly! I'll have to open it. I'll do it on the QT when it suits me."

"I just hope for your bleedin' sake it doesn't all go pear-shaped, yer can't run forever, cocker."

"Nah, yer right. It starts and it all ends 'ere! I just need to play it smart."

"By the way, any feedback yet on that Callaghan geezer?"

"Strange you should mention that! As it happens, I've been busy feeding him bent phone calls recently, hoping that he gets to Rossetti before I do, know what I mean?"

"What about the wooden tops on the beat?"

"Not even a sniff, I reckon he's gone to ground, he ain't that stupid."

"Hold up, Harry, I think I'd better do the same, there's a

few nosey bastards about! Soon as yer know something, let me know, yeah? Be lucky." The line went dead. Dawson wore the look of a man promoting grief. Sighing, he pocketed his mobile and headed back to the office wearing the composure of a much-troubled man. Hollins looked up as he walked through the door; he'd already written his script.

"Everything alright, Sarge?" he asked, picking up on Dawson's disjointed demeanour.

"Alright?! Why shouldn't it be?" His reply was about as convincing as a one-armed juggler.

"Gotcha!" murmured Hollins under his breath, and made a visual indication toward the package, which still lay on the table. His reaction enticed Dawson to look away as his face contorted with anger. Snatching the package in his hand, he stormed out of the office. In psychological terms the rest of the shift belonged to Hollins. Mentally, he'd won a silent battle in bringing about Dawson's downfall. Selfish or what?! Somebody should have reminded him that there was a queue waiting in the wings to claim that chosen prize.

The harder he tried to combat his nerves, the less he succeeded. Both hands were trembling as a copious amount of brandy hit the bottom of his glass. In one swift movement, he threw it down the back of his throat, and just as quickly relined his glass again before placing the bottle to one side. A compulsive shudder died a death as the desired effect kicked in. "Christ, I needed that!" he uttered in desperation and made a move to sit down. Even within the confines of his flat that same evening, Dawson found himself struggling to relax. The amount of brandy he'd consumed now seemed superficial. Unlike his inheritance, the package appeared to scream out reality. It now lay on a nearby coffee table, taunting him from every angle, mocking his sanity. Due to circumstances beyond his control, one particular wheel in his sordid life was about to turn full circle. Déjà vu ruled the moment as the paper knife in his trembling hand ripped through the jiffy bag.

The contents that spewed out onto the table were not unfamiliar and their significance locked into his semi-deranged mind. The moment created an adverse effect as an unexpected feeling of relief swept over his numbed body. In one sense, he felt purged of his demons by the evidence lying in front of him, leaving him transfixed. Whoever sent the package had been generous to a fault simply by enclosing two items to consider, both relative to his ever-diminishing future; a bonus indeed! Through sightless eyes, Dawson retrieved a CD disc from the table, his hand still trembling uncontrollably. If the object had been a stick of gelignite, he would have been blown to smithereens. Who gives a shit anyway? His face now matched his glazed eyes as the blood rapidly drained from his cheeks.

He needn't have bothered playing the CD back; he alone recalled the poison he knew it represented word for word, letter by letter. Indeed, he still retained a replica of the disc, although the bonus ball this time around lay in the form of a hand-written message which, when read, detailed the beginning of the end for him, prior to his inevitable death knell! The CD fell away from his slippery grasp as his eyes rested on a card exposing a message, hand written in capital letters. It was simple, it was ultra-believable, it would be his death knell!

DAWSON! YOU ALWAYS PLAYED ME FOR A FOOL. BIG MISTAKE! AS FROM NOW, YOU'RE A DEAD MAN WALKING! DO NOT ATTEMPT TO FIND ME (AS I HAVE FOUND YOU). DON'T EVEN CONSIDER LEAVING STONEWATER. THE ENCLOSED CD IS MY INSURANCE AND EITHER WAY IT WILL BE FORWARDED TO YOUR SUPERIORS. ROT IN HELL,

DAWSON, YOUR BED IS PRE-BOOKED.

YOURS IN BLOOD… R!

With the message firmly embedded in his addled brain, Dawson took on a begging posture. His situation had finally become untenable. The half-finished bottle of brandy appeared to be his only solace. He savagely gulped it down his throat almost as if it had been water.

It became all too easy, but by now his mental state had become devoid of any feeling as we know it. Calmly, he allowed the empty bottle to fall from his grasp as he half stumbled toward a nearby writing desk. The drawer he chose glided open unheeded; any other time it would have been a problem. *Strange*, he told himself. *The grief I've had in the past opening it.* When considering his current situation and the evidence, his statement was as surreal as it gets. Zombie-like, he removed a 9mm semi-automatic Glock 26 revolver and checked the magazine for live rounds. Satisfied it was full, he pulled back the safety catch. Gripping it tightly, he walked into his bathroom.

There, he positioned himself on the edge of the bath facing a floor-to-ceiling mirror. Holding the weapon in both hands, he forced the barrel upward, directly under his chin. The next procedure was rudimental. Taking one last pitiful look at his futility, he geared his head backward and simultaneously pulled the trigger. The weapon exploded in sympathy and recoiled upward in a final gesture of victory. Its job was now complete. Dawson's defunct lifeless body jolted backward as if kicked by a horse. He now lay in a disheveled blood-sodden heap in the bath. He'd become a designated dead man the second his eyes had left the mirror.

A recipe of blood and brains readily combined to decorate three walls and part of the ceiling. The blood created grotesque patterns from hundreds of rivulets now cascading down the white tiles that formed a macabre backdrop to the scene. In terms of unsolicited artistry, the scene was not far off the work of Picasso. Surely an epitaph to live with? Unfortunately, in Dawson's case he would only be remembered as just another bent cop.

## CHAPTER 13

# CONCLUSIONS

Hollins stood apprehensively in the corridor adjacent to where Dawson had lived prior to his death for the short time he'd reigned in Stonewater. His thoughts on the tragedy swung one way only as he witnessed the grim removal of Dawson's body from the flat. In a sense, he provoked a selfish attitude. It wasn't that he was a hard bastard, certainly not in that sense, but because he felt cheated by the man's unexpected demise. From what he could glean thus far from his guv'nor, everything now pointed to suicide. Going on the strength of certain evidence coming to light in the flat, they implicated a third party as a motive for his drastic actions. Another lead in the form of a CD disc was found, assuring the investigating team that the contents held the key to his misfortune, pending forensic results.

His indifferent thoughts were shortly brought down to earth by the DCI leading the investigation. "Barnes! Hollins! You can both go in there now. The place has been dusted. Remember, we're looking for anything that might have links to a conspiracy, and one other thing, you do not talk to anybody, especially the press boys. They'll have a bloody field day as it is." Apart from anything else, everything pointed toward the disc and what it might contain. The case in itself was without doubt a delicate one, and the police involvement went beyond the manor. A press report had been issued a couple of hours after the discovery of the body by the caretaker doing his rounds, at 12 noon, the day following the alleged suicide.

If feeling 'cheated', to quote Hollins, was an epidemic then Rossetti would have been on a life support machine if he'd been made aware of the drama instituted on the strength of a whim. Even he couldn't have envisaged the outcome that one small package could evolve into. Basically, it was the start of a campaign aimed hopefully at softening up Dawson into a state of insecurity, thereby creating his careless actions. He'd obviously underestimated Dawson's ability to come to terms with his track record.

Put simply, by putting the frighteners on the guy, he'd unwittingly made a rod for his own back, while at the same time an unwanted coffin for Dawson. On reflection, ensuring that the police were in full possession of the crucial evidence, namely the goods package, was the least of Rossetti's problems. He'd simply roped in the services of a regular punter, using the AA to deliver it for a couple of quid. Anybody else would have got nicely pissed up knowing that the world was well rid of another asshole. Not so Rossetti! His motive remained exclusive; he'd have called a foul by stating his act was personal and backed up with a nice wedge. Well, there's an argument for consideration. As paymaster for the firm, Frankie 'the Rinse' might also be justified in crying foul as well on a certain technicality.

Not long after the press report went public, he made his case quite clear. "Okay! So Dawson may be brown bread, but I've got a verbal contract written in lead. To my mind, Rossetti hasn't done the business first hand. So therefore the firm could now be looking for a refund on their alleged deal. Should at any time ifs and buts plus personalities clash, that amounts to one treble you wouldn't want to lay odds on! Although it isn't over just yet."

Stonewater nick was still reeling from the aftermath of the Dawson affair. Anybody associated with the case could never have envisaged that there could have been a sting in the tail. And long before any final forensic conclusions were finalised. Hollins knocked on the Super's door; his free hand held an envelope, the contents of which, unbeknownst to him, would turn the nick upside down on its head. For Hollins' role in the charade, poetic justice had conveniently stepped in, giving him exclusive rights to hammer home the last nail in Dawson's coffin.

"Come in." The Super glanced up from what he was doing. "Oh, it's you, Hollins. Problem?"

"Not as I know of, sir. I've got the forensic report back on the CD that was found."

"Good man. Should make interesting reading no doubt, close a few doors so to speak." Hollins appeared reluctant to leave and it showed.

"That's all, Constable, run along, I'm sure you can find plenty to do."

Hiding his frustration, Hollins slunk off. He stopped short as the office door suddenly burst open. The Super began acting crazy as he brandished the forensic report in the air. "The stupid, stupid bastard! Blew his brains out and for nothing!" Hollins was left floundering midstream.

"Sir?!" The guv'nor chose his words well before spelling it out.

"The disc! The disc is bloody well clean, Hollins. Dawson must have assumed that it was verbally loaded, how could he have got it so wrong?!"

Just for the record, apart from a few drops of brandy, and Dawson's fingerprints surfacing, the disc itself was branded as of negative value. Elsewhere, the tabloids would have ample fodder for the next few weeks' press once the disc disclosure was made available. For the time being, Dawson would have his 'fifteen minutes of fame' by headlining the local rag.

Rossetti slammed his bedroom door behind him, not bothering to lock it. Whatever assets he possessed, monetary or otherwise, could be found on his person. Stumbling down the stairs he entered the bar below. It took him a few seconds for his eyes to become accustomed to the sparse lighting, although in retrospect it was a damn sight better than the murky confines of the poolroom he'd staggered out of some hours earlier. "You've got no flaming chance with the breakfast, Rossi, so what's it going to be, wetwise?" The barman's attitude toward Rossetti had remained unflinching since their recent altercation. Not that he gave a shit, but Rossetti was under the impression that everybody acted in that way. Rifling around in his pocket, he managed to locate enough loose change to pay for his beer.

"I'll use yer paper if yer don't mind, see what's going down in the world."

"You obviously don't know then?" enquired the barman.

"Know? What's to bleedin' know?" Rossetti fired back.

"The bloody suicide! The Old Bill and all."

"No, you ain't making any sense, who's topped who and what?" The barman started to lose it, and shoved the paper in front of him.

"Christ's sake, Rossi, read the bloody paper yerself… and I want it back!" Momentarily ignoring the paper, Rossetti grabbed his beer and offered the bottle of salvation up to his mouth. Taking a long swig, his eyes skipped over the front page of the newspaper. As yet, his dour facial expression gave no indication as to his reaction to the blaring headline which threatened to jump out at him and consume his being. His body suddenly stiffened as recognition slowly set in. Lowering the bottle onto the bar top, he looked away briefly before returning to the paper, to satisfy himself that the barman wasn't winding him up. No, there hadn't been a mistake. The glaring headline said it all and was not about to go away, unlike Dawson, of course, who by now was probably making his bed up in hell.

The headline read:

SUICIDE TRAGEDY OF LOCAL DRUGS SQUAD COP!

and the article went on to describe in detail the circumstances surrounding the case.

Much was made of the reference to the blank CD on which the case pivoted. Furthermore, the case would be ongoing, involving a possible breach of security by the victim and persons as yet unknown. Rossetti's anger welled up to incensed fury as he spoke through gritted teeth. "You gutless bastard, Dawson!" The barman who was hovering forced him to tone down his voice. His face contorted and screwed up in temper as he reflected on what might have been, plus the ramifications that would undoubtedly follow from another source as a result.

He now found himself struggling to keep a check on his uncontrollable anger, but without success. He couldn't hold it in; it needed to come out. Emptying his bottle, he slammed it down onto the bar top, and spoke as if in conversation. Like it or not Dawson, even in death, had managed to get back at him.

"Don't think for a second you've won, asshole! You had it coming anyway, you might have kippered me up but you got yours, and..."

"Another beer, Rossi?" the barman interjected. Strangely enough, Rossetti declined his offer.

"Nasty old business that, Rossi!" the barman exclaimed, and nodded at the paper. "But I can't help thinking..."

"Yeah. What exactly?!"

"Well, why can't the Old Bill be honest and say the guy was on the make? It's bleedin' obvious he was bent!" Rossetti didn't even offer an opinion, his mind was elsewhere. *Bent? What would he know about bent? Fucking no good barman.* Breaking off from his ranting, he ordered a large Scotch and leaned up against the bar to continue his sordid thoughts.

"I'll tab then, Rossi, along with the beer, okay?" the barman stated. He then glanced down at the paper once more. His eyes glinted as he pointed to the headline. "'Ere, mate, I'll have money that you knew the guy." Calmly and collectively, Rossetti took the top off his Scotch and fixed the barman, eyes blazing.

"Know him?!" Fucking know him!" he exclaimed. "I killed the bastard!" Laughing nervously, the barman backed away.

"Yeah, yeah, Rossi, I'm sure yer did, and I'm bloody Mickey Mouse." Rossetti shook his head as if to justify a previous conclusion, and replied with a sense of conviction, "Like I said, fucking no good barman." And promptly downed the rest of his drink. You wouldn't need a fortune teller to forecast how the rest of his day was going to wind up.

Meanwhile, not a million miles away, Ronnie Callaghan could be heard in conversation with Siddie Levy. The reason for his call stemmed from an incident that had occurred some four hours earlier. Granite, the market inspector, was full of it when relating his version of events at five o'clock that particular morning whilst in Toni de Angelo's watering hole. Unlike the majority of the public, his source of information was first hand from a face anon who just happened to be in the vicinity when the news broke of his death. Ronnie couldn't wait to chip in with his opinion.

"Can't say I'm surprised, Granite. You know what that type is like, there was more to the guy than meets the eye!" The inspector's face lit up.

"Yeah, so are yer saying that yer knew him, or what!" Siddie immediately shot Ronnie a sidelong glance and motioned with a shake of his head.

"Nah, not really, just a stupid rumour, you know what people are like!"

Siddie heaved a sigh of relief; the less anybody knew of their previous involvement regarding the late Dawson the better. Little did Ronnie know at the time, but his integrity was on the line at downtown police HQ. Dawson wasn't about to go away gracefully; he'd become an undeniable asshole right to the bitter end. Not only had he fucked Rossetti by choice but looked to repeat his downfall by implicating Ronnie on demand. It was just after one o'clock that same day when the local plod decided to make themselves known. Ronnie felt under pressure the minute they approached his stall. It became a case of, 'If you don't, you will be arrested on…' Ronnie made it easy for them by deciding to co-operate. Siddie, on the other hand, took their advice badly.

"You schmuck!" he swore. "What about the business already?" The term 'helping with our enquiries' would never sound the same again. Long after his private ordeal was history, Ronnie would say, "But it wasn't your stall that was affected, mate." And in return, Siddie would enlighten him by replying, "What difference? Your loss is my loss, and that's family. So don't kvetch, my friend, tonight we get shickered!" Meanwhile, in the real world, Ronnie found himself banged up and under orders in the statement room. From the beginning, the investigating officer emphasised the point.

"You're free to go whenever. You're not under arrest at this point, do you understand?" Tutting, Ronnie smiled with conviction, nodding his head as he acknowledged the question. His body language radiated confidence. He'd been in tougher fights than this and come back.

"Absolutely. Let's get on with it," he replied.

"Fine, let's see now, how well did you know Dawson?" Simple enough question, requiring an even simpler answer.

"Dawson? I never met the guy in my life," replied Ronnie adamantly.

"Uhm, trouble is, Ronnie, like it or not, we have reason to believe there was a link between yourself and the deceased." Ronnie laughed at his suggestion and quipped, "Flowers have a tendency to die on people, especially when they're not watered. I guess he went to the wrong stall!"

The officer felt the carpet of suspicion lift from underneath his feet, only to disappear out of the window, although he did hold one last trump card of sorts. His damning question, when it came, hit below the belt, forcing Ronnie to sit up and take notice.

"Tell me, does this happen to be your landline number by any chance, Ronnie?" The sudden change in tactics monetarily threw him off course, although he still remained positive as he swiftly gathered his wits.

"You know it is! So do I! Where is this line of conversation heading?" The officer leaned back in his chair wearing a supercilious smile.

"Okay, let's move on, shall we? What can you tell me about this, Ronnie?" he enquired with a ring of confidence. At the same time, he produced a small note pad, which he placed on top of the desk separating them. Shaking his head, Ronnie hardly gave it the benefit of a glance.

"Doesn't mean a thing to me, I've never seen it before in my life, end of!" Suffice to say, the officer didn't appear impressed by his reply, and wouldn't be outdone.

"Would you mind turning the page over when you arrive at C?" Ronnie duly obliged and then wished he hadn't. There was no mistaking his own number staring back at him.

Based on what he already knew regarding his previous phone grief, the reality of the situation caused his body to stiffen. The officer, being old school, had read into his reaction and continued to pursue the current line of enquiry.

"So it's obvious to me that you do know something." Ronnie held back before replying. This latest revelation needed thinking about. Siddie had got it right all along: the bent phone calls he'd received, the Rossetti connection, it all began to make sense now. Ronnie was convinced that it was indeed Dawson who was responsible for the calls. But even more important would be the fact that Dawson knew something that the police didn't, insomuch as the letter R signified it could only have been Rossetti who sent the implicating CD, along with the damning letter.

There and then, Ronnie considered there was no point in harbouring vital information just for the sake of gaining a few brownie points.

Sooner rather than later, the Old Bill would put two and two together and arrive at Rossetti, the latter being Dawson's motive in the first place. Not only that, as a pawn in the ultimate conspiracy, Ronnie would need to come clean by exposing Dawson as the instigator from the moment he walked into the market that fateful day. Convincing the Old Bill that the bent phone calls were genuine wouldn't be a problem. They would have been timed and registered on the day. The ironic part of the whole damn mess was that Rossetti, despite his intentions to frame Dawson and then subsequently murder him, remained totally unaware of Ronnie's presence during the whole rotten sequence of events. More than anything, Ronnie needed to offload what he already knew.

"Know anything?! I got plenty to say, how much time yer got?" He then went on to relate his side of things, without missing a trick. The officer sat back in his chair, his face wearing a mask bordering on satisfaction.

"Well, I guess that puts that you in the clear, Ronnie."

"Clear! Clear of what, precisely?!" Instinctively, Ronnie's face tightened. The officer then chose to use a different angle.

"Not that you were ever thought of as being a suspect, you understand?"

"Obviously not!" Ronnie fired back. The officer rose up from his seat and proffered his hand.

"Thanks for your valuable assistance, it hasn't been an easy case to live with, you understand?"

"On the contrary, mate, I do understand. I know exactly where yer coming from. Life goes on, right?" They shook hands warmly and Ronnie departed on his way. Once outside the station, his initial instinct was to contact Siddie as a kiosk loomed large.

## CHAPTER 14

# DEAL OR NO DEAL

Excluding the fact that he was an eighteen carat public nuisance, you could at least always bank on his consistency. It appeared that Rossetti, yet again, had another problem. This particular one could be classed as habitual, and if challenged he would be more than likely to say, "I simply put the glass to my mouth and swallow, no problem!", which would be acceptable within the confines of one's privacy. But not when holding centre stage by mouthing off, especially when in the company of lowlife in the squalid settings of a Docklands drinking den! Even without the quality of booze, it could only be a recipe for grief, the problem being that how and when it arises controls the number of times you can hope to get away with it just to prove a point.

Even a past master like himself had his limits; suffice to say he didn't need to practise at it. On the back of the Dawson disclosure, Rossetti had decided to linger on at the AA until closing time, commiserating on the loss from a personal hit and the glory that he'd missed out on. He was hurting badly, as was his wedge as note after note was exposed to daylight. Finally, something tripped his mind and he ordered a cab. The barman duly obliged and engaged in conversation with another regular punter. "I swear I don't know how he does it. You'd have thought he'd had enough for one night, and as for that wedge he carries about with him, I reckon that could tell a tale or two."

The punter looked long and hard at Rossetti before remarking, "I'd like to know how his bleedin' mind works!" The barman responded with a negative shake of his head.

"You'd need to do a bloody post mortem on him to answer that one!" While he was waiting, Rossetti began to question his spontaneous decision to hit the town. He'd certainly pushed his luck in China Town recently, when the Rinse fortunately managed to bail him out. Any further reasoning faded into obscurity as a mental image of Dawson took over, forcing him into a verbal rant. Nobody was more relieved than the barman when the cabbie finally put his head round the door. He wasn't impressed, his jaw dropping as the barman indicated Rossetti, who by now was beginning to show signs of neglect in the leg department.

"Shit! Just my poxy luck to get that tosser for a fare!" he exclaimed. "I'll make double sure I make it into a nice little earner, the state he is in." Having negotiated his 'bloody nuisance' into the back seat, he was eager to get on his way. A few minutes later into the journey he checked on Rossetti through his rear mirror, just as a red light began to emerge in the distance. It quickly became obvious that his fare was well and truly out of it, so any form of conversation at this point went out with pink socks. Breathing a sigh of relief, he remarked, "Just as bloody well!" as the lights then changed in his favour.

Fortunately, the barman at the AA had forwarded the destination anyway, although he was forced to question the initial option and replace it with "Fucking Beachy Head, if I had my way!" Some ten minutes later via Canal Street, the cab eased to a stop outside the Miami Club, this side of China Town. "Wakey wakey, Rossi! End of the line," the driver shouted. It took a minute or two before he connected with the real world as his bleary eyes struggled to co-operate. *Never fails*, the cabbie assured himself, and turned his torch off. "Miami Club as ordered, guv." Rossetti stirred and endeavoured to sit up.

"Huh! I suppose yer looking for some poxy dough?" he slobbered.

"That's the general idea, mate. 'Ere, allow me." By this time, Rossetti had pulled out a fistful of notes from his inside jacket pocket and began to flaunt them at the cabbie. The driver's eyes popped as he swiftly relieved him to the tune of two £20 notes. "There yer go, mate, sorted! That'll cover it, don't worry about a tip." Having struggled to get his fare as far as the front door, his job was now over. Besides which, the £40 he'd lifted had begun to burn a hole in his pocket. He walked across to his car without looking back. A mask of satisfaction creased his face as he turned the key in the ignition. *There's one born every minute, the guy's a bleedin' loser*, he told himself. The engine burst into life; he slid away from the kerbside. Booting the accelerator, he sped off. One thing he could bank on would be knowing that his night would be better than most.

Since leaving the sanctity of the AA, things had moved very quickly. For the time being, Rossetti wasn't about to go anywhere as he stood lost in a stupor outside the entrance to the club. His current situation, had he been aware, now came under scrutiny as self-preservation hung in the balance. His addled mind began to swirl around as the atmosphere of the locale gripped him, while seemingly taking over his whole body. Considering the time of night, the streets still bustled with revellers and the traffic still flowed. He appeared to be transfixed by the noise and the interactive lighting that engulfed him. On a scale of 1 to 10, he'd have readily qualified as a legless bastard with honours! But then, he did have this gimpy leg to contend with. On top of that, whatever sensibility he had left badly needed reviewing. At the moment, it was working on automatic or, in the real world, nowhere bloody fast.

Just then his body shuddered spasmodically as the cold night air injected his pathetic frame. For some unknown reason, his actions caused him to involuntarily check out his wedge. Suffice to say, it was a token gesture of self-survival, when associated with monetary terms. Knowing how to hang on to it for what it was originally intended for would be crucial to his uncertain future.

The £10,000 down payment via the Rinse had been eroding on a daily basis, with booze being the prime investor, but sadly, with no return. As yet, his obsolete reasoning hadn't registered the fact that his windfall just might revert to a results-only policy, with an inclusion clause regarding suicide now meaning 'all bets off and monies refunded'! Gritting his teeth, he half stumbled through the club door. Whatever opinion you might hold, you could always rely on the man to make an entrance wherever. In this particular case, it came at the expense of a table and a couple of chairs he'd collided with. I mean, c'mon, who'd be stupid enough to place furniture in a bar? At least the experience had the desired effect of sobering him up to some extent.

A mental vision of his wedge flashed through his mind before he collided with the floor, and with good reason. Any third party assistance meant arms, and arms had hands on the end! All he had to do would be to get up and talk a good drink.

I mean, how hard is that?! Some six years ago, the club became a second home to him when affiliated to the Terry Winters regime of old. At that time, it was a convenient safe house patronised by a clientele ranging from chancers to full-time villains. The minute you walked or staggered in through the door, you became rubber-stamped as a victim of circumstances, and then paid for the privilege it offered by way of your pocket. But that was then and this now! As clubs come and go, the Miami hadn't really moved on, apart from the furniture that appeared to move now and then. The booze was still as wet as the floor, and the alcohol content in the optics was found to be debatable in the spirit world.

Rossetti steadied himself before venturing any further. Still, with plenty of shit flying around in his head primed by the Dawson saga, an altercation no matter what could prove to be his premature downfall. As it was, instinct cut in, making decisions without him having to think. He shook his head, then narrowed his eyes to counteract the subdued lighting confronting him. The lack of punters in the bar area told a story. Squinting at his watch confirmed his thoughts. "One o'clock, early days yet," he muttered. Slowly, familiar images materialised as recognition set in, considering that his situation began on the strength of a mad whim, born out of habit. He felt that he hadn't really been away from the place. Just then, his space suddenly became invaded by a nearby figure who'd witnessed his dramatic entry.

"Excuse me, sir, I presume yer a paid-up member?" Fair question! Over to you, Rossetti. For once in his torrid life, he now found himself stuck for a reply. The undeniable statement had blitzed any protocol hidden away within his twisted mind, leaving him to fire back in his own self-ordained way.

"A member?!" he retorted. "I've bought this poxy gaff twice over! So what's yer bleedin' problem?" Diplomatic as ever, the bouncer proceeded to do his job.

"I don't happen to have a problem, sir, but if you're intent on having a drink, you'll need to sign the visitors' register please."

"Hold up, so what are yer saying? You want my fucking autograph?" Right answer, wrong context! Forced into a corner, the bouncer motioned toward the exit, and took hold of his arm as he spoke.

"If you can't hold yer drink, then yer can't hold a pen! Let's go." Rossetti felt stunned by the bouncer's reply; all things being equal, he'd have settled for a smack in the mouth. His solitude didn't reign for long; his shocked exodus became history as his brain engaged, and he exploded into a verbal rant.

"Get out of my face, you know nothing, asshole! D'ye know who I am?" Their altercation ground to an unexpected halt as a third party emerged from out of the gloom. Confronting Rossetti, he released his arm before speaking.

"Relax! The guy wouldn't know yer from a biscuit barrel, but I would, Rossi!" His sudden statement hit him between the eyes, leaving him dumbfounded. For the second time in five minutes he'd been wiped out, all due to a situation he couldn't control. Not that he needed to, the voice in itself would have convinced him; it was the coolness of the man that wrapped it up.

"Frankie?!" The figure stepped forward into the light. Rossetti heaved a sigh of relief. "Shit, man! What the fuck are you doing 'ere?!" The Rinse appeared to be unmoved by his disclosure; instead he turned to the bouncer for conversation.

"It's okay, Jackie, I'll sort this one out. 'Ere, go get yerself a drink at the bar," and handed him a £10 note. Looking at Rossetti for a few seconds, he chewed on his lip before finally speaking. "Firstly, I'll tell yer why I'm 'ere, Rossi. On a need to know basis, it's because I happen to own the gaff! And secondly, you're getting to be one very bad fucking habit!" It's been said that coffee can have a sobering effect on some people. Frankie 'the Rinse' did it with the use of words, causing Rossetti to smart. He continued, "Anyway, I'm glad that you've called in, so to speak!" and continued patronisingly, "At least that's one phone call I now won't have to make!"

Putting it mildly, Rossetti's brain was like a roller coaster: up one minute, down the next. Then just as quickly, a breakthrough occurred. The alleged phone call had now triggered positive thoughts – money included. An image of Dawson had entered the equation. "Of course! The stupid bleeder thinks I'm 'ere to claim the balance on the contract, what a result!" he assured himself. The Rinse interjected, swiftly bringing him back down to earth.

"We can do all the talking we need to in my office, just follow me, Rossi." The room in question could be found at the far end of the bar and at the bottom of a flight of stairs leading into the basement area. The Rinse unlocked the door and ushered Rossetti inside. He stopped short as the room offered up its full potential. From then on, Rossetti's eyes did a full three-hundred and sixty-five degree turn, as he attempted to take in the room and all of its contents.

"Stone me! He's got a right little Aladdin's cave 'ere!" he mused. Old Masters dripped off the four walls, in turn complementing the plush, antique furniture and fittings. The thickness of the lush carpet he was standing on spoke volumes. Even with his gimpy leg, he wouldn't have had a problem skiing. The Rinse observed that his pension had made an immediate impression on Rossetti and broke his train of thought.

"Make yerself at home, Rossi, grab a seat." He concluded, "You seem to like what yer see, Rossi, nice eh?" So it was only small talk, but also with an ulterior motive pending.

"Yeah, yer could say that! If yer ever had to sell it, yer looking at a nice bit of wedge, right?!" In reply, the Rinse went for the verbal jugular.

"Exactly my sentiments, Rossi. Which brings me to the crux... Dawson!" Rossetti began to fidget as their strained conversation switched rails. *Where's he bleedin' going with this,*

*I wonder?* he thought. Picking up on his body language, the Rinse continued. "Tell yer what, how about a drink, Rossi? Scotch, I believe?" Currently that was the best offer he'd had all night. Besides which, he felt an air of uncertainty on the loose, making him feel somewhat uneasy.

Glancing upward, an original Constable hanging on the wall caught his gaze, causing him to reflect that a large Scotch in his hand would be a far better proposition from where he was sitting. "Cheers, Rossi!"

"Yeah, same as that," replied Rossetti, making the most of his first gulp. Meanwhile, the Rinse had eased himself back into his dimpled leather seat and proceeded to toy with his Martini. In spite of an injection of Scotch, Rossetti's confidence level started to ooze away quicker than the second hand of the carriage clock situated on a nearby card table.

Breaking off, the Rinse looked up. "I'll get straight to the point, Rossi, I've seen a seat that I like, right? In fact, it matches the one yer sitting on, trouble is, we're talking a nice few quid, know what I mean?" By now, Rossetti was close to freaking out. *Poxy chair? The geezer's lost it. We should be talking about our contract instead of bleedin' mind games!* he told himself, but decided to stick with the level of conversation.

"Yeah well, how much exactly for the chair?"

"£10,000 to be precise, although right now I don't seem to have that sort of money available." Leaning forward, he rested his arms on the table in front of him and gave a meaningful look. "But you have, Rossi!" Rossetti now felt slaughtered by the implication alone. The man had handpicked his words very carefully, leaving him wandering in no man's land, screaming for survival.

"We had a deal! I did the fucking business by getting the asshole off yer back, so what are yer laying on me?" The Rinse gave a cryptic smile before replying, "Unfortunately, Rossi, the firm don't see it like that! A blank disc and a poxy get well card just don't run to a £10,000 investment!"

"I fucking mullered the geezer, what d'ye want from me!" he spluttered. Rossetti was losing it fast; in contrast, the Rinse remained calm as he pressed a button hidden underneath the desktop.

"You just don't get it, Rossi, do yer? You aided and abetted a bent cop into blowing his fucking brains out, right? But at the end of the day, your finger was no more on his gun trigger than mine! As a result, the firm are now rightly saying that the original contract is an aborted deal. All they are looking for is their £10,000 back, end of story!"

"You bastard, Frankie, you've had me over, you can go to hell!" By now, he was on his feet and screaming threats, oblivious to the figure entering the room from behind him.

From then on, any form of resistance was futile. For Rossetti, it felt as if the two opposing walls had filled in around him as two massive arms encircled him from behind, before finally lifting his body completely off the floor.

He felt his chest begin to close down as he strenuously fought to regain his breath.

"Thank you, Donna!" The Rinse seemed totally unaffected by the drama unfolding, and jabbed his finger at Rossetti as he spoke. "One week, Rossi! You have the benefit of one week to get the money together, d'ye understand?! When yer do, you know where to find me. I'll advise you again to be sensible about this proposition." Rossetti's attempts to retaliate ran to zero as a hand the size of a shovel blotted his mouth out, rendering him verbally useless.

"Where to boss?" the gorilla enquired nonchalantly.

"Oh yeah, obviously the back way, Donna. Ideally into the alleyway, and make sure the fire door is shut when you return." He made three or four sweeping motions with his hand before continuing. "Just get the fucking loser out of my sight!"

With Rossetti off the scene, it was time to relax once again. Removing a handmade silk handkerchief from his top pocket, he began to wipe his brow, and replenished his glass from a nearby solid silver shaker resting in an ice bucket. "Uhm, nasty business that! So unnecessary," he concluded as he sipped his Martini, pausing only to replace the glass on the table, every movement he made as methodical as it was intended to be, leaving him to savour the remains of the drink.

Reaching out with one arm, he manipulated a secret drawer built into the desktop; methodical as ever, he removed a black leather address book. Flicking the pages, he stopped at the letter J. Removing the antique handset from its rest, he carefully dialled the appropriate digits for Jersey – 01534 – plus a private number. Speaking out loud seemed to be a requirement. "It's such a pity it had to come to this, but the asshole was going nowhere, he just can't be trusted anymore..." His private speech was curtailed as the Jersey connection came through. Five minutes later, he replaced the handset as a broad smile embroidered his face.

"Sorted!" was all he said, and made his way upstairs. He still appeared to be smiling five minutes later as he began to check the bar till.

CHAPTER 15

# A WAKE-UP CALL

The faceless recipient in Jersey also had a valid reason to smile, although, unlike the Rinse, his was as exclusive as it was false, when linked to his ongoing thirst for, or rather sadistic pleasure in, bringing about 'death-on-line'. His toneless voice would be the only sole form of bodily contact, from the beginning through to the end of any agreed contract. In the underground world of shadows and false identities that surrounded his macabre existence. His professionalism as a paid hitman derived from a long and successful career. "Experience," as he would explain, "is simply a 'body' interrupting my line of fire", proving that the wealth and property he'd amassed over the years derived from unswerving reliability! On the business side, the Rinse connection had been the third enquiry inside of three months. The last two were fortunately fatal in their singular expedience, and simply classed as being a 'termination agreement', or to the underworld, a 'contract'. Like any other business, certain conditions prevailed, which made for a joint understanding between buyer and seller. This applied mainly to the contract, enabling the fee to be fully paid up prior to him proceeding. All things considered, it's fair to say that in over twenty-five years in business he never had a bad payer.

Moving on, he did hold a no-fee-no-win file on prospective 'victims', until such time that a particular contract became tenable. Amongst others, his files contained the available SP on two prospective victims, both of whom claimed to have strong links to Stonewater UK. Unfortunately for one of them, a contract would become reality within forty-eight hours, and then, quote: 'at your convenience'. Replacing the phone, Buffy Manilla crossed to a bureau and removed a file marked 'Pending'. From amongst the contents he removed a mugshot photo. Once again he smiled insidiously as a feeling of recognition set in. Nodding confidently, he looked up from the photo. His eyes narrowed as he came to a conclusion that had remained dormant for some time inside his calculating brain.

Eventually he spoke. "Interesting, two different sources, but both for the same victim! Ah, just as I thought, he's obviously upset a few more faces along the way. I think I'll treat this particular one as personal!" His intended victim should be congratulated on the manner by which Manilla had influenced his would-be executioner. Having replaced the file in its original order, the relaxing ambience and solitude of his luxury integral swimming pool beckoned. The time in Jersey was approaching 1.45am, but time to him was meaningless, with no set pattern to his torrid existence. According to Buffy Manilla, a clock just counted as a function of life that happened to be there. After all was said and done, his prime role in life would be to eradicate the latter, and not to gratify it!

Inside the following twenty-four hours or so, one particular tax exile residing in Spain would be making the headlines for all the wrong reasons. The intended scenario would entail another day in the office, or business as usual for hitman Buffy Manilla, as he was known by Interpol and New Scotland Yard alike.

In terms of preservation, Rossetti was hurting badly... again! In both body and soul. So nothing new there then! Except to say, the consistency of his deadbeat existence had now moved up another league in intensity. Meanwhile, his fantasy alter-ego had dramatically nosedived, but this time around lower than the bottom step of the fire exit from which he'd been surgically ejected a few seconds previously. The grotty surface of the cobble-lined back alley gave a whole new meaning to the term 'discomfort' as beleaguered flesh and blood made contact. The inevitable pain that followed was briefly lost as a surge of torment racked his pathetic frame. And he in turn became consumed by overriding hatred directed at both the Rinse and the world at large; why not?

Given time, the pain would eventually become redundant, leaving only self-ordained misery as his only ally. Slowly, and cursing inwardly, Rossetti struggled to regain his feet. Raising his head, a volley of abuse spewed from his twisted mouth. He could have saved his breath as his ranting fell on deaf ears, and in turn was swallowed up by the environment he felt himself cocooned in. He shuddered involuntarily as the keen night air colluded with the untimely shock of realisation as to his situation. An adjacent waste skip afforded him a moment's reprieve as a means of support, enabling him to take stock of his plight.

Unaided, his inferior brain swung into play, targeted by a distant image from the remnants of his ego ladder screaming out for belated attention. He shook his head vigorously in a vain attempt to merge his deluded feelings. The moment became all bets off as any ambitious cravings were swept to one side. Slowly, rung-by-rung, his doomed vision disintegrated into an abyss of self-destruction. His body suddenly stiffened as a cold wave of fear took hold, putting his situation into perspective. It was simply reminding him that, as from now, he'd become a marked man. Frank 'the Rinse' had stated his case in no uncertain terms as to his immediate future. The moment had become a wake-up call.

Coupled with Dawson's demise, a strange turn of events had now transpired to heap on his misery. Dawson had unwittingly left Rossetti a legacy beyond his control. His untimely suicide, selfish or otherwise, was classed as on the house at the time, with all outside interest barred, leaving Rossetti a victim of circumstances by a quirk of fate. He now found himself saddled with £10,000 worth of blood money, now firmly attached to his own precarious future. The down payment he'd secured had now become a number one interest-free transfer account, and the premium to be paid in blood via a bullet unleashed from a covert assassin.

On the plus side, at least the keen night air was free. Breaking off, he took advantage of it by inhaling deeply for a few seconds, mainly to regain composure. Adjusting the sleeve of his jacket, his watch happened to catch his eye. "Just after twelve o'clock," he muttered to himself, and continued, "It's only time lent, d'ye hear me, Rinse? I'll have my day, and when..." He stopped short as a scavenging rat emerging from within the bowels of the skip suddenly caught his attention as it chose to linger and sniff the air. For some unknown reason, Rossetti felt drawn to its presence as he stood trance-like watching its performance. Three or four times, the vermin disappeared, only to return from amongst the trash. At length, it emerged once again, this time clutching the remains of a half-eaten burger which it subsequently set about devouring. There and then, the affinity that Rossetti felt toward the rat became cemented as the rat briefly left off to eyeball its inquisitor. Finally, the deadlock ceased, but not before Rossetti had spoken his mind. "Yer a game little bastard, I'll give yer that! You got what yer wanted by trying. We're two of a kind, you and me, two bleedin' rats together. It's all about survival in the end." The rat gave him a quizzical look and vanished in the trash before he could finish.

*Ah, what's the poxy point?* he asked himself. *Besides, he got what he was after, nah it's my turn!* In a final gesture to endorse his burst of newfound egotism, he raised a clenched fist skyward, venting his feelings in the process. "Rinse! Callaghan! It all starts 'ere and now. It took a rat to show a rat the answer, I'll see yer both in hell before it's all over!" He could still be heard ranting to himself as he skulked out of the alleyway. Having paid the cabbie off, the entrance to the AA loomed large; pulling himself together, he lost no time going in. Apart from a few regular stragglers, the bar itself appeared to be deserted. The regular barman glanced up as Rossetti approached. Discarding the remnants of his cigarette in the trash bin, he decided on a conversation of sorts.

"Blimey, Rossi, I didn't expect to see you until tomorrow. What happened? D'ye get blown out?" For a few seconds, a stand-off situation left Rossetti's thoughts to go into overdrive. Slowly and deliberately, his eyes dropped floorwards, narrowing as they did so. The barman, sensing a backlash, reached out for a nearby pint glass in anticipation of a likely confrontation. Rossetti looked up with enflamed eyes. The leer on his face complemented a threatening reply.

"Just do yer poxy job and stick a Scotch in a glass for me, and for the record, I don't do bitches, asshole!" There and then, the barman decided that his job was bigger than his mouth, and duly obliged by fixing him a double, sighing with relief as he did so.

*That could have been a bit nasty*, he told himself. *Saying that, I'll be bloody glad to see the back end of him, the geezer's impossible!*

Rossetti glared in response as he weighed him in, and made himself distant by taking a corner table in the bar. Changing the habit of a lifetime, he elected to place his drink to one side as he contemplated instead the events of the last few hours. His addled thoughts swung one way and then the other, before finally descending into the bottomless pit that was his mind. He buried his face in his open hands in an attempt to escape his thoughts. Who was he kidding? You can't buy circumstances off the shelf; like it or not, they just happen to come with the turf. Putting it mildly, he'd had one hell of a shit day! So welcome to the real world, Rossetti!

Breaking off for a second, he averted his gaze towards his glass of Scotch. That too had somehow begun to lose its appeal, tempted as he was to down it. It would seem that just for once in his indecisive life, a nomadic section of his brain had suddenly started to register positive. Time and time again, his clenched fist made contact with the table top in frustration; eventually he spoke. "I gotta get focused, there's too much shit going down, I have to deal with it!" Conclusion chased conclusion as he sought a deal with reality inside his troubled mind. At least there was something on offer. In retrospect, twenty-four hours ago his distorted brain would have obliterated any form of logical reasoning out of sight.

So here we are, and another wheel in the life of one Paul Rossetti had once again turned full circle, in the process condemning his future existence to an acute case of survival. He of all people understood the rules; now would be the time to deliver should his ongoing and personal vendetta ever materialise. Unfortunately for him, fate would need to be consulted; the fact that Dawson was now out of the equation had inadvertently left him holding a passport to eternal grief. Consequently, this last altercation with the Rinse contained serious undertones, climaxing in a permanent penalty clause.

Time itself is endless, until analysed of course, assuming that you have it to spare; failing that, it can become a bore. In his case the luxury arising from a week's reprieve was already starting to ebb away minute by minute as he sat deliberating over a game plan based on the evidence surrounding his dilemma.

The fact that he appeared to be oblivious to a form of contract that lay in the offing courtesy of the Rinse gained no more credence in his impending security problem. Fortunately, a vision of Maltese Pete entered his mode of thought. Glancing upward, lips pursed, he nodded conclusively as the hint of a vengeful smile slowly lit up his face. He'd been thrown a delicate lifeline which he desperately needed to capitalise on. *I need to get myself tooled up, no question! Besides, the geezer owes me. Yeah, I'll get it sorted!* he convinced himself.

Elsewhere, the barman felt bored and tired; luckily another ten minutes would see him finished for the day. With nothing to lose, he looked across in Rossetti's direction; picking up on his twenty minutes or so of sobriety, he decided to go for bust. "Hey, Rossi, you gonna drink that Scotch before it goes off?!" he shouted. His line of sarcasm fell on deaf ears; Rossetti appeared to be unmoved. In its place, a form of sensibility had kicked in. It seemed that his borrowed existence had finally hit base, although there were two other factors that would need addressing: namely, the residue concerning the £10,000 blood money, the effects of which could result in a knock-on effect as from now. He realised that a change in address would have to become an absolute priority. The all-too-convenient lifestyle given up by the AA had, in the short term, run its course. The time was ripe to evolve by creating a covert existence, but under an alternative roof. As for the money, its ownership had never been contentious from the moment it formed part of their deal, although retaining the wedge as a whole would far outweigh the grief it could create in the long term.

Easing himself back into his seat, he reached out for his Scotch, as yet untouched. Caressing the glass, he began to ponder over what dregs of thought remained, any of which could enhance the outcome of the decisions he'd arrived at. Finally, the curtain fell as his brain shut down, leaving him a determined man. Raising his glass, he ogled the contents for a few seconds as if mesmerised and uttered, "Here's to you, Rossi." The Scotch never touched the sides as he promptly threw it down his throat. Gritting his teeth he winced, the drink having left its mark.

Rising from his seat, he crossed the floor and made for the stairs leading to his bolt hole. The barman glanced across and shouted out a token, "Goodnight". He needn't have bothered as Rossetti chose to ignore the interruption as to his future welfare. "Please yer bloody self," the barman remarked casually, and considered an alternative option before continuing, "Now there goes a man with half the bleedin' world on his shoulders. Me? I'm only married!" A percentage of people could say that one man's observations needed a reversal in terms of truth. But, whichever way you played it, Rossetti's fate was placed directly at his own front door. Only time itself held the key to that line of thought. Needless to say, he slept like a baby that night.

## CHAPTER 16

# RESULTS ALL ROUND

Living with an image of his nemesis Ronnie Callaghan proved grief enough in terms of contradiction. Putting it mildly, Rossetti's view of the world in general wouldn't have changed one iota, even if he were to wear rose-tinted glasses. His infinite urge to intern the ghost into a permanent fixture, care of the local graveyard, had now become an overwhelming obsession due to his new take on life. Even his dented mental status had been granted a reprieve, and could now be found hovering between the borders of insecure stability and a mockney version of sanity! It reflected the profile of a desperate man living on the sands of borrowed time. But at least he was on the case; the last twenty-four hours had proven to be fruitful. When locating the whereabouts of the illusive Maltese Pete, the overriding fact that he was even on the manor gave Rossetti a glimmer of hope.

As it was, there were untold hurdles placed in his path, but his feet firmly gripped the starting line in a fresh bid to become the running man. Acting on the information he'd fortuitously gleaned via his fragile link to the local underworld would now see him out of the starting blocks. His only problem, should it arise, would be confronting the only person who could effectively get him over the first hurdle. *The guy is like a bleedin' bomb waiting to go off!* he reminded himself. *And that's on a good day, at least I've got the wedge to bail myself out if it all goes belly up.*

The sudden downpour he'd been experiencing left off as quickly as it had started. "Not before poxy time, bleedin' weather!" Rossetti expressed his displeasure and hesitantly emerged from the shadows of a shop doorway where he'd been forced to seek solace from the unexpected downpour. His hands dug deep inside the pockets of his Crombie overcoat as he digressed. Standing on the edge of the kerb, he peered across to the other side of the road. Through the misty light, he could just make out a solitary doorway. The dismal display above the transom, dark as it was, gave him cause to relax for a minute. "Uhm, the Officers' Club," he convinced himself, and mumbled, "At least I've got something right!"

The coldness of the night air penetrated his body, lulling him into a final decision. *What the hell! I've come this poxy far!* With that, he made his way across the road. Faltering briefly, he nervously checked his watch before entering the club. If the information he held proved to be kosher, there was more than a chance he could be tooled up before the night was through. The first unforeseen hurdle he encountered came by way of the resident bouncer who made it quite clear by getting busy. It was a knock back Rossetti hadn't allowed for as the Muscle quizzed him for a form of ID, leaving him to pale at the thought of being ejected. His only trump card was one of bluff as he rifled in his pocket for a £20 note, pleading as he did so. "Maltese can vouch for me, we got some business to sort out. 'Ere, this should make it easier to find him."

The Muscle never moved a hair as the sweetener was thrust into his top jacket pocket. "I didn't see that!" he responded, and continued, "But if there's a next time, then the ante goes up. In the meantime, behave yerself otherwise yer out on yer neck!" The moment became a war of attitudes as Rossetti fired up inwardly and just as swiftly opted to bite his tongue. He realised there was far too much riding on the outcome and that grief wasn't on the cards. He uttered a token thanks under his breath, and made his way into the smoke-filled bar. Once inside, he couldn't wait to have a passing dig at the Muscle when out of earshot. "Flash bastard! The Traveller would have mullered him six years ago, and saved some for breakfast!"

Through the palls of haze created by the habitual smoke, the optics hanging behind the bar beckoned him, and like a magnet began to draw him in. Grabbing a bar stool, he plonked himself down and ordered a large Scotch. The past incident and the conclusion it provoked faded rapidly as he scanned the faces sitting around the bar; in the event Maltese had made an appearance. Further investigation drew a blank, and a seed of doubt entered the equation. "Shit!" was the best he could offer, though his Scotch helped offset a distinct mood of pessimism. Time began a war of nerves as Rossetti toyed with his third Scotch. He momentarily broke off to check his watch. The mask of disdain that crossed his face spoke volumes.

Even his drink had lost its flavour and become a non-runner! He felt gutted; he'd paid out good money for information that now looked likely to come to nothing. His mind churned one way and back again as he recalled the verbal attached to its source. "You ain't got a problem, take it from me he'll be there. He'll be involved in a big card school that's going down, and I mean big! He jumped up when I had to pull out, the money involved was too heavy for me." Trouble is, that was then and this was now. Suddenly, and without warning, his elbows collapsed on to the bar top from the weight of an alien hand descending on his shoulder. His gut tightened as a cold wave of fear impacted his body.

For a few seconds his inanimate frame lay sprawled across the bar. As the pressure began to lift, he instinctively spun around in retaliation. A mask of disbelief locked horns with premeditated intentions as the two faced off.

Immediate recognition set in, leaving Rossetti only too eager to back off. "Fuck's sake! What the hell you playing at, Pete?!" he gasped. Relieved as he was, there was no way he could let Maltese think that their untimely meeting was anything less than coincidental. "How did yer know it was me anyway?" Maltese jutted his jaw as he eyeballed Rossetti before replying.

"Simple!" he exclaimed, laughing deeply from the back of his throat. "Yer the only bleedin' cripple in 'ere, right?" His implication forced Rossetti to squirm inwardly in a vain attempt to conceal his reaction. There was more to come as Maltese pressed home a verbal advantage. "Bit off the manor ain't yer, Rossi? You must have pissed somebody off!" Once again he found himself off balance as the proverbial knife went deeper, finally twisting in his gut.

Money, it has been said, talks in any language and Rossetti quickly reminded himself that the wedge he'd got stashed in his pocket would hold up for a thirsty oration if and when push came to shove. "Money! Let's talk money!" When considering his delicate present situation, Rossetti, nevertheless, remained calm and collected as he spat it out. The reaction it evoked from Maltese forced Rossetti back onto an even keel. "I owe yer, remember?" he reminded him. "For the shooter, that is. Where do we go from 'ere?"

"As it happens, Rossi," Maltese replied, "we can talk some business. Yer lucky, yer caught me in a good mood."

"Good!" exclaimed Rossetti. "Fuck, you're in a bad one!" Okay, so it appeared to be patronising, but coupled with a result as Maltese sealed a verbal deal.

"Tonight I'm feeling lucky, Rossi, so I'll overlook the afterhours intrusion this time around. By the way, I managed to get the right tool and ammunition yer after, so let's talk some money." Rossetti heaved a huge sigh of pent-up relief before replying.

"Fine, it's as good as sorted from where I'm standing. You can have the £400 balance I owe yer, here and now." A pregnant pause set in, making him feel him somewhat isolated for a second, and he needed to deal with it. "Surely that ain't a problem?!" he retorted. Shaking his head, Maltese effected an insidious smile.

"Not from where I'm standing, Rossi, but I think the Rinse might want to run with a different version. From what I've heard, you ain't exactly flavour of the month just nah." This latest revelation came like a bolt out the blue, leaving Rossetti feeling slaughtered. He now found himself struggling to deal with the implication.

"The Rinse! What's that asshole got to do with the deal we made?" he snapped back. In reply, Maltese laid it on the line.

"It seems yer can't afford to fuck with me, Rossi. So I'll level with yer. I happen to know that the geezer wants you removed permanently by way of a contract. Meaning that the shooter is the only friend you've got, at an adjusted price of £800! As for the information I've given yer, you get that for nothing." Rossetti was now rendered speechless as Maltese did a demolition job on him, at the same time hanging him out to dry in the process. He knew it, and the rest of the world knew it: he'd become an outsider in a three-horse race he was never going to win.

His hands were shaking with temper as he peeled off the £800 in blood money from his ever-declining wedge. He felt gutted, and Maltese was well aware of the fact. "Just look on the money as an investment, Rossi. Yer broke the bloody rules and now it's come back to haunt yer. From now on, yer need to start looking over yer shoulder if you want to stay healthy."

"So what's bleedin' new?!" questioned Rossetti, not that Maltese could give a damn anyway.

"Ain't my problem, Rossi, although me and the Rinse, we go back a long way so I know what the guy's capable of. I'm only telling yer this cos the asshole ain't exactly on my Xmas list, know what I mean?"

"Huh!" snorted Rossetti. "I've got nothing to lose, he doesn't frighten me!"

"Whatever, Rossi. Look, why don't yer lose yerself for a while? 'Ere, tell yer what," fumbling in his back pocket he produced a tatty calling card which he thrust into Rossetti's hand, "for what it's worth, you might wanna ring this number. Do yerself a favour, the guy is a pal of mine, he runs a safe house in town."

"Yeah? I might just do that, thanks for the SP."

"No problem. In the meantime, we need to sort out a meet for tomorrow morning, and you can pick up yer insurance. Now let's have a fucking drink! I've got a date with a pack of cards and four losers in twenty minutes."

Early next morning, as arranged, Rossetti could be found lurking underneath a convenient flyover in possession of the security he'd craved. Personalities apart, business is business the world over, and for his part of the deal, Maltese had been on the case and delivering. "There yer go, Rossi, yer pays yer money yer gets a result! Okay? You've got a .38 snubnose Cobra Colt, no ID attached, plus a dozen rounds. For what it's worth, the shooter is called a Snubbie in the right circles!" He pondered before continuing, "Used the right way, a man could do a fucking lot of damage with a tool like that!" Breaking off, his eyes narrowed, and he concluded, "But that's your business, right?!"

Rossetti was made up with his newfound toy, and it showed. "Yeah, I intend doing just that! And you can make a book on it. As from nah, this little beauty is gonna be my mouthpiece. Nobody will fuck with me anymore. Them days are antique, you'll see." Maltese appeared to be oblivious to his egotistical ranting.

"Yeah, yeah, whatever yer say, Rossi." His prime thoughts belonged elsewhere. As far as he was concerned, their meet had ended there, leaving Rossetti to continue issuing a one-man warning to the world at large.

The lust for more money kicked in, reminding him he needed to be long gone. A hasty "See yer around, Rossi" was lost in the roar of his car engine as he accelerated away in a cloud of dust, leaving Rossetti playing out his egoistic charade to an audience of one. At least he had something going for him, crazy or otherwise, which was a damn sight more than the phone situated in the downtown gym office. It had been sounding off for a couple of minutes, before finally being attended to by Dave Molloy. Fortunately, the door to the office had been left ajar, prompting him to act. Snatching at the handset, he made himself known.

"Hello... Molloy speaking... can I help?" The reply, when it came, was swift and laced with positiveness.

"Hopefully, I'm trying to contact Tommy Russell."

"Who's enquiring?"

"It's Charlie Cochrane, promoter!"

"Oh sorry, mate, I didn't recognise yer voice. Tommy's laid low at the moment, poxy flu I think. Hang about, I'll get hold of Ronnie for yer. He's bound to know the SP."

"Thanks, appreciate it." Molloy lowered the phone and beckoned across to the ring in an effort to gain Ronnie's attention. Calling time on the session, Ronnie climbed out of the ring and made his way over.

"Who is it, Dave?"

"Charlie, Charlie Cochrane, that is."

"Good news I hope! 'Ere, take over for a while will yer, this could take some time, please God!"

"Sorted, no problem."

"Charlie? Ronnie Callaghan, what can I do for yer, mate?"

"Hi, basically, it's what I can do for you. Molloy was just saying that Tommy is feeling iffy at the moment."

"Yeah, afraid so, is there a message I can forward?"

"I'm ringing to say that I've verified the contract concerning young Danny Simmons."

"That'll do for me, Charlie, that's the hard bit out the way."

"Exactly! As you know, we discussed the venue the other week that has also been finalised, so we're looking at the first week in September, Tuesday the 4th to be precise. Simmons will be on the back half of the bill, so don't break a leg to get 'ere, okay? In the meantime, keep me posted on the kid's progress, especially any untoward injuries whatever. I won't bother Tommy for a couple of days. I'll leave it in your capable hands, Ronnie, but let him know I called anyway."

"Sorted, mate, leave it with me."

"Oh, just one other thing. Is that sparring partner you're using earning his dough?"

"Absolutely! No question, mate. The guy has proved to be invaluable in Simmons' build-up, can't fault him. I can't thank yer enough for getting him involved."

"Only too pleased to be of assistance, Ronnie. Anyway, onwards and upwards, be in touch."

"You do that, Charlie. Be lucky, bye." Ronnie replaced the receiver with a look of approval. "Now there's a man I could do business with 24/7, best thing that ever happened for the stable." Any further sentiment died a death as Simmons caught his eye as he sparred. Checking himself, he reverted into spectator mode. *There's no question, the kid's beginning to look more fluent in the way he moves now*, he told himself assuredly, and continued. *Especially the way he seems to set Jenkins up for the big one!* He cringed as Simmons cleverly wrong footed his man while firing a full-blooded right hand to the side of the head. Impressed as he was, Ronnie could sense the makings of a gym war erupting between the two as Jenkins fired back in response.

Enthusiasm was one thing, but a possible injury arising from a moment of madness would become a trainer's worst nightmare. Even more so at this juncture in Simmons' pre-fight build-up. Ronnie had seen enough. Swiftly crossing over to the ring, he levelled his concern by bawling the two fighters out. As a sweetener, he pulled Simmons to one side. "I think we get the message, Danny," and added, "Do yerself a favour, and save it for the big night, son!" A shadow from behind then caught his eye, and he turned to acknowledge Mickey Gibbons who appeared desperate to air his views.

"Blimey! That could have been nasty, mate. You read that one about right, but I gotta say, the kid's come on a bundle since Jenkins came onto the scene. They definitely suit each other." He was referring to the fact that Jenkins found himself inducted into the stable via Charlie Cochrane. Simple reason being that Simmons' next opponent was a Southpaw the same as Jenkins, hence the need of his services.

"Ouch! I felt that too," Gibbons again remarked as Simmons off-loaded another good shot. Ronnie grimaced.

"Yeah, you and me both, Mickey, but I've yet to meet a Southpaw who wasn't a sucker for a right hand!"

"I ain't about to argue with that! It's just the gift of knowing when and how to set yer man up."

"Exactly my sentiments. Oh, before I forget, Charlie's been back in touch, Cochrane that is. In fact, I've only just come off the blower."

"I thought you were looking pleased with yerself earlier on," exclaimed Gibbons.

"Yeah! That and the kid's performance tonight. Anyway, Charlie's put a cap on the deal, it's all set to go for the 4th September."

"And the venue?"

"Southend Leisure Centre." Gibbons paused before replying. A quizzical look brushed across his face.

"God! That place brings back a few memories." Ronnie could also feel a pang of nostalgia creeping in as he recalled a distant chapter entering Gibbons' previous career. The man could never be denied his moment of fame, when as an amateur he'd beaten the best that Europe could offer. Unfortunately, a murderous intervention by Rossetti at that time had culled any promise of a professional nature, reducing his status to an advisory position.

Ronnie broke the deadlock, and returned to business mode. "You know what they say, Mickey, if you ain't done it, yer can't talk about it! And you… could waffle for hours." Gibbons grinned and nodded for England.

"Bloody good game, innit?!" he fired back.

## CHAPTER 17

# DOING IT BY THE LETTER

The clatter of the letterbox opening and shutting caused Ronnie to look up from reading his morning paper. "Blimey! They're getting earlier every day." His observation was directed toward Mickey Gibbons as the two sat having their morning breakfast together. Squinting, Mickey shook his head before replying.

"Who the hell's early? The post?" He could be excused for his lack of enthusiasm; the big fight live on Sky had monopolised the early hours of that morning. Under the circumstances, he'd opted to stay over, although whatever sleep came his way was riddled with the aftermath following the peak viewing. Yawning, he stretched his flagging eyes. "You expecting anything, mate?" he enquired.

"No, only poxy bills, I expect," Ronnie grunted, and quipped, "About time Ernie came up trumps. The last time I had a win, there was a bleedin' king on the throne!"

Mickey, couldn't help but grin, and caved in.

"I dunno how yer do it, mate, eight o'clock in the morning and yer full of it! At least you've woke me up now."

"And not before time. Tell yer what, put us in for another cuppa, while I grab the mail." Within minutes he reappeared as Mickey finished pouring. Glancing up, he gestured toward the pot.

"Bit weak I'm afraid, mate, that's the last of it." Engrossed as he was in dealing with the mail, the remark went clean over Ronnie's head. Any thoughts he may have spilled on the matter were on a level plane.

"As long as it's wet," he replied in a nonplussed voice. It became evident that something was bothering him. A prolonged silence reigned as he scrutinised the one remaining envelope clasped in his hand. Mickey's cup hovered at half-mast due to the look of conjecture now etched on Ronnie's face. The question needed to be asked.

"Is there a problem, mate? The letter, I mean." His enquiry fell onto deaf ears, leaving Ronnie to toy around with the offending letter. The ongoing silence began to leave its mark, forcing Mickey to tinker with his cup in an effort to distract him.

It seemed to create the desired effect as Ronnie broke the spell. "Ere, what d'ye make of this? I can't seem to get my head round it." A couple of seconds followed by a sympathetic nod summed up Mickey's hasty reply.

"I see what yer mean. There's no address, not even a stamp, apart from the letter C written on the flap. He shook his head again in mock defeat, before stating, "Doesn't run to much, does it?"

"At a guess, I'd have to say it's a bleedin' wind up' and I ain't impressed," Ronnie concluded.

"Well, you haven't opened it yet. That'll tell yer what you want to know, but I take yer point." Without hesitation, Ronnie savagely ripped the envelope open. Swiftly he removed the contents consisting of one sheet of note paper, noticeably as cheap as the message it spawned. In a split second, Ronnie's body stiffened, his eyes now transfixed in a blend of total shock and anger. Fully focused, he lip-read every single poisoned word. The depth of the implication contained in the message far outweighed the number of words.

The text of the message comprised a mixture of single

letters, obviously selected and cut out from various newspapers. These, in turn, were set at random spaces, apart from one in particular. The word on closer examination undoubtedly alluded to a bygone chapter in Ronnie's life. It read:

CaLL A g HAN

I G iIVE YO U NOt IC E T HE PHOENIX HA S RiS E
N
Fr om TH e AS hes

It was crude, it screamed a threat, and moreover, it was in his face! Any notion suggesting the contents could have been a wind-up were instantly discounted. Ronnie had now seen and read enough. His hand shook uncontrollably as he handed the letter over to Mickey. "So help me! That bastard's gonna pay for this!" he remarked grimly. Strong words indeed, although his clear-cut response certainly

"The fucking psycho might just as well have signed it ROSSETTI, care of Slatteries' gym! It all makes sense now, Mickey. It's obvious, he must have somehow managed to escape from the inferno all those years ago. Yeah, it has to be Rossetti who's responsible for this shit!" Mentally drained, he dumped himself down into the nearest chair and shot an appealing look at Mickey in an effort to gauge his reaction.

Mickey wasn't short in replying. "Bloody hell! Six years on and the asshole is still intent on making a name for himself. Yer gonna have to take this creep serious. Yer talking Old Bill involvement 'ere, you do realise that?"

"Poxy legal? That's the last thing I want, mate," he groaned. "Besides, the situation as I see it has gone further than personal, know what I mean? Trust me, I'll sort it!"

"I'm not doubting yer for a minute, Ronnie, although two major problems spring to mind."

"Go on."

"One, the fact that he's undoubtedly putting himself about on the manor, and two, he obviously knows where to find you. Believe me, Rossetti has got nothing to lose. He's in this for the long haul and you need to accept that!" Wiping his brow, Ronnie sighed deeply.

"Yeah, yer right of course. I need to get my head straightened out, even get Siddie involved." Mickey nodded briskly in acknowledgment, and continued.

"By the way, the envelope, I presume you found it on the doormat?"

"Funny you should mention that, but yeah, it was lying underneath the rest of the mail. Why d'ye ask?"

"I'm just thinking, I thought as much, otherwise you would probably have been on to it right away, correct?"

"Fair comment, and yer point being?"

"It just proves that whoever pushed the letter through the flap must have done it late last night on the quiet!"

"Yeah, I'll go along with that. Blimey, you'd put bleedin' Columbo out of business, you would!"

"Saying that, the difference is…"

"Is what?" Ronnie intervened.

"… is that it could have so easily been petrol, and not a letter!"

"Christ's sake! It's beginning to be a ruddy nightmare. Maybe yer right, if I…"

"Right? About what exactly?"

"I'm thinking Old Bill as you suggested."

"Nah yer thinking straight, mate." He left off to check his watch. "Look, it's eight thirty already. So why not give the market a swerve today, and give 'em a bell?"

Ronnie was forced to smile.

"You're getting to sound more like Siddie every day, but yeah, it all makes sense. All they want is the SP from me, and then they can act accordingly on it."

"Precisely, you don't need the bloody grief. The sooner that asshole Rossetti is banged up then so much the better!" Twenty minutes and a shower later, Mickey left for work with Ronnie's parting shot still ringing in his ears.

"I'll be in the gym tonight if yer around." Minutes later, the phone grabbed his attention. The dialling tone seemed to have a mind all of its own. "C'mon." Patience was at a low ebb. "Somebody... anybody... Oh, hello, Stonewater nick?"

"No sir, this is Division, hold the line and I'll put you through."

"Damn! Not another bleedin' wait." He was still cursing long before the connection was finally made.

"Stonewater HQ, Sergeant Bryan speaking, how can I help?"

"Oh, er good morning! Yeah, I've got a mail problem." He couldn't have been more abrupt; at least the sergeant had a sense of humour.

"Is that in human terms, sir, or postal?"

"Bleedin' typical," muttered Ronnie under his breath.

"You were saying, sir?"

"Right! What I meant to say was, I've had a letter delivered and I ain't happy about it."

"I really think you need to contact the GPO, sir."

Ronnie shook his head and blew hot air before replying. "Not in my case, mate, the letter I'm talking about happens to be ruddy exclusive!"

"Aren't they all, sir?" the sergeant persisted drily. Personality battles didn't exist in Ronnie's makeup; he decided to jump the verbal queue.

"Only when they ain't poison pen, sunshine!" he volleyed.

"Now that, sir, is an altogether different kettle of fish. Meaning, I'm going to require some details from you." Ronnie duly obliged on the premise that a visit from a DC could be on the cards shortly, pending availability. Replacing the handset, his mind reflected on the content of their conversation. One aspect he found he could bank on: it certainly hadn't starved him of his exclusive wit.

"Bleedin' good job I hadn't murdered somebody. I'd have spent three days convincing him!" Approximately an hour later, his mood had swung from humour to headache, leaving him less than happy. One other bodily function in particular had caught him with his pants down. Literally. "Coming, coming, just give the flaming door a day off will yer!" he shouted, and concluded, "Can't a man have a shit in peace?!" The answer to that question came via the determined asshole hanging onto his doorbell. Fumbling with his trouser belt, he finally made it to the end of the hall. Negotiating the front door, he found himself confronted by a youngish member of the local plod flirting with an ID card.

"And you are?" demanded Ronnie, deciding to get in first, an undying habit from his ring days. Caught unawares, the caller duly responded.

"The name's Hollins, sir, DC Hollins that is, Stonewater Central. You're Mr Callaghan I believe? I'm here regarding your mail problem."

*Mister*, Ronnie mused. *Got a nice ring to it, been a bloody long time since anybody called me that!* "Yeah! Guess you'd better come inside, son." The DC brushed past him, leaving Ronnie to put him at ease. "By the way, the name's Ronnie, I don't do Callaghan, okay? Make yerself at home, mate, through there, look," and indicated toward the lounge. Finally relaxed, the two settled in for a form of conversation.

"You obviously know why I'm here?" Hollins enquired.

"Yeah, I explained the situation to your colleague. Bryan, I think his name was. Bit of a character the geezer."

Hollins chuckled and added, "Old school, Ronnie, you know how it goes. Anyway, back to this letter you've received."

"Sure, I've got it right 'ere."

"Do you mind if I see the contents?"

"Fill yer boots, mate, that's what yer here for. I've obviously got my own ideas about it though." Handing the letter over, Ronnie studied Hollins' face as he absorbed the alleged poison it contained. Slowly, he lowered the letter as he digested the contents. Deep in thought, his face screwed up as he drummed his fingers on an adjacent coffee table. A sustained silence followed for a minute or two before he would part with anything less than conclusive.

"Phew, that's a tough one, only a dozen or so words, and yet a hundred or so permutations. What's your overall view on it, Ronnie?"

"Permutations eh? I hear what yer saying, son, but I reckon I've got it in one!" voiced Ronnie.

"Well, that more than narrows the field down. Are you suggesting that you actually know who could have delivered it to you?" Nodding emphatically, Ronnie replied, "And more!"

"Really? At least we're bound to agree that the second line statement is nothing less than a threat of sorts."

"That's putting it mildly, mate, we're talking a vendetta 'ere."

"What, as in 'Goodnight, nurse'?"

"Huh," Ronnie snorted. "That wouldn't even run to a contest. I'm talking as in bloody terminal!" Hollins frowned heavily at Ronnie's theory.

"That's quite a statement, Ronnie." He hesitated slightly before continuing, "I can see that you're really serious about your beliefs."

"You'd better believe it too, son. So with that in mind, let me ask you something. Were you in the force locally, say, some six years ago?"

"God no! I wasn't even thinking about becoming a copper."

"Uhm, so the gangland murders wouldn't mean anything to you then?"

"Heavens no, besides, I was living in South East London at that time." Ronnie went on to explain the shootings, and the aftermath of what was once Slatteries' gym. Plus, the fact that the remains of only one victim were ever found.

"So yer see, son, this letter is a giveaway from where I'm standing." Hollins appeared to be taken aback by Ronnie's disclosure of the facts, but at the same time eager to digress.

"This Paul Rossetti guy, I just get the feeling that his name has cropped up recently down at the nick. One thing is for sure, I'll do some digging in the records department and hopefully obtain a profile read out. From what I can gather, he sounds like a right basket case, and dangerous with it!"

"That's something else we can agree on then," expounded Ronnie. Nodding conclusively, Hollins produced a calling card.

"Here, you'd better take this for what it's worth. As for me, I'll let my Super dot the i's on this one. I can see him going public with this case."

"I don't think you've got any choice, son, it ain't gonna go away overnight, not at least until the fat lady sings, know what I mean?"

"Right! Well, thanks for your help, Ronnie, it's been quite an education, and don't hesitate if you need to get back in touch at any time." There and then, they shook hands and he departed. For Hollins, this latest revelation had been a learning curve in disguise. On the flip side, Ronnie had been left staring at his first monumental hurdle.

## CHAPTER 18

# SAFETY IN HOUSES

At some time or another, certain types of people tend to play with fire when confronting that well-worn adage, or so we're led to believe. In Rossetti's case, the act of flirting with death just proved to be another aspect of his indifference. His current sadistic pleasure now entailed the personal comfort he derived from five rounds of 9mm fire power, each of which would prove to be more than capable in bringing about death by design! This, in turn, coins the term, 'You only get what you pay for'. Having said that, the unfortunate recipient would rush to say, 'I beg to differ', metaphorically speaking of course!

The corners of his mouth contorted to suit each unique situation as he ogled the full clip of ammunition. One by one, he released and proceeded to reverently caress each round of death between his fingers. The verbal diarrhoea that spewed from his mouth summed up the inevitable climax of his macabre delusion. "Nah let's see, which one of you little beauties is gonna do the business for me? Will it be this one? Maybe not, how about this one then? Uhm, possibilities of course, then again I like the look of this one. Ah, what the hell, they've all got Callaghan's name written all over 'em. Besides, it ain't as if I'm selling bleedin' tickets, he's gonna get his anyway!"

A look of sheer hate on Rossetti's face turned into dented sadness as he proceeded to reload the magazine. With just one to go, he stopped short, speaking to the bullets as if they were family. The lesson came across as firm, with a hint of an apology. "I'M SORRY YOU'VE GOT TO GO, BUT DADDY INSISTS ITS BEDTIME. IF YER GOOD, I'LL LET YER OUT SOON, AND YER CAN PLAY AGAIN. AND IF YER GOOD… VERY GOOD… WE'LL LET MR CALLAGHAN JOIN IN, WON'T THAT BE NICE? BUT WE NEED TO KEEP IT A SECRET FOR THE TIME BEING, YOU UNDERSTAND."

As he started, so he finished, his mania now teetering on the edge of insanity.

Not that he was aware, of course. His present mental state, devoid as it was of common logic, only required a shove to access the realms of utter madness. In retrospect, the sudden switch in relocation to a safe house via the AA had been intended solely as a ploy to gain respite linked to self-preservation. Maltese Pete put the move into context during a conversation a week after Rossetti had taken up his offer to chill out. "The way I see it, yer get unbalanced! Raving mad! Nutters! And then yer get fucking Rossetti! He's definitely got a death wish, the geezer. What worries me, though, is who he takes down with him, cos he'd still be a bleedin' nuisance brown bread!"

"You sound as if yer regretting getting him tooled up," remarked his drinking partner.

"As it happens, yer probably right. I'm thinking it was a bad call on my part."

"I did 'ear a whisper that the Rinse ain't a happy man either."

"Happy?! That's putting it mildly, seeing as Rossi turned him over for a nice few quid, and I think the penalty clause has run out!"

"Fuck's sake! No kidding, well we all know how that's gonna wind up."

"Yeah, exactly! And not forgetting this Callaghan guy he's always mouthing off about. I can't see him sitting around waiting for it to belly up, can you?"

"Huh, I can see firework night coming early this year. Nice to be bloody normal, innit?"

"Yeah, gotcha. Oh, which reminds me, you still owe me a carpet for that Charlie you had off me last week." Like the man said, quote, 'If normal is staying healthy on a diet of underworld activity and cocaine, I'll more than settle for marriage as a pastime', unquote! So the story goes or, as they say, 'You make your bed, you lie in it'. In Rossetti's case, his bed consisted of an overused mattress, ably supported by the floor it rested on. At least he had an option of moving elsewhere should the situation arise. The actual layout of his newfound bolt hole appeared spartan to say the least, in this case comprising a kitchen and debatable lounge/bedroom. The toilet was bookable in advance, and there was a strong rumour going around that a bathroom could be found on the third floor… somewhere!

The building, as a whole, fell into the category of an oversized 'town facility' shortly after its conversion from a 60s bonded warehouse into numerous 'bedsits'. From a detailed construction point of view, the only thing holding the building together was countless coats of paint over the years. It also housed an intriguing assortment of tenants. It certainly wasn't the best that Docklands had to offer, for the simple reason that there was no best! As a result, the illicit atmosphere that blanketed the immediate area had unwittingly created a world of seclusion and, in turn, comparative safety for some. 'Home is where you lay your problems' comes to mind.

As things stood, Rossetti's current credit rating wouldn't have run to a mortgage on a park bench, let alone the last chance saloon into which he'd now found himself incarcerated. Also, his approach to survival would need updating outside of the twilight world he'd foisted upon himself. Even his prehistoric attitude had now succumbed to alarm bells causing him to take stock of his renegade existence. In short, he'd become a marked man by design within the confines of the local underworld, all due to the Rinse scenario.

Then, of course, there would be the untimely presence of the local plod to contend with, this being in relation to the poison pen letter he'd conveniently dumped on Ronnie Callaghan. That in itself could create ripples. More than enough to pursue a far superior vested interest which, in turn, could earmark his now tentative future. Question! How does one begin to evaluate the word 'safe' if and when asked? Based on the given facts, and Rossetti's dire circumstances, you could almost be forgiven for excluding the obvious, and run with the lesser definition: a strong box containing money and effects. And so to another safe house, but this time set at the opposite end of the spectrum.

Siddie Levy practically flung himself at the door as the bell sounded. "Come, come in! Get yerself inside, mate, and out of that lousy rain. Rachael!" he yelled. "Ronnie's here, stick the kettle on, Bubbulah."

"Grrr, poxy weather!" Ronnie growled. "And bleedin' cold with it." Siddie nodded aggressively and quickly ushered him inside.

"Ere, let's take yer coat, mate, it's going to take some drying out." In spite of the warm welcome he'd received, the pensive look that clouded Ronnie's face alerted Siddie to hone in on a particular problem when on the phone earlier. Certain elements of their heated conversation were still alive in his thoughts. Regretfully, each issue had been firmly rubber-stamped and under the heading ROSSETTI! Just then, Rachael appeared on the scene.

"Oh cheers, Rachael, nobody can make a cup of rosie like you do." Taking a swig of his tea, Ronnie shifted his attention Siddie's way. "I thought I'd better save the worst until last, mate, knowing how yer would react. 'Ere, this is what it's all come down to." Reaching inside his inner pocket, he withdrew a photocopy of the poison pen letter in question. Grim faced, he handed it over for scrutiny. Leaning back in his chair, fists tightly clenched, he awaited Siddie's interpretation.

He could almost see the blood drain from his face as he meaningfully digested the contents. Ronnie winced, fully expecting a verbal outburst; he wasn't about to be denied. Following an extended couple of minutes' deliberation, Siddie glanced up, his face registering positive as he responded with conviction. Sitting bolt upright, Ronnie listened intently, totally lost for words of his own. Was he confused? Maybe even relieved in more ways than one? He soon realised that for reasons of his own, this wasn't the Siddie of old speaking.

The ghost of Rossetti, it seems, had somehow been resurrected, and in so doing enabled a veil of uncertainty to be lifted from his thoughts. In an instant, the seeds of pacifism were blown away as he stressed his point. "No more questions, no more holding back anymore! It finishes right here, my friend. The man has obviously flipped," and concluded, "As a result, he will make mistakes, and that will be his eventual downfall!"

"Please God!" echoed Ronnie. "And bleedin' sooner rather than later."

"Yeah, whatever! But we will get through this mess, trust me. I should lie to you of all people." There and then, the subject appeared to be closed as they shook hands in a gesture of loyalty, although Siddie still continued to have the last word and strongly emphasised his point.

"You're more than safe 'ere, but then you knew that already."

Easing himself back in his chair, Ronnie stretched out his legs. Totally relaxed he gazed around the four walls of the room. Any underlying fears or hidden issues were mentally blown away. "Yeah, yer right, mate," he concurred, "this is what yer call a safe house', ain't it?!"

## CHAPTER 19

# WINNERS AND LOSERS

All things considered, their inauguration trip down to Southend proved to be an uneventful journey. Acting on the advice of Charlie Cochrane, the promoter, any hint of traffic was nonexistent once clear of Stonewater. Checking his rear view mirror one more time, Ronnie slid the gear stick into top gear, at the same time easing the car into the fast lane. The clock on the dashboard told him that it was fast approaching 4.30pm. He nestled back into his seat, feeling completely relaxed once more as the M23-25 interchange rapidly faded into the distance. He then broke off to make conversation. "That's handy, it ain't half as busy as I thought it would be," he stated, adding, "no reason why we shouldn't make good time."

Mickey Gibbons, who was in the front passenger seat, nodded in agreement and looked over his shoulder. "Youse two alright in the back? Yer a bit quiet." His observation was met with a chorus of banter from Danny Simmons and Siddie Levy. From the outset, the evening had boded well, and confidence prevailed as they continued to head for their destination. For young Simmons, it could well be a night to remember and savour in more ways than one.

The blood, sweat and tears arising from the last five weeks had finally culminated in a make-or-break situation, pending the legitimacy of his arduous pre-fight programme. In a little over three hours' time, the simple task of raising a weary arm with the help of a benevolent referee could signal a climax to end a perfect day. Should he succeed, his win could well kick-start a successful career.

Ronnie, meanwhile, was forced to ease back on the pedal. The traffic, he observed, had begun to gridlock as the Dartford Bridge loomed large. Once safely across, he negotiated junction 30 in favour of the A13 and Southend direct. "You can all relax now, guys, the heat's off," he readily assured them. "Especially you, Danny," he ventured.

"Huh, don't worry on my account, Ronnie," Simmons piped up. "The only pressure coming my way I'm saving for Richards!" He was alluding to his forthcoming opponent. Ronnie took it in, smiling discreetly at Simmons' brashness.

*Cocky little bleeder*, he mused, although deep down he secretly admired his charisma. Personal triumphs filtered through his subconscious, notably a faint recollection of his own initiation into the 'world of leather', and then encompassing the paid ranks. *Yeah, it's all coming back*, he convinced himself. *Christ, was I pleased to hear that final bell ring!* A sudden abrupt intervention from Gibbons quickly brought him back down to earth, although a grain of nostalgia still managed to hold on.

"Keep yer flaming eyes on the road, mate, yer bloody well miles away," he reminded him.

"It was a whole lot further than that, Mickey, and I got a result," he fired back with conviction. Gibbons appeared to be momentarily perplexed at his reply.

"Have I missed something 'ere?" he asked.

"Nah, it can wait. Ah, not far to go nah, Leigh-On-Sea coming up." Ten minutes or so following their arrival at the venue, the relaxing trip down reverted to history. Notably, the heated atmosphere that lined the leisure centre spilled over into the main dressing room as they entered and, in doing so, created an adrenaline-charged atmosphere. With ample time for respite on their hands, the three found a convenient corner, enabling them to chill out and relax. Meanwhile, Siddie had been left to his own devices, namely by circulating and ensuring that the bar wasn't losing any money. In due course, the formality of Simmons' weigh-in and medical had proven successful, so any time left now became a bonus.

Ronnie began to stir in his chair and checked for time. The acute expression masking his face quickly grabbed Mickey's attention. Inwardly, Ronnie remained on a high as he relished the in-house buzz, but at the same time remained methodical as true professionalism came to the fore. Rising to his feet, he confirmed Mickey's thoughts as he spoke for both of them. "Time we got this show on the road, mate," he emphasised. Indicating Danny with a nod, he continued, "And you'd better give Danny a bleedin' shove while yer at it, he thinks he's sleeping for England."

The minutes were slowly ebbing away for Danny who, by arrangement, would be opening the second half of the bill following the interval.

Procedural activity took over; having dressed down into corner garb, it was left to Mickey to bandage and tape Simmons' hands prior to him being gloved up. Above the banter resonating around the room, the exclusive voice of Big Tommy Russell alerted Ronnie that a pre-fight get together was on the cards. In no time at all, the two were engaged in a verbal shakedown. As per usual, Russell threw himself into the heart of things, and Ronnie... was just Ronnie.

"So how's the kid handling the situation up to now, mate?" he queried. "Any qualms I should know about?"

"Trust me, Tommy, yer gonna have more bleedin' grief paying me out later than worry about young Danny," Ronnie jested. "But seriously, for his first outing he's on the case and well focused, so yeah, no problems."

"That is reassuring! A win tonight will do him a power of good, especially appearing on Charlie's bill," Ronnie replied adamantly.

"As I say, mate, we ain't in this business to take prisoners! Know what I mean?" Tommy was forced to chuckle.

"Should have known better than to have asked. Anyway, I'm gonna grab a ringside seat. Tell the kid be lucky, yeah?"

The walk from the dressing room to the ring itself seemed like an extended marathon to Simmons. In fact, it was a little less than two memorable minutes. Once he'd emerged from behind the velvet drape curtains and into the public domain, he was met by the deafening tones of the inimitable song, 'Simply the Best', as it reverberated around the packed hall, and not before he soaked up the sound of the baying crowd. His initial reaction to the response led him to momentarily falter in his stride, allowing his brain to kick into overdrive.

Elation left its mark as his subconscious took over, one fantasy scenario overlapping the other, before stalling. *This is real. This is happening now. This is all for meeeeeee!* it screamed out, inwardly.

"You okay, Danny?" Ronnie quickly brought him back down to earth. "C'mon, mate, we've got a job to do." Along with a house steward back and front, and flanked by Ronnie and Mickey, they slowly headed off toward the ring.

In a later conversation, according to Danny's reckoning, "It felt like the ring was a million miles away at the time, somewhere!", although in the real world it roughly evaluated to no more than fifty-odd yards. Through a sea of haze and distorted faces, recognition kicked in. Danny shot a searching glance Ronnie's way, swiftly followed by a reassuring wink and matching grin.

"This is your time, Danny, so milk the moment, my son!" he stated firmly. From then on, his body actions became robotic as Mickey ushered him forward. A wave of awareness for the occasion surged through Danny's body and limbs, allowing his head to roll in unison with his arms as they collided with fresh air. He could almost hear his heart beat, but for all the right reasons as the ring apron confronted them.

Ronnie lost no time in reaching the top of the ring steps. Once on the apron, he toed the middle rope to ease access for Danny's ring entrance. With all three now in their respective corners, it was open for business time. "Keep on the move, son, yer need to keep warm," Ronnie stated. Shadow boxing on the spot, Danny reminded himself he'd heard the same order a thousand times before, although this time it had a double edge to it.

"Shit!" he told himself. "It's finally happening at last." Glancing round, he observed his opponent, Paul Richards, limbering up in the opposite corner while glaring ominously in his direction. Meanwhile, Ronnie had other ideas.

"Okay, Danny, let's get yer disrobed and yer war paint on." Mickey deftly fingered the last of the vaseline off the back of his hand, and smoothed it over Danny's eyebrows and cheeks. The MC then took over and introduced the two. With final instructions ringing in his ears, the referee motioned the two fighters toward the ring centre. After reading them the riot act, they retreated to their respective corners to await the opening bell. Mickey slipped Danny's mouthpiece in place while giving some extra advice.

"Work him onto yer right hand where yer can, but don't..." He was cut short as the bell sounded and no man's land beckoned. With two contests already secured under his belt, Richards was only too eager to open up his account once again, and began to leave their mark in his pent-up aggression.

Intent on carrying the fight to Simmons, he systematically unleashed three punch combinations as he came forward in a square-on attitude, relentlessly driving his man backward into his own corner. Any premeditated game plan became nonexistent as the ropes claimed full ownership of his back. Bobbing and weaving purely on extinct became a no-brainer as Richards' punch routine continued to hone in from all angles. Leaning on the ring apron Ronnie, meanwhile, could be heard screaming at him from under the bottom rope. Not that Simmons was party to his utter frustration. Selfishly or otherwise, Ronnie had briefly found himself catapulted back in time, returning as a 10-year-old kid again, parading on the streets of his own generation, where everyday existence became a lottery in will power.

Meanwhile, Richards appeared unstoppable as he hooked at will from every angle, working in selective mode on Simmons' lower body. From somewhere inside Danny's fuddled brain, a dormant sixth sense connected to a grain of survival, and in turn released an untapped power surge. From a one-man workout, the scenario confronting him was turned on its head as he dug deep into his own resources. Retaliating with short sharp punches from behind closed gloves held high suddenly proved to be a turning point. It was evident that Richards was showing signs of rapidly tiring, while Danny's upsurge in work rate began to tell, and in so doing, forcing Richards to grab him and hang on.

By now, the frenzied crowd were on their feet, alive to the fact there was more than one round now left in the contest. At ringside, Ronnie's face dropped lower than the ring canvas as the ref suddenly intervened in their private war. Eyes blazing, he turned to Mickey. "You thinking what I'm thinking, mate? Surely he ain't gonna stop it!" In reply, Mickey was adamant.

"No way, Ronnie, there's only fifteen seconds to go to the bell by my reckoning." Their joint fears were swiftly allayed as the ref prised the two apart. But not before he made a point of checking out a notable swelling on Danny's cheekbone. Fortunately, time had run out before the two could square up again as the bell sounded the end of round one. A cat on a hot tin roof couldn't have bettered Ronnie's instinctive reaction as he leapt through the ropes before it had died away.

It became the shortest route available, and Danny wasn't about to argue as his battered body slumped down on the corner stool. With mouth agape and lungs clawing air, Mickey hastily removed his mouthpiece and forcibly spread his leaden arms to rest on the middle rope. Ronnie, meanwhile, lost no time applying an over-wet sponge to the nape of his neck. The prominent swelling on closer inspection now became a priority as Mickey cautiously proceeded to iron the bruising using a metal compress. Just then, the ref intervened in a bid to stamp his authority.

"If that swelling becomes a problem or, worse, splits, the kid's in for an early bath night. You know the rules, guv."

"Not if I can bleedin' help it!" he muttered under his breath, but dutifully acknowledged the ref's concern. At least a form of respite was on hand in the shape of a water bottle. Simmons, on the other hand, held his own theory as the water hit the back of his throat.

"That was bloody nectar, Ronnie!" he gasped, after reluctantly having to spit it out. Ronnie raised a digit and put things in perspective.

"It don't come for free, son, yer gotta bloody well fight for it, right?!" Discarding the bottle, he rattled out fresh instructions. "Stay calm, and for Christ's sake get yer jab out of retirement. When he feints left then you nail him with a right cross. Just imagine yer working out in the gym. Nah get up on yer bleedin' toes and move!" Mickey swiftly slipped his mouthpiece in position before he could fire back. "Think like a fighter," was the last Danny heard as the timekeeper curtailed Ronnie's verbal recipe.

His gainful advice had left its mark; Danny appeared to be reluctant to leave off battling as the bell called the second round to its conclusion. On returning to his corner, Danny flatly refused the inclusion of the stool in displaying an attitude of self-confidence. Nobody could be more relieved than Ronnie as he went public. "Good work, son, nah yer getting it together. I'd say that round was even."

"I'll go one better than that. I reckon Danny shaded it," Mickey concluded with added conviction. As before, he was forced to break off from working the compress due to the ref's continued interest in Simmons' cheek injury.

"You're doing a good job there, guv. It appears to be holding up. I'll give him another round on the same basis." Mickey smothered his obvious relief, and nodded back in reply as Ronnie marked Danny's card.

"As from nah, you raise yer game, son. Richards is a round to the good. Press forward and up the ante with the leather, let's see if he can take a dig!" Seconds later, it became a spectator's vision of appreciation as the two stood toe-to-toe slugging it out as the round gained an upturn in momentum. Once again, the ref became forced to intervene, this time having to pull both boxers apart. Well inside the last minute, it was noticeable on sheer aggression alone that Danny was getting the best of the exchanges as he continued to take the fight to Richards who, by now, found himself forced to cover up as telling punches began to leave their chosen mark.

At the ringside, Ronnie was struggling to keep his nervous system on a damper. "Take it from me, Mickey, I'm telling yer nah, Richards has shot his bolt, the guy's got nothing left to offer, wotcha think?" His opinion, if shared, could have been heard at the back of the hall as Simmons instinctively morphed into a one-man mean machine. Mickey winced as Danny caught his man with a full-blooded right cross as he came off the ropes. The impact of the blow, plus the added impetus given out by Richards as the two made a connection, deemed conclusive. The outcome of the fight had now risen to a new level.

In Richards' case, the circumstances had signalled the beginning of the end. Any immediate resistance ran to futile. For a split second, his numbed body seemed to hang suspended in the air as his feet left the canvas behind. The force of the blow in question was enough to send his mouthpiece spewing out into fresh air. His eyes glazed over in sympathy as his nervous system automatically shut down. Luring his dysfunctional brain into irreversible submission, he was unconscious before he hit the canvas. The ref immediately waved Simmons away to a neutral corner as he prepared to take up the count.

A token twitch at eight determined Richards' inert prostrate form, and then it was all over as the ref indicated 'nine and out!'. The world embraced a winner, and Simmons finally found himself in the frame as a living testament.

The sweet smell of success ran riot throughout his body, causing him to leap off the canvas and continually punch the air in a bid to sanction his validity. Within seconds, Ronnie and Mickey had joined him in the ring to bolster his emotions. Meanwhile, Richards' seconds had succeeded in bringing their man back to normality, albeit totally fazed and dejected. For his part, the referee lost no time in declaring Danny the winner, and raised his hand aloft as a formality. The onlookers rose as one, and not before a shower of nobbins began to rain down onto the ring canvas as a plaudit for their appreciation of a gutsy performance.

The trek back to the dressing room could be measured in seconds from Simmons' point of view as Ronnie hurried him along in a bid to evade a gauntlet of back-slapping well-wishers and fervent fans. "God! That feels so good!" Danny stretched his fingers as Ronnie cut the last of the bandages away from his hands.

"Not half as good as the verdict though, my son. You proved to yerself tonight you've got it in yer to bounce back while under pressure. That is special!", a statement later echoed by Big Tommy Russell and Charlie Cochrane alike when airing their views at a post-fight autopsy. Cochrane was also quick to cement any further ongoing business relationship with the stable to procure a vested interest in Simmons', quote, "promising future", unquote. The point had been made, and in turn sealed the cap on a night to remember. In spite of the razzamatazz that came linked to his glory, Danny was quick to convey his interest in Richards' current welfare.

Any fears he may have held thankfully proved groundless when exchanging their goodbyes later. All things considered, their journey back to Stonewater appeared destined to be a blend of variable points of view and radical humour. On the strength of a few beers, Siddie put the whole episode into context. "That one particular kosher right hand that Danny threw, the one that did the damage, was to my mind bloody sweeter than any apple I've sold this week!" And that from a man regarded by the majority as a nominated terminal pacifist!

## CHAPTER 20

# NO STAMP REQUIRED

As far as situations go, Rossetti was slowly being dragged downward into a whirlpool of overwhelming frustration and added torment, whereby the only means of escape would be to succumb with dignity, and then to go under. All in all, an agreeable result when considered on merit, leaving the world to breathe a huge sigh of relief in response. Dream on people, we're talking Paul Rossetti here, first cousin to a sewer rat! Allegedly, I hasten to add on behalf of rats everywhere. It would seem that his present survival potential was beginning to show flaws as the four walls he'd loosely inherited of late began to threaten and engulf his sicko mind, body and soul. On a par with the real world, his situation could readily be tagged as being 'a shit day at the office'.

As it was, the irresistible urge to break free from his self-induced exile was proving to be untenable when pitted against the cut and thrust of a regime synonymous to his type. Even his latest play toys were showing signs of losing their appeal. Let's face it, you can only count so many bullets at any one time in any one day! So maybe that was the root of his problem. If he hadn't got them to hand, then they wouldn't become a subject for debate. *It all boils down to allocation, a time to offload*, he convinced himself as, once again, his homicidal tendencies were allowed to surface.

Selecting a round at random, he studied it at length,

reminiscent of a hundred times before. His face registered a mask of pure evil, at the same time allowing his poisoned mind to collude with a sickening conclusion. "Of course! You selfish bastard!" his voice erupted. "What took yer so bloody long?" His impromptu outburst was over before it had even started as he continued to rant, but this time in a meaningful vein. "Yer bleedin' well right, yer know," he said with conviction, and continued, "It ain't mine to keep any longer. Callaghan needs to know that the investment in his future has been reviewed!" A maniacal laugh came into play as he made the point. "The least I can do is to fucking remind him." With that in mind, the next few hours were taken up devising a fabricated letter simply by utilising the countless outdated newspapers that littered the floor. Satisfied with the content of the letter, Rossetti double checked the poisoned verbal contained in Callaghan's update, also ensuring its safe keeping by lining the brown envelope with a single nominated round as a companion, before finally sealing it. An impromptu decision came to nothing as his current thoughts tended to waver. "Nah, it can wait, it'll give him something to chew over when he's having his breakfast. With a bit of luck, it might be the fucking bullet!"

Brain exhausted, he fell back on his bed as tiredness blanketed his corrupt body. His head sought refuge on what once resembled a pillow, which in turn played host to his wavering security which was now lying dormant underneath the butt-end of his shooter. This, in turn, caused a bulge to connect with his cheek. He noted how good it felt, and made no effort to move. The warmth it generated allowed his security zone to feed off its awareness. Without prompting, his head began to move in a perverse manner, enabling his cheek to caress the bulge. *God! A pillow never felt so good*, he convinced himself. Whatever inner thoughts remained became more personal as a vision of Ronnie Callaghan drifted into play.

Finally, his perversion matured as he spoke softly but with conviction, directing his illicit fantasy to filter down through his pillow. “Sleep well, baby, be patient, we’ll have our day, it won’t be long nah.” In contrast, the shooter shifted slightly to one side, almost as he finished speaking. Rossetti, in his madness, would find comfort in believing that the movement was just more than coincidental and readily embraced the moment as a form of acknowledgment.

And so it was over. Heavy eyes ceased to flicker as sleep finally washed over his corrupt frame. Within seconds, a deep and numbing slumber set in. Meanwhile, the real world could breathe a huge sigh of relief, until such time as his stupor had run its course. A few hours later, brain now rested by design, found Rossetti in a more resolute frame of mind, albeit to his erratic standard, when finally awakening. Any harboured doubts swiftly evaporated as a feel-good factor raided his body. Any resident demons had now ceased to exist and were long gone.

At least, the welcome hiatus had now created an opportunity to put himself about, and Callaghan figured highly on his mailing list. It was also important to remind himself of the need to operate fast whilst the high remained intact. *It’s only bleedin’ lent, they’ll be back!* he convinced his hidden fears. A casual glance in a nearby wall mirror confirmed his reasoning as the face of a man on a mission appeared. “I like it!” he exclaimed, and then proceeded to check his watch. “Yeah, reckon I couldn’t have timed it any better,” he murmured confidentially. It was telling him that it was fast approaching 2am.

A hasty cold wash in the kitchen sink proved sufficient to remove a mask of uncertainty about the next hour or so. It was time to make his move. He shivered slightly, and took note of his bedraggled Crombie 'hanging up' on the floor. Throwing it around his shoulders, his attention was drawn toward his pit. Pulling his alleged pillow to one side, he removed the exposed shooter and housed it inside his inner coat pocket.

An insidious smile took out an option on his face as he took possession of the brown envelope with its macabre contents. "Shit! Couldn't leave that behind, could we nah!" he stated firmly, and continued to patronise his *pièce de résistance*. "We're in this together, baby, nothing's changed, you get to spread the gospel, and me?! I get to blow Callaghan away when the right time comes along." A hideous laugh ensued as he ogled the symmetry of the envelope once more. Finally, he thrust it inside his coat pocket. Two or three minutes later, and akin to a rat deserting a sinking ship, Rossetti slunk out of the safe house. Momentarily, he was forced to pull up short as the chill of the night bit into his face, causing his body to stiffen in sympathy.

Cursing in his own exclusive manner, he made a beeline for the resident shadows and melted into the foreboding night, surfacing some five minutes later within the proximity of a taxi rank. Even operating under the blanket of the present twilight zone, his movements nevertheless retained complications. Rossetti was aware that he could ill afford to compromise his covert actions. On the contrary, his very existence would be deemed vulnerable if under the scrutiny of an over-zealous police patrol car. Madness, or so we're led to believe, has its own degrees of performance when analysed, and Rossetti's manic behaviour, it would appear, gave him carte blanche to acquire the full rights to madness perse.

In direct contrast, his overriding desire for ambition and self-preservation had more than stood the test of time. His proven ego had achieved more than a blazing inferno could ever have done. He was, in theory, a class act all on his own.

The fact that he was labelled dangerous also rendered him clever too, in an abstract sort of way.

The knowledge that his arch nemesis Callaghan could define his ultimate hurdle in the course of time only served to fuel his eternal lust for complete self-satisfaction. Ironically, Callaghan, through circumstances alone, had attributed the very key to maintaining Rossetti's survival. As for the hurdle in question, if and when confronted, he would require that certain panache enabling him to match the height of the bar. Currently, as things stood, a distorted leg combined with an over-inflated ego ran to a bookmaker's holiday money should you become a gambling man!

On the flip side, quote, 'It ain't over until the fat lady sings'. A well-worn adage indeed, but it could prove to be a cop-out when grief became imminent. Putting it bluntly, while in the same vein, just removing the 't' from 'can't' means you could be left with Rossetti! Maybe? Out of sight and out of mind fitted his present situation. Opting for the sanctity offered by a convenient shop doorway, with no sell-by date attachment and an adjacent taxi rank, was the best he could hope for on a safety basis, but with a price. He once again found himself forced to rearrange his overcoat collar as the overspill fog rising out of the nearby basin, due to the late tide, swirled crazily around in the dank night air, now adding to his self-imposed misery.

Shivering was compulsory as he vented his feelings. "Poxy weather!" he snarled through gritted teeth and shifted the weight of his body from one foot to the other in an effort to keep warm, cursing again in the process. "A taxi! Just one lousy bleedin' taxi, ain't a lot to ask, is it?" He made a halfhearted attempt to peer through the darkness and beyond. Apart from the odd drunk reveller or two, the night totally belonged to him as he strived to collect his beleaguered thoughts. Uppermost in his mind, the inevitable showdown with Callaghan remained a permanent fixture.

In the meantime, the poison fodder due for delivery was burning a hole in his pocket. "Shit! I must be out of my skull," he ranted, which just about summed up his present situation. *Yeah right, Rossetti! I mean c'mon, two thirty in the early hours and freezing bloody cold, lurking in downtown planet Zob! Just to offload a poxy letter! Okay, I respect it's your call, and for once in your lousy life you got it right.* Meanwhile, the genuine article had been asleep for nearly four hours, well cosied up and oblivious to your current nightmare. *So what d'ye want Rossetti, a poxy medal?!*

Seconds later, the distinctive drone of a car drawing close proved to be his salvation, due to the welcome sight of a cab coming into view. Without hesitation, he made the road his own, and in so doing forced the cab to a premature halt. Slowly the passenger window slid down as Rossetti edged closer. The less-than-amused driver lost no time making his point. "You got some sort of a bloody death wish, pal? Wotcha think yer playing at? The rank is the other side of the road, besides, that's me finished nah for today." At this point, Rossetti appeared impervious to the driver's reaction and thrust a sizable wedge in his face.

"Look, I need to get into town. I'll more than make it worth yer grief. Can we do a deal?" Fortunately for Rossetti the amount on offer spoke volumes. The driver was under orders and wasn't about to argue his case. He was at the wrong end of a shit day, and a fistful of folding would go a long way to compensating him.

"Tell yer what I'll do, seeing as I live on the manor, we'll call it £40 for the round trip, yeah?" Rossetti heaved a sigh of relief, but still demanded the last word.

"I thought they'd hung Dick Turpin years ago," he said from out the corner of his mouth, and swiftly joined the driver up front.

"Right, so where we headed to, mate?" demanded the driver.

"Bottom end of Bloomfield Terrace, back of the Queensway, d'ye know it?" replied Rossetti.

The driver half turned toward him and replied drily, "For £40 I bleedin' do! Typical Rossetti replied in the only way he knew how.

"Yeah, in that case, boot it, I ain't got all night." Fifteen minutes or so later, his intended destination became a reality. "Anywhere 'ere will do, mate, here's a pony. Lose yerself for five minutes, then pick me up 'ere again, right?!"

"You're paying, guv'nor, so five minutes it is!" Nodding, Rossetti alighted and lingered briefly until the cab had become a memory. He then approached the doorway of his hocus-pocus delivery. The house in question was situated some fifty yards or so away, and converted into flats at some stage in its life. He soon realised that it was essential he move fast to ensure his cover was kept under wraps by making his pickup point in time. The less the cabby knew about his whereabouts the better. And then there it was: the doorway that stood between himself and his nemesis. In spite of the chill carried on the night air, he felt a sudden rush of heat consume his frame.

The moment came alive as obsessive hate threatened to run riot, and in the process obliterate his intended game plan. Through blurred vision laced with temper, the door began to disintegrate. In its place, the spectre of Callaghan now appeared, mocking his frustration. By now, Rossetti's homicidal demeanour was registering flashpoint on a thin red line that ran from zero to zilch. Meanwhile, his head began to pound mercilessly, forcing him to screw his eyes shut in a pathetic gesture of defeat. And then just as suddenly, his nightmare was over, allowing his demons to give up the ghost.

The induced sequence had only run for a few seconds. Even so, the letter clasped tight in his hands now jolted him into action.

Hands trembling, Rossetti slowly eased the door flap open and inserted the envelope, pausing for a split second before finally lowering it back to its original position. His breath came in short stabs as the delivery reached its hightened climax. "Screw on that, Callaghan! There's more where that came from," he uttered with a sense of certainty. He glanced around in a furtive manner; satisfied, he made his way back to the end of the road.

There was no disguising the smug look imprinted on his face, which remained until the cab swung into view moments later. It became evident that the driver was eager to get back to Docklands and home as was his fare. "I presume we're heading…"

"Yeah!" Rossetti intervened. "Docklands and step on it."

"The rank?" questioned the driver.

"Nah, the basin end of Wharf Road will do."

"Sorted!" the driver replied, and sped off. Quarter of an hour later and having been paid what was owing caused him to remark further, "Please God all my punters are as good as you."

"Huh!" quipped Rossetti. "But then they wouldn't all be as fucking mad as me!" The cabby shrugged his shoulders in response before replying, "Yeah, know where yer coming from, mate, but it's still the easiest £40 I've earned all week!" Grunting a hasty, "See yer", Rossetti made his way over to the safe house. Whatever his failings were, you could always rely on him to put things in perspective as once again his mission toward madness came to the fore.

## CHAPTER 21

# SECOND HAND MAIL

And yet it still continued to bleed! You would have thought that with over forty years in the fight game, and a renowned cut man to boot, he would surely have found a clue by now. Ronnie's mediocre attempt to staunch the blood flow arising from a cut lip whilst shaving that particular morning wasn't the start to the day he'd envisaged. For a man whose exclusive life ran by the minute, any errors would have completely derailed his harmonious approach to life.

*This is really pissing me off! I can't believe it's happening*, he told himself again as his latest futile attempt to stem the flow ran to nothing. *Ain't your day, mate, is it?* his reflection in the mirror confided in him as once again another droplet of claret sought refuge on his vest. *Shit! That does it, you won't bleedin' beat me*, and he reached out for a bottle of 1000-1 Adrenaline in his medicine cabinet.

Even without the grief in hand, he was running late in terms of setting up his pitch at the market, all on the strength of a sleepless night. He shook his head in despair as he checked the time. Even the clock appeared to be mocking his performance. *Blimey! Five forty-five. It won't be worth going at this rate. I'd better give Siddie a bell, he'll be wondering where the ruddy hell I am.* Unfortunately, with Lady Luck deciding to have the day off, there was no way he could have prepared himself for the next unexpected event that would continue to plague his precarious day.

He happened to be standing at the end of the hall, when his vision became distracted by the buff-looking object lying on the doormat. A cursory smile took over his face, and not before he expressed his distaste. *Poxy bills! Don't yer just luv em?* was his first reaction. Glancing at his watch, he succeeded in confirming another train of thought. *Six o'clock! The postman must have shit the bed, nah, that can't be right.* Shaking his head, he approached the end of the hall. Seconds later he wished he hadn't as a familiar gut feeling came home to roost.

*Strange, even with a reminder, you get the benefit of a bloody stamp!* he told himself.

His body froze as he bent down to retrieve the alleged letter lying sunny side up, and the only identity it carried reflected in his acute anger. His gut immediately told him that it wouldn't take a stewards' enquiry to discover its source. The significance of the single capital C more than indemnified his awareness that the person responsible for the drop lay directly in Rossetti's stable. Steeling himself, Ronnie breathed deeply before ripping the suspect envelope open, his hands shaking in temper as the contents came to light. It took him a few seconds to assess the poison it contained due to the layout. But the significance of the postscript single bullet didn't warrant an interpreter, and only served as a wake-up call alluding to personal security.

He felt numb and shook his head again in total disbelief, feeling totally eclipsed by the events as they unfolded. By his own omission, round two belonged to Rossetti! His intrepid moonlighting had paid dividends in the psychology stakes. Not only had Rossetti succeeded in putting the knife in twice, but he'd managed to twist it as well.

*The bastard's done it in style this time around!* as Ronnie would say when summing up, his riveted eyes once again taking in the poisoned threat. It read as follows with the format in the same vein as its predecessor. In stark contrast, the sicko inclusion, namely the .38mm round, came across as a promotional bid. In the event a get out clause should come into play.

The poison pen letter read:

CA LL-A-GH-AN

YOU R IN TER ES T I S GRO W I ING O N ME CHE C KYO U R

INS R ANCE C OVE R FO R UN FI N ISH ED BUS IN ESS PHO E N IX

Meanwhile, at the market, Siddie was dutifully engaged taking money from a punter, when Ronnie's call came through, which was also why he chose to ignore it. "It's a simple case of priorities and economics, mate," he argued. "The difference being that sterling has got a more positive ring about it, if yer know what I mean!" which couldn't be said for Ronnie's wilting patience. Being cajoled into a spectator's point of view only increased Siddie's concern as the poison pen letter was exposed moments later.

Problem! It was 6.30am in the morning. It was also proving difficult to get his head around the scenario, and just to add to his frustration it was costing him money as a potential punter moved on from his stall. Annoyed?! You work it out. Meanwhile, any attempt on his part to collaborate on the subject was suffocated as Ronnie persisted in making the line his own. Once again, Siddie winced as one expletive toppled the other, forcing him to hang his mobile out to dry in the knowledge that Ronnie would take the bait. A second or so later, his forecast delivered as an aborted silence kicked in at both ends.

Siddie could be excused for thinking that his mobile gave out a sigh, although any would-be reprieve became short lived as Ronnie found his second wind. "So where in hell do I..."

"Ronnie, shut it!" Siddie's well-timed intervention was short, sharp and needed to be aired along with his own views. Being well pissed off one minute and peacemaker the next became an asset that commanded respect. And Siddie happened to be a past master when it came down to logic. "For Christ's sake! Keep calm already, you ain't gonna win any medals mouthing off. You need a rational approach to what's going down. I understand where yer coming from, but there's a right and a wrong way of dealing with the situation. Firstly, working as a firm we stand a far better chance of sorting it. So, as from now, you think chutzpah, my friend. Don't let the schmuck wind yer up, because this is what it's all about! He's priming yer. In the event you lose it and come running. Leave that option in his court, and I swear to God, his poxy nerve will become his eventual downfall."

"Please God!" exclaimed Ronnie vehemently. Their heated conversation continued for a short while, but on a mediocre level, ending with Ronnie agreeing to disagree. On the flip side, the two arranged a midday meet in Toni de Angelo's market café to pick over the bones and further discuss the probability of a game plan.

In retrospect, this latest ploy by Rossetti to once again attempt to undermine Ronnie's stability had, in effect, created a double whammy in terms of direction. Mentally, the chilling letter had rocked his fiery demeanour.

Alternatively, one particular overriding factor would lie directly in the face of the bullet and how well he handled the extreme need to err on the side of caution, before rushing headlong into a one-man vendetta as an excuse for dented pride.

"Looking back on it nah, it was almost like the creep was standing in front of me, and dictating the verbal shit. And me?! I was just bleedin' powerless to do or say anything. I felt absolutely gutted."

"And the bullet itself, how did yer handle that?"

"Nah that was scary, mate, and the crux of the matter. Okay, so the verbal shit in the letter I can live with. But I tell yer, that poxy bullet is something else. It could well turn out to be part of a bigger package deal, know what I mean?"

"Precisely!" Siddie echoed. "And that is why yer can't afford to do a solo act. As you say, words are only skin deep. On the other hand, who's to say the putz ain't tooled up and binding his time to break out?"

Sitting in Toni's café a few hours later, over a light lunch the two were heavily engrossed in deep conversation whilst drinking copious amounts of cappuccino. It was no coincidence they had met up within minutes of each other, such was the importance of their prearranged meet. Ronnie took off the top of his drink before replying, hesitating slightly. Siddie had obviously hit on a raw nerve. "Shit! If, as you suspect, he's tooled up, that's a whole new ball game. I mean we know the asshole is an absolute nutter, which means anything is possible."

Siddie breathed easy; suppressing Ronnie's urge to blindly pursue a dangerous liaison with Rossetti was now put on hold, pending any further unwanted grief. What his hands couldn't say was left to his mouth as he expressed his immediate relief. "Nah yer making sense, mate. You have to believe the guy, like it or not, has got access to a shooter. So yer need to start to respect the quality of fresh air, it ain't a game anymore!" A cool silence followed, in which time Ronnie digested the truth of the matter before concluding.

"Thanks, mate," he nodded. "I just needed to be told."

"And likewise the Old Bill," Siddie promptly reminded him. "The slant on the bullet moves everything up a league. They've got the resources, so take any advice on offer, right?

I'd better make a move, I need to snatch a few quid while I can, and you?"

"All things considered, I reckon I'll open the gym up earlier tonight, and have a row with a fucking punch bag, and imagine it's Rossetti I'm hammering. That'll do wonders for my system. Anyway, I'll bell yer later tonight. Be lucky." Siddie smiled ruefully,

"Lucky! I bloody need to be, my money pouch thinks it's on a diet. Which means I'll have Rachael on my case, and you reckon you've got problems?!" Once outside Toni's they shook hands and went their respective ways. Wandering back towards his stall, Siddie thought he'd detected a few scattered rain drops in the air. Glancing upward gave him carte blanche to curse the world at large, including its maker, as the heavens opened up, forcing him to take whatever refuge he could.

An hour or so later, soaked to the core and the day's takings just short of the floor, he slunk from out of the market, heading for home with a view to shared sympathy. Who was he kidding?! At best, the only reprieve on the cards would entail a Rachael 'domestic'. "Can you get that, Bubullah? It's more than likely Ronnie." Siddie was halfway between having a shave and a shower, when the phone happened to kick off that evening. Not that he even qualified for a shave, but the sanctity of the bathroom seemed a far better deal than a stewards' enquiry into the demise of his stall wedge.

Marking Ronnie's card, plus the overlap from the unexpected rain, had resulted in a double you wouldn't put odds on as Siddie pleaded his case earlier. In reply, Rachael appeared adamant. "Loss! So explain loss! In business the word doesn't exist. I tell you, money should make money," she scolded. In Siddie's case, the money in question represented a stall full of unsold fruit and veg. And still, Rachael would insist that loss meant Spanish for 'the'!

Snatching at the receiver on a pretext it could have been Ronnie indicated concern linked with added affection for the man she regarded as family. "Eh, Siddie? It's Ronnie. What's occurring?"

"No! This is Rachael speaking. How was your day?"

Ronnie hesitated before replying, and hoped it wasn't too obvious.

"As good as it gets, I reckon. Make £5 spend £6, you know how it is."

"I'm pleased for you. You should be so lucky." He felt unusually uncomfortable having duped her in conversation but decided that discretion was the better part of valour. Having just spent the best part of an hour of extensive grilling via the local plod, Rachael was proving to be a breath of fresh air, but with reservations. "You'll never know the half of it, sweetheart," he told himself quietly, and continued.

"Yeah, thanks for that, Rachael, we really need to catch up sometime over a salt beef supper maybe?"

"Now that would be kosher! See you soon, please God," she concluded. "Oh," she cut back in, "Siddie would like a word."

"Hi mate, I couldn't help overhearing. I don't suppose you've got the time for a waffle tonight?"

"Sorry, I'll have to give it a swerve tonight, I'm afraid."

"Damn!"

"You say something?"

"Nah, just me thinking out loud." Deep down, Siddie felt gutted. In the absence of Ronnie's company, the rest of the evening would become monopolised by earache, with no known antidote besides. As for Ronnie himself, the mere thought of punching six bales of shit out of a bag trading under the name of Rossetti had a certain ring attached to it. No pun intended of course.

## CHAPTER 22

# HARDWARE AND A GORILLA

Elsewhere, Rossetti could also be found to be targeting options, but in an illicit context, not surprisingly. The idea of adding an extra to his 'hardware' department gave credence to detail, if, and when, a wisp of opportunity should arise to resurrect and put into play the only asset that reigned over his present life expectancy. In hindsight, the expression 'jumping the gun' seems to fit the bill in his case.

The deal that he'd previously struck, or should I say, steamrollered into via Maltese Pete, had left his judgment somewhat flatfooted by not considering the implication of noise when using his .38 Cobra. The benefit of securing a silencer would ensure a more personal touch simply by allowing him the freedom of choice to strike to order. *Fine, I can see where he's coming from. Unfortunately, it all comes down to paying the piper for the privilege.* In this particular case, the price would be too high to accommodate the likes of Rossetti when considering his alien track record.

From a seller's standpoint, it was an open and shut case: 'You want it! I can supply it! This is what it costs!' Problem! From where Rossetti was standing, the top half of the £10,000 he'd inherited from the Rinse had now been placed on the missing list, whilst the balance was currently under 'antibiotics'. In short, the residue of his ill-gotten wedge was looking a bit sick. If ever there was a plus to consider, then pinning the elusive

Maltese Pete down would be the very least of his problems. As for location, the word on the street pointed to one particular gaff in question, commonly referred to by losers and gamblers alike as simply Shuffles, the name synonymous with playing cards as opposed to Rossetti's exclusive mode of walking. The obvious difference was that his gimp was the product of his own hand rather than from a card dealer!

The haunt in question had been favoured by Maltese of late, notably due to the lure of big money associated with the lucrative in-house card schools. For his part, Rossetti's only interest featured in negotiating a deal to somehow obtain a silencer of sorts, which also entailed using the best part of his beleaguered wedge. The requirement to be minted up should an offer become available was deemed imperative, allowing any personality clash to be brushed to one side when folding money came into play. Money, first and foremost, reigned superior as the plasma of the underworld. With it, a substantial wedge carried respect and standing; the lack of it created a breed of underdog that snapped at every morsel for survival. At least Rossetti could be classed as being exclusive. His current status now placed him midway down the road to perdition on a one-way ticket.

The clock set in the dashboard was timed at just after midnight. Moments later, the taxi pulled off the ramshackle road and came to rest on the fringe of some wasteground adjacent to a dated second hand car lot. The surrounding area set over a two-mile radius was riddled with kerbside garages and car breakers alike. The obnoxious stench of disused oil and burnt rubber hung on the night air, ably supported by the resident fog. At varied intervals, disused warehouses and the odd office block still remained prominent on the skyline as an epitaph to a once-thriving commercial industry.

Situated on the east side of the basin estuary, the locale

had become the last bastion of Docklands, and therefore long overdue for regeneration, mainly due to its accessibility which, in turn, was limited by an out-dated toll bridge. Because of its shady links with the motor trade, the area as a whole came to be known as the Isle of Wheels. It would be fair to say that from a postcard perspective, the area looked a far better proposition by night than it did by the light of day!

Emerging from the cab, Rossetti lost no time in making himself scarce as he headed towards a distant light set in the bowels of a cul-de-sac. Visibility, or the lack of it, became a case of what you see you get. Briefly he faltered in his step to avoid the relic of yet another burnt-out car. "Shit!" he exclaimed. *I don't bleedin' need this, I only hope the geezer's given me the right SP*, he confided in himself. Acting on loose talk derived from the depths of a bottle of Scotch, and via the AA pub, was the best he could hope for when Maltese and timing came under scrutiny. Any confidence he may have generated was now hanging on the door hinge of despair. His body language spoke for him as he tentatively picked his way through a carpet of debris. Eventually, the entrance to the building came into focus.

He checked himself before hammering on the door. Reaching inside his Crombie, he reverently patted the bulge in his inner pocket to ensure his wedge was still intact. Breathing more freely, he took possession of a small hip flask. Throwing his head back, he forced the contents down his throat, which caused him to shudder. Using the back of his hand in lieu of a hanky, he wiped his mouth; it gave him a moment's reprieve to gather himself. Gritting his teeth, he steeled himself and banged on the door. A minute or so later, the door slowly eased open. Any form of light was obliterated by the oversized figure confronting him. Rossetti immediately took a step back as the gorilla facing him made the running.

"Yeah, what yer looking for, business or pleasure?" he

demanded, and leered, or maybe it was just him! His enquiry was short and to the point. The first half of the question he could equate with Maltese. But pleasure?! *He's having a laugh*, Rossetti told himself.

"ID, you got any ID?" The gorilla soon brought him back down to earth.

"Eh? Nah, not as such, look, I've got some business with Maltese Pete. I've been told he'll be 'ere tonight."

"Yeah, looks like you got lucky, pal. There's a big card school kicking off shortly and I know he's involved. Chances are he's in the bar. I'll flush him out for yer. A name? I don't know yer face, who shall I say wants him?"

"Uhm, Rossetti, Paul Rossetti, he'll know." The gorilla smiled – or was it a wince? – as the name made an instant impact on him.

"What! *The* Rossetti?" For once, he was lost for words and floundering as their conversation continued. "You've got some front, sunshine, putting yerself about. There's out-of-town interest riding on you!" Rossetti paled as the implication came home to roost. He'd heard undisclosed rumours recently, now they ran to a headline review. Shrugging his shoulders, he fired back in desperation, "Ah, whatever." It resulted in a vain attempt to gloss over what he already knew to be true. The gorilla grunted – they do that, don't they? – raised his eyebrows and gestured.

"Your funeral, mate. I'll fetch Pete, you wait 'ere," and promptly slammed the door in his face. Rossetti now found himself taking stock of an uncensored nightmare. The world can be a lonely place, especially at 12.15 in the early hours marooned in no man's land feeling bloody cold and sober, and with a possible hiding to nothing in the offing. Nothing new there then! Apart from the sober aspect. Without warning, the door swung open, and a more-than-relieved Rossetti found himself ushered into a spacious, smoke-ridden, dimly lit room. It was finally left to the gorilla to put the house rules into perspective as Maltese motioned him over to what appeared at first to be a makeshift bar.

"Any hint of grief, sunshine, and I'll make it as painless as possible. I ain't paid to mop up blood, do yer understand?" Rossetti's blood ran cold, and colder still through fear as his gut tightened in sympathy. *Fuck's sake! That ain't a warning, it's a bleedin' death threat!* he convinced himself.

"Well, well, well! Look what the cat's brought in. I gotta hand it to yer, Rossi, you must think terminal is the name of a racehorse!" and concluded, "Right nah yer more sought after than flaming Jack the bloody Ripper!" Rossetti felt way out of his depth the minute he kissed the cab goodbye.

"Yeah, nice to see yer too, Pete," he replied in a semi-friendly patronising manner. Maltese chose to ignore the obvious undertones in favour of intrigue.

"Nah what in hell's name would yer want with me?" Rossetti fidgeted as an image depicting a treble Scotch, closely followed by a one-way ticket to Brazil, flashed through his distorted mind. "Well?"

"Yeah, eh, bit of business I hope." He stopped short and cleared his dry throat. "It's important, know what I mean?"

"Spit it out then, I got a big game kicking off shortly. What are yer after anyway?"

"Basically, I need some extra insurance," he blurted out.

"Namely?" His ragged nerves got the better of him as he forced the issue.

"A silencer! Yeah, that's what I need, a bleedin' silencer!" His unprovoked outburst left him sweating and feeling uneasy as Maltese glared intently while considering his latest demand. In retrospect, the possibility of seeing money and daylight coming together somehow appealed to him, besides which, it would give his own ante a boost with the big game in mind. *Not only that,* he mused, *who's to say that Rossetti will still be around when it's time to collect his insurance? Nah. I'll string him along, it's money in the bank for me.* Without fear of being sued, the expression 'No honour amongst thieves' had been aired and co-written by Maltese when summing up his latest win. *Could well be an omen for later,* he assured himself, and nodded confidently before deciding to speak. "Okay, Rossi, let's talk. I presume yer carrying a wedge?" Nodding aggrievedly, Rossetti patted his Crombie. His actions sent out the wrong signals, and were quickly seized upon by Maltese.

*Could be the little shit's carrying a shooter for all I know. Mind you, there's one way of finding out,* he told himself. "Tell yer what, you pay for the drinks, Rossi, and we'll talk some business!" He motioned the barman over. "Set 'em up, Harry, doubles all round. Scotch and my usual." His cold eyes never left off as Rossetti reached inside his pocket and produced a sizable wedge. "Yer wouldn't be carrying a shooter in there as well, would yer, Rossi?"

The ringed statement was brash in content and was quickly followed by a sarcastic laugh. Rossetti had been done up like a kipper and it showed in his face. "Cheer up, Rossi, for fuck's sake, it ain't all bad. Yer silencer shouldn't be too hard to come by." Switching alternatives led him to digress briefly. "If I remember rightly, the last time we had a deal I left yer for a card school, and wound up winning a nice few quid. So I owe yer. Give me a monkey deposit and the remaining carpet when I deliver, wotcha say?"

In a word, Rossetti was left feeling slaughtered. The idea that Maltese was doing him a favour merely by quoting telephone numbers was no different to karma turning full circle and biting his arse in the process. Impatience appeared to be short loaned. "That's the deal, Rossi, take it or leave it!" Downing his drink, he caught the barman's eye. "Same again, Harry," he bawled, and gestured in Rossetti's direction. "Better make his a treble, he don't look too kosher to me. Oh, and by the way, he's fucking paying for 'em!"

Rossetti's face remained blank; he felt utterly destroyed.

In the final analysis, it became a case of pay up and look good. In return, the Scotch beckoning in his glass never touched the sides in a quick-fix effort to regain some sort of composure. In spite of the content, his hands visibly shook minutes later as the initial monkey instalment changed hands. As usual, Maltese had the final word when checking the wedge. "It's only money, Rossi, besides, where you're going it ain't compulsory! By the way, you still banged up in that safe house?" Like a puppet on a string, he nodded to order. "Right! In that case I know where to find yer then." Their one-sided conversation suddenly ran dry as two mean-looking faces approached and interrupted Maltese's verbal assassination.

It immediately became clear to Rossetti, merely by their body language, that they were no strangers to Maltese as they passed. "We'll be in the back room, Pete. You've got fifteen minutes," the shorter of the two stated and indicated with his head. Maltese nodded back in response.

"Yeah, no problem, Previous. Just keep my seat warm, will yer?" Rossetti's curiosity then got the better of him.

"What's all that about then, Pete?"

"Oh, the game, the big card game, they're both involved."

"I didn't recognise any of 'em."

"Well, yer wouldn't, would yer? You've been off the manor too long," he remarked drily.

"Yeah, that figures. So what's with the guy nicknamed Previous then?"

"Ah, just a name he inherited from the Old Bill. At one

time, he was rated the best burglar in the business. His name is Freddie Bash!"

"You said 'used to be'?"

"That's right! He knocked thieving on the head some time ago. He now runs a moody security business to blag a living."

"Blimey, yer don't say. Mind you, with a name like that!" Maltese nodded.

"It's a long story. But at one time, he had more form than bleedin' Red Rum! He had more charges set against him than a supermarket's got punters! Hence the nickname Previous!"

"And the other face?" Maltese chuckled – or maybe it was the sound of somebody being throttled – leaving Rossetti feeling agitated.

"Did I say something funny?"

"Nah, yer alright, Rossi, I was thinking out loud."

"Yeah?"

"About Fat Louis, the other face."

"Fat! Yer having a laugh, ain't yer?"

"As it happens, he used to top about eighteen stone at one time. But he lost it all doing a twelve stretch in Bellmarsh."

"Seems a bit bleedin' heavy to me. So what's the SP?"

"Fat Louis was the best getaway driver in the business bar none! That is, until he fucked up big time!"

"Go on."

"Him and four other faces had planned a bank heist in the City. The day before the raid, he nicked a Jaguar off a driveway and, would yer believe, it had a full tank of gas!"

"Sweet, he must have thought he'd won the poxy lottery!"

"Anyway, the following day they hit the bank about right, no problem. Fat Louis, as usual, was outside giving it large on the pedal." He stopped short and stifled a laugh. "… I think," he concluded, still sniggering.

"So what's so funny about that?!"

"Funny! I tell yer what's fucking funny, Rossi. The motor takes off like a bleedin' rocket with 'em all inside, well wedged up of course, and comes to a dead stop 200 yards down the poxy road!"

"No shit! Don't tell me, fucking road block, yeah?"

"Nah, nothing like that! The tosser had run out of juice!"

"Hang on a minute, you said the guy had a full tank of gas."

"I did! But what Fat Louis couldn't have known was that the bleedin' gas needle had previously got stuck, and that the AA were on their way to fix it ten minutes after he bloody well nicked it!"

"Stone me! So the only juice he had in the tank meant the wheels were running on excitement."

"Exactly!"

"How unlucky is that? If it was raining lager Fat Louis would have had a fork in his hand!"

"As long as it doesn't rub off on me tonight, I don't give a shit! Anyway, win or lose I'll be in touch in a couple of weeks' time, if yer still around that is. Oh, one other thing, my surname is Castelli, with two Ls, in the event yer thinking of making a will out!" Forced to stand in silence, Rossetti wore a mask of despair. Finally, he shrugged his shoulders in a hopeless gesture as his frame adopted the spirit of a broken man.

"Drink?!" The barman logically invaded his private space.

"Yeah, I think I'd better, and a cab while yer at it." Minutes later he was back.

"There yer go, and the wheels are on the way." Rossetti weighed him in, and stood silently toying with his Scotch.

"He's a funny geezer, that one." Still feeling wiped out, Rossetti looked up.

"Who is?"

"Maltese. I couldn't help earwigging. He's got a funny way with words, know what I mean?"

"Tell me about it. That's why I drink Scotch, it don't bleedin' answer back!"

"Knowing him, I wouldn't make a book on it, he'd find a clue around it." Just then, the distant tone of a car horn broke their conversation up.

"I'll see yer around, Harry. Be lucky."

"Who fucking knows?" replied the barman. "Small world, innit?" Rossetti forced a smile and turned on his heel to leave. Without any prompting, the gorilla came out of the woodwork and made himself busy opening the door to let him out. Rossetti couldn't resist the chance to have a final pop at him.

"None of my business, sunshine, but what sort of dough are yer on working 'ere?" The gorilla drew his chest up and squared his shoulders.

"Dough? I'm on a nifty a night, the management look after me 'ere."

"Really! A nifty, eh? Well, look, I ain't supposed to tell yer this, but I happen to have the SP on a nice little earner. It's twice the money and less hours."

"Sounds the business. Is it kosher?" Slowly, Rossetti began to reel the gorilla in, and continued.

"You gotta believe it, sunshine, the job itself is in jeopardy!" His eyes began to light up, realising he could be on to a good thing.

"I don't suppose you've got a phone number to go with it?" he enquired.

"Nah, sorry, pal, not on me. If yer that interested, I've left a contact number with Harry behind the bar, he'll sort it for yer. Be lucky." Struggling to keep a straight face, he managed to stifle a grin and lost himself in the increasing gloom of the night. Strangely enough, the carpet of debris he'd encountered earlier on failed to become an obstacle as he made his way back to the main road. He was chuckling when the cab dropped him off some ten minutes later.

He paused briefly before turning his key in the lock. A sudden hint of nostalgia had crept in unexpectedly, and in the process opened up a meaningful door from way back. *They just don't make 'em like the Travelling Man anymore*, he exerted. *Gorillas these days ain't got no bleedin' class!* Continuing to snigger, he offered the key up and let himself in.

# CHAPTER 23

# STIRRING PROBLEMS

The distinct aroma of designer coffee wafted through the kitchen area, almost eclipsing the smell exuding from a hard-done-by slice of toast fighting for its life under the grill. As if to order, an arm reached out in a desperate attempt to put it out of its blackened misery. "Shit! You'd have thought I'd have got it right by nah," Ronnie scolded. At least the coffee in his cup looked a far better proposition, even though his opinion would come across as somewhat tainted should it become an issue. Glancing up, a mental picture of a cappuccino filled his thoughts. *Nobody does it like Toni de Angelo, the man's a bleedin' icon!*

Without doubt, and given the time, that would be one of the better conclusions he would be led to make that morning as he went through the motions before facing the rigours of market trading. Then again, it wasn't as if he even liked coffee! "It's wet, and it keeps me awake!" Quote, "Stick at what yer know, because at five o'clock in the bloody morning, yer wouldn't even know if you were drinking poison!", unquote. Having said that, the majority of people, given the knowledge it was a Monday anyway, would have plumped for the easier route and accepted a peerage in the sick club.

"Damn it!" The hot coffee scalded his mouth, and forced him to make a final decision. "Ain't exactly happening for yer, old son, is it?" he asked himself and lowered the cup. If only he'd taken Rachael's advice, given on numerous occasions. "I tell you, Ronnie, coffee only becomes coffee when the water is just off boiling. Trust me, that is kosher." Even Toni would have sanctioned her reasoning. He knew it and the world knew it, leaving Ronnie to accept that Rachael was always going to be right.

Finally, his frustration caved in to a war of mundane verbal, forcing him to form an illogical opinion. "Hell! Why does life have to be so bleedin' complicated? You've got up and down! In and out! Stop and start! Left and right! And poxy hot and cold! I ask yer, all I want is a lousy cup of coffee!" Fair assessment; on the other hand, he could so easily have been married! Adding more milk to his problem only prompted more grief in knowing the damage had already been done. Under the circumstances, calling time on his meagre attempt proved to be the best result all round. "I guess there's only one place left for that!" he concluded. The nearby sink offered no resistance as the alleged coffee became history in seconds. "Just wasn't meant to be," said it all as he placed the jinxed cup into the drainer. *I might just as well leave earlier while I'm in front*, he confided in himself. Under the circumstances, it seemed to be the best deal on offer given his morning track record, which only left Toni de Angelo to take the brunt of his short-lived patience some twenty minutes later.

Glancing up from preparing the soup of the day, Toni did a double take. "Ronnie?! You shitta the bed, huh? You not happy man, mebbe I help." His larger-than-life Latin overtones humbled Ronnie into submission.

"Please God! Would you believe, a real coffee?" He was almost pleading. Toni waved any doubts to one side on size alone as a huge arm clasped his shoulder and meaningfully guided him into a seat.

"No problem, my friend, you wanna da coffee, I makka

the coffee. Now please to relax, okay?" It turned out to be the longest three minutes of his life. He'd swear to it. Toni returned and placed the coffee down on the table in front of him, leaving Ronnie to his own designs. When you know somebody that well, you can afford to give them the space they crave. "There's a lot more going on inside that head that I know about," would have been Toni's answer if an opinion came under scrutiny.

All facts considered, he would normally have been on his second cup by now, giving Toni the hurry up in the bargain. Unfortunately, if there had been a script involved, then Ronnie sure as hell forgot to bring it along with him. As it was, a full five minutes later found him still doing a good impression of somebody who'd completely lost the plot, but at the same time continuing to stir the original cup and obviously content to do so in a blasé manner. Whatever appeal it had going for it now only registered as solace as he sat staring into an unclassified pool of semi-cold liquid. And yet, he still persisted to stir.

His demeanour, for whatever reason, appeared plagued with doubts.

On the flip side, there appeared to be one thing you'd willingly gamble on: that from the moment he'd woken up that particular morning, it was going to be the best he was going to feel all day! Unless...

"Hey, Ronnie!" Toni had once again picked up on his current posture and hopefully thrown him a lifeline. "You wonta find what you look for in the cuppa, my coffee is for drinking, huh?" Oblivious to his reasoning, Ronnie nevertheless carried on stirring. Shrugging his shoulders, Toni reverently crossed himself. There would have been no way he could have known by body perception alone, even though he'd now become alive to a problem of sorts, just how far-reaching Ronnie's inner warring with Rossetti in mind had evolved. The key to that equation was now secured in Ronnie's unsettled mind.

On reflection, Siddie's preconceived notion, as good as it was intended to be at the time, namely, to tough it out, appeared to wear thinner than a Scottish cheque book, leaving Ronnie knocking on the door to never never land. Putting it mildly, his highly charged demeanor was now on a 24/7 roller coaster to God only knows where! And the rails it was running on had been substituted for Ronnie's entangled nerves. And just to exasperate his misery, Rossetti was in the driving seat holding a full-blown licence in one hand and a one-way ticket to hell in the other.

For whatever reason, Ronnie suddenly ceased stirring to mutter under his breath convincingly, "He's in there, yer know. I can see the bastard, yer can't kid me!"

"Of course you can, Ronnie! But no other bleeder can, now get your head sorted!" It was a desperate attempt by a second hand brain to bail him out. It wasn't to be. He continued to blabber on as a mental image of his nemesis appeared in the reflection of his now defunct coffee. Concern was briefly shelved as Toni became distracted by the appearance of a hungry market trader requesting the eternal full English.

"I serve you two minutes, okay, Mickey?" he said, flustered.

"There ain't no rush, mate. Besides, I'm waiting on a delivery anyway, take yer time." From out of the corner of his eye, Mickey caught sight of the huddled figure seemingly heavily engrossed in the far corner. He was forced to look twice to allow recognition to set in. "Wotcha, Ronnie," he stated cheerfully. "Good day for the race, mate." Ronnie never flinched; his face remained completely passive; any outside interest washed clean over his head. Looking perplexed, Mickey glanced back at Toni with raised arms and gestured in Ronnie's direction. "Blimey!" he retorted. "There's got to be more life on bloody Mars! It ain't like him, I hope it ain't catching." Toni had heard and seen enough. "Excusa me one memento." Hurriedly reaching for his mobile, he selected a specific contact number.

Ronnie was still stirring his alleged coffee a little later when Siddie burst through the café door. If by chance, stirring a cup of coffee became an international pastime hinged on an alternative meaning, namely a wake-up call, then professional hitman Enrico Maniella, alias Buffy Manilla as he was known by New Scotland Yard and Interpol alike, would surely have been found guilty on both counts. Of late, his hermit-oriented existence was in dire need of a fresh makeover, namely, kicking the arse of complacency in exchange for a taste of freedom. Even a working break would more than suffice for an acute case of utter boredom.

His illicit profession had been ignited by the hand of terror and then fuelled by assassination to order, when, as a young man, he was forced to witness the execution of his political and wealthy parents. From out of that locked-in moment, the cocktail of circumstances surrounding their horrific demise addled his brain into a futuristic desire to bring about death on demand. On that particular question, sheer fascination dispelled the trauma of seeing flesh and blood entertaining a hail of designer lead. Like puppets, their redundant bodies writhed and kicked involuntarily as the hands of the Grim Reaper worked the strings of impending death. And then it was over as the gunfire reached its climax.

Throughout this induction to hell on earth, his inner emotional senses had never wavered. Unblinking eyes appeared transfixed by a misshapen and grotesque mound of broken bodies. Apart from the odd twitch arising from tormented nerve endings, the useless flesh and blood that once resembled the fulfilment of life had now become just another statistic. Upon leaving the scene of carnage, he chose to never look back, and this also applied to his newfound career. Through unforeseen circumstances associated with his first kill, he had become permanently based in Jersey. His chosen profession had given him access to infinite wealth and unlimited property, culminating in a multimillion-pound state-of-the-art villa. The additional asset of an F430 Spider Ferrari gracing his private driveway gave merit to his ongoing prowess as an international hitman over the years. And yet, he still found himself bored.

Maybe a predetermined decision to take time out of late had momentarily influenced his memory and timing regarding a recent phone call, the latter coupled with a 'business' arrangement on the mainland. The question was now, had Buffy Manilla genuinely forgotten one particular contract in hand? Or had the lack of motivation in his life caused a rigid regime to falter? For the time being, the rest of the world, as far as he was concerned, could willingly go to hell as he nonchalantly sauntered toward his study.

It soon became the third time in as many minutes. His over indulgence in imbibing his best Napoleon brandy partly arose from an inner restlessness. In return, the connoisseur would argue strenuously in defence of the pedigree brandy. Moments later, the sweet aroma of a King Edward cigar formed the backdrop to the lustrous veneer-panelled study in which he now lay at full stretch on a dimpled chaise longue. The ice in his Waterford glass chinked as he offered it up once again. Stopping short, he methodically stroked his chin with his free hand whilst contemplating an immobile situation.

A look of concern flitted across his face. It became evident that something untoward appeared to be bugging him. Rising from the comfort of the chaise longue, he approached an oversized bullet-proof window which ran the entire length of one wall. It gave out a panoramic scene capturing views of

Roque Point and St Clement Bay beyond. The wistful look on his face as he took in the view slowly creased into a mask of realisation tinged with acute satisfaction. "Of course!" he exclaimed solidly as his fist slammed down onto the sill. Affording a half smile to justify his outburst, he rebuked himself, before uttering, "The Rossetti contract! How in God's name could I have let that slip?" The immediate conclusion that sprang to mind only ranked second to his black sense of humour. "I've been getting away with bloody murder just lately," he quickly reminded himself, and delayed a false grin. Ironically, a fly-on-the-wall copper wouldn't hesitate to agree unreservedly with his testament.

Moving away from the window, he crossed over to a Chippendale walnut bureau; carefully, he pulled the roll-top down, removing a pure-leather-bound diary from an inner sleeve. He proceeded to study one particular page for a few minutes, then nodded to himself before speaking. "Uhm! Thought as much, the name alone should have meant something. It just didn't register when the call came through. I definitely need to close the book on this character!" Pausing briefly, he digressed, allowing a larger image of Rossetti's past status to emerge. He then continued talking in the same vein. "Well, Mr Rossetti. It appears that you have this nasty habit of upsetting people, period! Something tells me you've led a very charmed life from way back. First off, it was a certain Terry Winters, and now this latest episode concerning a certain Frankie 'the Rinse'," he tutted. "Time I reviewed your file, my friend."

Sifting through the exposed contents strewn in front of him, one particular mugshot caused an immediate response. "I should have known better. How could I have possibly forgotten a face like that?!" Holding the photo up at eye level, he continued his appraisal on a mock one-to-one basis. "As I recall, some six years ago, I allowed you the privilege of a fool's reprieve, all due to Terry Winters' unforeseen death. I couldn't see the point of putting you down at the same time though, even knowing that the contract monies had been honoured. The same concession also applied to a Mr Ricky Peters. As for Tito 'the Butcher' Santini, he obviously caught me on a good day. Or coming from him…" he stopped off to smirk, "… one hell of a lousy day! In retrospect, I particularly relished that contract. I seem to recall that I extended my patience when delivering his coup de grace, not that he would have thanked me for it of course!" Sighing deeply, he continued in the same vein. "As for you, Mr Rossetti, the sooner you're wasted the better all round all things considered. damn, I almost forgot myself! The pleasure, of course, will be all mine. All I require now is a certain sum of money to clarify your absolute termination!" Strange! The remaining brandy in his glass had a defining sweetness as he readily knocked it back. Placing the glass down, he reached for his phone.

For whatever reason, stirring as a pastime was now fast-becoming fashionable from every angle. In Rossetti's case, there was a solid reason why his undying thirst to take his revenge on the world had taken a fresh slant. In this case, deriving from the old adage 'when thieves fall out'! This, in turn, had resulted in a crisis even he couldn't ignore. With this in mind, he would now be forced into continually looking over his shoulder 24/7, purely as a security aspect. Failure to comply could eventually become his 'swan song'!

Even the added rider attached to the alleged safe househad now inherited a sell-by date, all down to the cost of one lousy bottle of Scotch! "You mix with yer own, you down with yer own! I don't make the fucking rules, bring it on." Quote! And that from the bent mouth of the asshole in the adjoining room. Christ's sake! How pissed did he get that night when acting on behalf of the Rinse? Honour amongst thieves went out with pink socks the minute Rossetti was fingered for a postal address. He now found himself banged up like a rat in a corner that could only spell convenience for the likes of anyone with a grudge against him. If, and when, push came to shove.

Living like he did in a manufactured world of arch villains and Jack shit alike was now proving to be untenable. His plastic lifestyle, as of now, was hovering precariously somewhere between 340 and 360 degrees, leaving an impatient piper with his hand out and expecting to be paid. Not the best legacy on offer. But we are talking Rossetti here, clamped to a situation that was now spiralling out of control, and in the process leaving him with nowhere else to run, with all options barred. He'd been damned from day one as he continued to drift into a self-imposed existence, fraught with grief. Confronting his initial problem, bearing in mind he'd taken on the mantle of a marked man, would undoubtedly place the emphasis on time, an aspect of which lay well beyond his control, and could prove to be a commodity that even money couldn't buy in the real world. That being bullshit!

Everything and everybody has a price, and hitman Buffy Manilla would argue his case, especially when acting as an agent for the Grim Reaper PLC. The universal adage, 'What you don't know about, you can't worry about', appears to have surfaced, possibly favouring Rossetti and concerning a timely reprieve. Is it remotely possible that through a blend of arrogance and delayed ignorance, he'd unwittingly exposed a loophole via the alleged contract on his head? That being the case, then Rossetti had no way of knowing whether or not a settlement figure had been established, or even paid.

Working along those lines, then Manilla could be suckered into making a move based purely on a verbal agreement alone.

Nobody works for nothing! Leastways yours truly. Not that money would always sustain an incentive to murder. The answer to that mode of thought would become unravelled in time to come, directly by Rossetti himself no less. Working on assumption alone, the latter had to believe that the all-important monies affected were now registered in Jersey.

With that overriding fact in mind, he decided to go for the jugular, simply by taking the Rinse out of circulation as a token gesture of his underlying hate of the man. The heat would then diminish and, likewise, another hurdle would be crossed. Whatever time remained could now be used to bring about the long-awaited outcome of a personal vendetta, fed by a malignant tumour of unparalleled hate. In the meantime, coffee problems apart, Ronnie Callaghan would have to remain stolid until such time as Rossetti's torrid destiny came under question. Or would he…?

## CHAPTER 24

# DEADLY THOUGHTS

"So what's the quack have to say then? Couldn't have been all bad, could it?" Siddie Levy was desperate for some feedback regarding Ronnie's unrehearsed lapse in time, acting on a call from Toni de Angelo. Under orders, and flying a distress flag, Ronnie found himself forced to bite the bullet and a tablet or two by visiting his doctor and hopefully levelling his suspect sanity. Ronnie was adamant in reply to his plea.

"Stone me! I dunno what all the bleedin' fuss is about. It's nothing I can't handle, trust me."

"That's not what I asked yer," Siddie promptly fired back. But then he should have recognised the symptoms. Any form of supposition had to be deemed as flawed when tackling the truth.

"Stand on me. I appreciate yer concern, mate. Okay, I fucked up for a spell. I should never have let it happen. Even now, I can't believe I allowed that asshole to get to me, it's just that..."

"Yeah, what? Go on." Siddie decided to jump the gun. By maintaining interest, the possibility of Ronnie opening up any further might just provoke the response he was gainfully seeking. "Well?!" Ronnie could be seen to be hedging, but nevertheless continued.

"He did happen to mention..."

"Who, what?"

"D'ye really want to know?" Immediately, Siddie sensed a wind-up might be on the cards, and swiftly cut short his current interest.

"I'm listening already, yer know I do."

"The doctor said…" At this point, Ronnie's face creased and he was bent double laughing. Siddie felt slaughtered and held his head. A reply didn't come easy.

"I should have known better. You've done me up like a kipper! Sometimes, you can be such a putz, Callaghan, d'ye know that? So tell me already."

"He said…"

"I'm sure he did!" Siddie fell into line.

"He said, 'If you ever get the urge or the need to boil over again, then give coffee a swerve and stick to tea'!" Minutes later they were falling about and laughing for England. When we laugh, the world, as a whole, tends to laugh with you, so people would have us believe! Alternatively, at the opposite end of the spectrum, should you find yourself hell bent on pursuing the audacious act of cold-blooded murder, the world and its wisdom are denied the privilege that freedom of speech can offer. Or so Rossetti would have us believe. Strictly from a victim's point of view, you understand. No argument there then!

On reaching a critical chapter in his inconsequential life, he'd succumbed to taking the road to wherever fate had decreed to lay down its roots. There could be no turning back in this exclusive game known as FINALE, or the additional bonus from within a Community Chest to aid or abet his manic fantasies. The remnants of his subnormal existence now chose refuge in the obligatory pack of Chance. Given an ultimatum, his present position might have been bolstered at the mere thought of being dealt a Go-to-Jail card.

At the very least, he'd exist in the knowledge there would always be a tomorrow in the offing. And the added option by way of a bellyful of porridge to consider its outcome. Forget it! That notion was never on the cards, if you'll excuse the pun! Besides, he'd come too far. And the road to perdition was fast running out. Having said all that, the ultimate prize of unfinished business was akin to the one remaining trump card left in his hand of destiny. If called upon, he wouldn't hesitate to produce a pair of would-be victims as his banker. How that sequence would rank along with other players now lay with whatever fate was willing to dish out.

Another consideration, of course, and one that couldn't be ignored, would be one of stakes. The majority of gamblers, if challenged with the situation, would no doubt err on the side of caution, safe in the knowledge that the stakes were higher than the odds were shorter. No takers there then, unless of course, you happened to have the brains of a rocking horse. Sound familiar?

At this moment in time, Rossetti could be found short on words, due to the gods on high previewing a final shopping list for his benefit:

HATE: A requirement he could always use more of, in spite of being weighed down with more than his share!

LUCK: Impossible to buy, even if obtainable, having now pushed his to the limit from the day he was born. Not to be confused with loser!

A LIFE: No point really at this stage; not only that, it wouldn't be right to offload Rossetti onto a clone, for the latter's sake, of course. Money well saved!

BLOOD: Only administered in a lifesaving emergency or opportune situation. Surely he couldn't get that lucky, could he?!

VENGEANCE: Now there's something he could afford to buy in bulk. But in exchange, the price might just cost him his life!

So who was the fool who suggested that life came cheap? When certain ideals kick in, there's more to a tailor-made murder than the involvement of money as an incentive. In his case, premeditated planning, linked to a glut of personal satisfaction, would be payment enough, end of! Coming to a clinical decision with the Rinse's future health in mind was paracetamol free and took all of two minutes. As of now, he was firmly in Rossetti's sights and labelled as a priority victim.

The overwhelming urge to blow away the guy necessitated a strict code of surveillance when acquiring specific times and dates relative to the would-be victim's movements. This, in turn, could only be executed under the cover of darkness. Even so, he would be no less vulnerable than at any other time. Any spontaneous showdown outside of planning, irrespective of the outcome, would result in total disaster, simply by bringing his nemesis Ronnie Callaghan in to avoid a bloody confrontation, and consequent death.

One murder alone was never going to be enough to sate Rossetti's greed for vengeance. He now had the incentive to prove something, having been thwarted by that, quote, "Selfish bastard, Dawson". They say 'There's none so blind as those who cannot see'. That particular endorsement now lay directly in the Rinse's stable. In a short space of time, he could well come to rue the day he inadvertently allowed Rossetti to merge into his life, and the circumstances beyond.

His first mistake centred on and around the Dawson contract going arse up, and in the process having no return on his outlay. The joker in the pack fell to Rossetti, who refused to budge when a certain wedge became an issue. The result was an aggressive attempt to humble Rossetti into submission by virtue of being unceremoniously dumped like so much rubbish into a rat-infested back alley, which only led Rossetti to rewrite the script in defence. The second mistake was to blindly underestimate the latter's exclusive survival rate. Love him or hate him, the tenacity of the man was never in doubt. Like a bad penny, he would bounce back to suit, and the outcome could well be costly.

This time around though, it would run to a one-off appearance with a calling card stamped 'death', and a shooter as a mouthpiece. In the meantime, the Rinse's planned demise would serve as a prelude and an induction into a reign of terror and violence, consequently surpassing the heinous murder and downfall of former gangland baron Terry Winters some six years previous, in conjunction with the arson attack he perpetuated. Which in turn rang the death knell on Slatteries' gym over at Docklands – scene of the crime in question, and the subsequent attempted murder of Ronnie Callaghan. Mayhem was at an all-time premium that fateful day as the flames of liquidation enveloped the stricken building. What little remained was finally razed, leaving in its wake the seeds of hate generated by a torrid association with nemesis Ronnie Callaghan.

Having lain dormant for the last six years, those same seeds were now primed and ready to blossom once again, this time in the form of an inevitable vendetta. Rossetti was now in a strong position to enforce a radical closure on the one account, after which the rest of the world could go hang. Assuming of course, the Rinse didn't intervene with ideas of his own. In the meantime, to achieve what Rossetti now regarded as death by default, i.e. the balance on the Dawson contract and the resulting grief when assuming that Buffy Manilla could be on the loose, would require the pressure of keeping a low profile. Time was now running out on the meter as a covert stake-out on the Rinse's playground, namely, the Miami Club, became an obsession when monitoring his twilight movements.

It was night four, and the novelty began to wear thinner

than a bottle of turps. The last hour had the beginnings and the ingredients of a self-imposed nightmare. If there had been a hell on earth, he'd have willingly opted for the genuine article, notwithstanding his current situation. The fact that he was in possession of a one-way ticket for either option did little to sway his judgment. His present status included an off-the-cuff cocktail of cold, damp and bleedin' miserable! Although not necessarily in that order. As a job lot, he would have readily settled for the proverbial 'well pissed off scenario'. Even the half bottle of Grouse whisky lining his coat pocket had begun to live up to its namesake by showing signs of wear and tear in the liquid department. And still he felt fucking cold!

His pathetic frame shivered involuntarily as the keen night air once again left its calling card. Constantly checking his watch had been the only form of motivation he'd allowed himself during the last half hour, which reflected in his nervous system trailing. Any kosher blood he may have retained in his body had done a runner an hour ago. What now remained had managed to bypass his gimpy leg, allowing it to fall into a deep slumber. He would pay for its resurrection some time later.

He cursed inwardly as only he knew how; he should have known better. The room for personal emotion had long been filled; now was the time to open the door and release a lifetime of pent-up retribution. For the present, patience was placed on ice in lieu of gleaning vital information that would topple one of two distinct hurdles that now stood between himself and a sworn commitment, to eradicate what ever threat stood in his way. In contrast, the unmistakable tones of an automobile approaching broke the stillness of the night. The intrusion immediately jolted his awareness, reminding him what the hell he was doing at two o'clock in the morning holed up in a rat-infested back alley of convenience along with an overused waste skip as a smokescreen.

The visible headlights levelled the far end of the alley as the car drew nearer, and just as quickly faded as it continued on its way.

Emerging from within the shadows, it soon became clear that Rossetti wasn't impressed. Highly frustrated, he vented his frustration. "Shit! It just ain't happening tonight! Where the hell are you, yer tosser?" Checking his watch only confirmed what he already knew. The last four nights had at least proved a valid point: old habits die hard! As a paradox, habit and the manner in which the Rinse would die now became something that Rossetti could savour in the interim. In retrospect, the feedback he'd managed to collate had proved to be conclusive as a distinct pattern now began to emerge.

At approximately 1.45am the Rinse's car would reverse down the back alley, some thirty yards or so to where the fire exit of the club was situated. Once there, it would remain parked for an average of ten minutes or so before the Rinse made an appearance. Rossetti figured the hit could be made within a twenty-minute period, fifteen minutes of which allowed for his car to show and the eventual departure. Any time remaining would be classed as killing time. Literally speaking of course, so with two victims in contention, he would need to act fast.

As an extra touch, the likelihood that the Rinse was moving money around gave credence to the briefcase he always carried, and the reason why he opted to use the fire exit when leaving the club. If his assumption held water then, ironically, Rossetti would be on all-expenses-paid hit, sponsored by his victim no less. On the flip side, the fly in the ointment, and a big bastard at that, could be his minder and driver, the lovely Donna. Rossetti had fixed ideas concerning the latter's future welfare. And it wouldn't have run to a counselling session.

Any headache coming his way would be classed as

permanent due to lead poisoning. His epitaph would also be arranged to suit his chosen gender, and would read: 'WASN'T LIFE A BITCH?!'. For the moment, his mode of thought became distracted by a small pair of bright, enigmatic, piercing eyes emerging from within the waste content of the overladen skip. In a split second, his body froze, whilst being lulled into a sense of déjà vu as the oncoming eyes turned out to be the front end of a large scavenging rat. From then on, the remnants of Rossetti's hyped and twisted imagination came into play as he focused on the intervention of a debatable and dumb ally. The moment became surreal as the vermin edged closer, to within a foot of his outstretched hand, constantly sniffing the air as if locating a safety zone. Once satisfied, it sat back on its haunches and began to eyeball Rossetti. In return, intrigue got the better of Rossetti, drawing him into a hasty conclusion. "Stone me! Yer a cocky little bleeder!" His imagination briefly got the better of him. "Nah, couldn't be, could it?"

On a more positive note, his mind flashed back to that uneventful night when Donna, acting under orders, had forcibly ejected him from the club, in the process dumping him like a bag of shit onto the hard cobbled alleyway. That, in turn, spawned a one-to-one counselling session with another particular rat deriving from the same skip. For once, Rossetti felt suitably relaxed as his madness demanded more. Speaking low, he applied a more positive approach: "You don't remember me, do yer? It's me, yer old pal Rossi. What am I doing 'ere, yer thinking? Well, I'm tying up a few loose ends, only this time tomorrow they'll be fucking permanent! You get the picture?!"

There was no question that the two had a distinct and defining rapport. The rat appeared to lean on his every word. Meanwhile, Rossetti continued to draw him in on a level plane. "Oh, by the way, I'm sorry about the intrusion, I realise the skip is your manor, but I was desperate for some sort of cover, yer do understand, don't yer?" Later, Rossetti would swear that the rat nodded in approval as its head twitched from side to side, finally motioning with its snout toward the skip as if to say, "What's mine is yours, feel free. We're in this together. I reckon you and me are two of a kind, and like you I have to find a means of survival as well. Just bear in mind that all forms of life are relevant insomuch as we all share that one thing in common: DEATH!" The curtain then came down as the rat suddenly turned and leapt back into his exclusive world of decay and disease. But not before a plan began to materialise in Rossetti's subconscious, the core of which highlighted the skip combined with the demise of the Rinse.

It would also serve as a gesture of allegiance toward the rat, in the shape of a body, but that would come later! The experience, overall, had only lasted a few minutes, although it was sufficient to give his dwindling ego a much-needed kick-start. His stake-out was finally over; everything now hinged on the Rinse making an appearance the following night. In any event, he needed to be prepared. Making the most of the darkness, he skulked out of the alley on one good leg. He paused momentarily to take one last glance back at the skip. A wry smile twisted the corner of his mouth as he spoke. "Rats! Fucking rats! Yer can't live with 'em, and me? I can't fucking live without 'em!" Food for thought maybe?

The species, taken as a whole, is very much maligned as vermin go, mainly through ignorance, so as an unlikely association what the hell is Rossetti's excuse? Answers on a postage stamp please! Lingering long enough to mutter a token, "I'll see yer around", he raised one hand in a gesture of friendship, before finally turning on his heel. Moments later, and still disturbed, he was swallowed up by the lengthening shadows of the chill night air, albeit the real world.

CHAPTER 25

# DEATH BY DESIGN

Once inside the comparative safety that four walls could offer, chilling out and taking stock of a situation that would demand total commitment in the hours prior to a premeditated bloodbath would necessitate assessment of the risk involved before, during and after such an undertaking. In Rossetti's case, a blend of madness and delusion far outweighed the need for any perspective. As far as he was concerned, a 9mm bullet lodged in some poor bastards head solved everything..

Any argument over and above would be short lived if and when confronted, his response being, "The asshole is bleedin' dead! End of, and that's a fact!" The price of chilling out was now running at a premium, with more shit than a corporation sewer could hold flying around in his head. Sleep itself was now neck and neck with wide awake. One scenario continued to exploit his psychopathic avenue of thought, causing an overwhelming surge of blood to consume him.

The contrived idea consisting of a ringside seat at the expense of the Rinse would surpass any form of Charlie, and the additional bonus of no cold turkey as a downer would be something to relish. Without warning, a mental image of Maltese Pete invaded his manic headspace. His addled brain reacted like a sieve as the buzz it generated attempted to drain his alter ego. The moment caused him to sit bolt upright as the image collided with a raw nerve. "Damn! Damn!" Frustration echoed through gritted teeth, leaving sanity to kick in. "Of course! How the hell could I be that stupid? The geezer still owes me for a silencer."

Not that it would mean a reprieve of sorts with the Rinse in mind, but in its absence, like it or not, Rossetti would need to review his exit from the intended scene of crime, bearing in mind any untoward noise could well become an issue. Any alternatives were soon swallowed up by tiredness as his body slumped backward in defeat. The only solace came from the comfort of his shooter, now nestling under his pillow while awaiting a summons for all the wrong reasons! One could never guess his present state of mind at this juncture; only an in-depth autopsy could clarify that position, although what sleep he'd managed to salvage at intervals hadn't remedied any misgivings he may have harboured. On the flip side, when he awoke at around 11.30pm, a stinking cold he'd inherited from the previous stakeout, including a poxy headache, wasn't exactly a gourmet recipe in the run-up to committing a cold, premeditated murder… or two!

At worst, he could afford himself a leer of satisfaction as he exposed the shooter to the daylight. Any personal issues were immediately sidelined as he reverently grasped the .38 Cobra. He gloated as he caressed his warm cheek with the butt end, and said with emphatic conviction, "I'm sorry you've had to wait this long, baby, it won't be long now. We're gonna have so much fun together!"

The distinct aroma of gun oil filling his nostrils together with the feeling of metal on flesh charged his addled brain. His torrid breathing accelerated and his heart began to race in unison as he slavered over the gun. Within seconds, his madness reached a new level as his reflection in an adjacent wall mirror began to morph into an image of the Rinse. His breathing, by now, had become more erratic as he levelled the shooter directly at the face responsible for inciting his dementia.

Repeatedly pulling the trigger, he acted like a kid at play, allowing his head to roll from side to side and chanting in a child-like manner, "We're going to kill you! We're going to kill you! We're going to kill you! We're going to…" Another aspect of his madness caused him to falter mid-stream as the charade finally peaked, allowing his torment to settle like a deflated balloon. Cold sweat oozed from his forehead, spiralling down in rivulets, prematurely checked by his prominent cheekbones. He shook his head in a bid to relieve the problem, while adjusting to a dead-beat breathing pattern.

For a short time, he chose to remain silent, intent on gazing into the mirror.

Finally, the vision faded into obscurity. But not before he said in a jaded tone: "Can yer hear me, Frankie boy? Yer a dead man walking! You and that asshole of a minder have been in my face for far too long." He suddenly left off as a further thought broke ranks. "Oh, by the way, don't forget the briefcase will yer? Yer know what they say: pay up and look good! Nice way to go out, Frankie baby, I'll be seeing yer shortly!"

Anybody with half a brain could relate to the meaning of the word 'composure', even if they couldn't spell it! For Rossetti, the definition ran to loading a magazine with six rounds, and not dropping one on the floor. Once satisfied, he spun the chamber of the Cobra and adjusted the safety catch. Taking a deep breath, he made a final sweep of the room as a matter of course. Had he overlooked anything? Who the hell was he kidding? All he ever owned was what he stood up in. Even his wrist watch could be living on borrowed time if the next few hours were to go belly up.

But for now, all the waiting he'd endured seemed redundant. Now was the time to call in the piper. Once clear of the safe house, he hailed a cab and alighted a street away from the Miami Club on the pretext of self-preservation. Five minutes later, furtive as ever, he edged his way toward the opposite end of the alley for all the right reasons. Once in position, it would enable him to gain some extra strategic cover to the rear of the skip, knowing that the victim's back would be facing him until such time as he made his move.

Every second became an eternity as time dragged by. "C'mon, Donna, where the fuck are yer?" He was getting agitated, and it showed. "Don't bleedin' spoil it for me nah, you asshole, yer owe me!" Briefly, a touch of optimism crept into the equation. Given the SP he held, the following twenty minutes or so could prove to be life changing in more ways than one. Unmistakably, if trading under the aliases of Rinse and Donna!

In spite of contending with the biting cold solitude of the night, he freely admitted to feeling good within himself as his chequered mind drifted back to Slatteries' those six years ago, swiftly reminding him that Terry Winters' demise had been a dress rehearsal for an occasion such as tonight. This was vintage Rossetti at his best. "Now I'm moving up!" he mused. "After what's going down shortly my hand will be on the top rung of the ladder. HELLO WORLD… PAUL ROSSETTI HAS ARRIVED!" His meandering suddenly became a no-no when it was interrupted by two bright reversing lights and the distinct throb of a car engine ticking over. He was beside himself as he yanked the shooter out of his pocket. Restraining himself, he spoke through gritted teeth as the car edged slowly toward the fire exit.

"Yeah, c'mon baby. Bring it on, don't fucking stall nah, you'll miss the show!" Moments later, the vehicle, driven by the unsuspecting Donna, ground to a halt. From his vantage point, Rossetti lay poised less than ten feet away. The driver's door opened to make way for a bulky figure, not yet recognisable. For some unknown reason, the car lights had been left switched on, hindering his view by creating shadows from every angle possible.

*It has to be Donna!* Rossetti firmly convinced himself. His reasoning became academic as the fire exit door flew open to release an opportune surge of light, exposing his problem in the process. *Shit! It doesn't come no better than this! It would have been a poxy shame to have wasted a bullet!* Meanwhile, the faint but unmistakable figure of the Rinse stood framed in the doorway, complete with a case of some kind. Up to now, what had transpired belonged to Rossetti. It was more than he could have envisaged; undoubtedly he was on a roll that could only end at his discretion.

For only the second time in his less-than-illustrious life, he would be calling the shots. And with a degree of luck, making them! By now, the knuckles on his hand were showing white as his grip tightened on the Cobra. Slowly he released the safety catch as he sighted the Rinse securing the door behind him. "Right!" exclaimed the Rinse. "Ready when you are, Donna, let's get the hell out of 'ere." Rossetti struggled to suppress a laugh.

"You got that part of the script right, you asshole!" And he emerged from behind the skip as Frankie reached for the car door handle.

Donna, sensing something amiss, whipped around quickly, his face etched in disbelief, and attempted to make a move forward. Leering, Rossetti shook his head and waved the shooter in response, stopping him dead in his tracks.

"Don't even think about it, sunshine! Unless of course you want it right 'ere and nah?" He then spelt out the options available. "Either way, yer get yours!" The Rinse might, as Rossetti suggested, 'read the script', but in the end turned out to be a lousy actor. Except to say that the look on his face in monetary terms was priceless.

"Rossetti? What the… this has to be some sort of a fucking joke!" He was struggling to find the right words as the situation unfolded. Unlike Rossetti, who by now looked fired up and well in control.

"Joke?" he remarked coolly. "A poxy joke! The fucking joke is on you, Frankie boy, cos you ain't gonna be around to bleedin' share it!" Sheer desperation called for a tactical change in attitude, as the Rinse cringed.

*The man's an absolute nutter, but even he must have a price*, he told himself, and continued to open up. "Nah let's be sensible about this, Rossi. Is it money yer after?" Rossetti was adamant in reply.

"That! And a whole lot more. Now throw the bleedin' case over 'ere."

"I'll see yer in hell first you bastard!" Screamed the Rinse. Rossetti replied with a hideous laugh.

"Yer seat's already booked, asshole, and as for yer fucking girlfriend Cinderella, she ain't going to no sodding ball tonight, or any other night! Nah bleedin' move it!" Never off the case, Donna spotted a chance, and made to move forward as the Rinse threw the case to one side. Instantly, Rossetti jumped the queue and retaliated.

"You'd better tell His Ladyship to back off, and while he's at it, start the car," his motive being to lessen the sound of gunfire if and when.

Apart from his life, Frankie's wellbeing at this stage now ranked less than a £10 note. He had nothing else left to bargain with… unless… An impromptu thought made a sudden breakthrough. "Look, Rossi," he said patronisingly, "it doesn't have to end like this, surely we can talk about it?"

"Talk?! You got a fucking nerve. The talking ended when

yer put a bloody contract out on me!" he stormed.

"But that's my point! Trust me when I say it never transpired. Yer off the hook, period!" Rossetti appeared to be unimpressed.

"Hook?! So is a bleedin' leg of lamb. You put me through hell, you bastard! Nah it's payback time."

"But, Rossi," he fell to his knees, pleading and snivelling like a baby, "I'm begging yer, don't do it, don't do it." His pathetic pleas went clean over Rossetti's head, who felt totally bored; he'd heard and seen enough, he just wanted out. The next few minutes were crucial in allowing him to place his hand on the top rung as a testament to his villainous prowess. Briefly, he seemed to be drawn towards the skip as a sudden rush of infinity flooded his manic outlook. And then it all made sense!

"You!" He nodded toward Donna. "Pick that little shit up now!" And indicated to where the Rinse was still grovelling on all fours. Donna looked bewildered as Rossetti continued to press him. "And when yer do, stick him in there with the rest of the crap!", tapping the side of the skip as he did so. His request became a reality as the scenario unfolded, leaving the Rinse a blubbering wreck as he was forcibly bundled onto a heap of decaying matter.

Rossetti milked the moment before continuing, "I've apologised to the crap yer in, but it'll soon get used to yer!" He was forced to break off while at the top end of degradation. Rapt as he was, he neglected to monitor Donna who, by now, was slowly edging toward him. The moment became do-or-die as he lunged at Rossetti. In the event, it was the last physical act he would perform.

The second that his semi-raised foot connected with a loose cobble, causing him to slip, he became a dead man walking. Or in his case, flying, as the top end of his doomed body collided with the side of the skip. As he descended, his head took the full impact. Twenty-odd stone of flesh and bone crashed down, catching the metal lip of the skip, in the process twisting his neck at a grotesque angle. He was dead before he hit the floor, his neck shattered beyond recognition as he lay chest down on the cobbled floor of the alley. Except to say, his blooded and sightless eyes were now looking down onto his massive shoulder blades.

Rossetti couldn't believe his luck. But at the same time, he felt somewhat cheated at his would-be victim's demise.

"You selfish bastard!" he ranted. "Why couldn't yer have waited for me?" He lashed out at the inert body with his good leg as his madness began to peak. "Yer see what happens when yer decide to piss on my parade?!" His bloodshot eyes began to well with temper as he turned his attention toward the Rinse, who was cowering like a baby and praying like it was all one big nightmare. He only succeeded in enticing Rossetti into further verbal degradation.

Taunting him into deeper submission, Rossetti continuously slapped the chamber of the shooter. "It was in 'ere all the time, just waiting for him. Couldn't Donna see that? He's fucking ruined it for me!" A deathly silence reigned, allowing Rossetti to take stock. "But you! You ain't gonna let me down, are yer, Frankie boy?!" He was almost pleading for an answer as he methodically stroked his victim's dishevelled hair from his grimy face, at the same time forcing the snubnosed barrel of the shooter against the middle of his forehead. "Oh, I almost forgot. Just one more thing, I know he wouldn't have minded, but are yer happy to take Donna's bullet as well?! After all, I can't see the sense in wasting it, can you?!"

The Rinse found himself in hell quicker than he could reply as two deadly rounds tore into his skull, primarily dispersing the back half of his shattered head into bloodied fragments of brain and bone, in turn, carpeting a large area of the backdrop of rubbish. And then finally it was all over as reality found a foothold. The deed was done; there was nothing more he could do as an encore. "Fuck's sake! That felt so good," he exerted. "Nah, it only leaves that mug Callaghan for me to deal with. Can yer hear me? Yer gonna get yours soon enough," he ranted.

Retrieving the case, he proceeded to turn the car lights and engine off, and finished by throwing the keys into the skip. Pausing, as he did so, he aimed one last verbal put down directly at the Rinse.

"Just thought yer might need these, I wouldn't expect yer to have to walk to hell!" As if by royal command, a rat suddenly appeared from out of the rubbish, and began to clamber over the defunct remains that once belonged to the Rinse, almost as if it intended to share Rossetti's moment of glory. Call it coincidental, or maybe even karma, but the rat's spontaneous intervention allowed a hidden infinity between the two to surface. Rossetti didn't require any prompting, and swiftly rose to the occasion. "I told yer I wouldn't let yer down, didn't I?" he grinned, or maybe it was something caught in his eye. "I'll see yer around. Be lucky." With the case firmly in his grasp, he turned and limped off into the cold foreboding depths of the alley.

## CHAPTER 26

# OUTSIDE INTEREST

A couple of hours later that same day, a call from the public domain was transferred to Stonewater HQ via New Scotland Yard; it was logged at 4.39am. The sergeant on duty at the time the call was registered had good reasons to question its validity. He was even less pleased when the caller gave his occupation as 'a full-time party reveller, looking for a short cut home'! Suffice to say, Jobsworth kicked in as the sergeant relayed the call to the CID branch.

"Yeah, well basically, that's all I could get out of the guy, Harry. Not even an address. That and a load of verbal crap. I think he had problems, sad bastard!"

"Sounds like a wind-up to me, Sid, although his timing is certainly in character for the time of day."

"Yeah, you're probably right, but I just can't help thinking..."

"You're obviously not happy, mate," his colleague suggested.

"Well, I don't know what he'd been drinking, Harry, but to get back to what I said previously he kept banging on about a couple of winos he'd come across in a back alley somewhere!"

"Huh! Sounds to me like the creep is off his face!"

"I should have hung up, especially when he mentioned the fact that two bodies kept blanking him all the time."

"Christ! What the hell was he on?" Harry blasted.

"Exactly! But he made such a big thing about it, makes yer wonder."

"So did he mention where these alleged bodies were that he came across?"

"No, not specifically, although I seem to recall he mentioned the Florida Club vicinity a couple of times."

"No! There's no such gaff. I happened to be with the drug squad at one time, so I should know. Could be the silly bastard got himself confused with the Miami Club. In which case, that does ring a few bells."

"You've got my interest, Harry, go on."

"That alley, the one you mentioned earlier, runs up the back of the club. I remember it well. It used to be a pickup point for smackheads, until we got involved."

"Uhm, maybe there is a connection between the two clubs as you say then!"

"Look, I'll tell yer what, I'll get a body up there to have a sniff around, okay?"

Within minutes of an investigation being carried out, the grim discovery of the late Rinse and Donna came to light, confirming the earlier suspect report. Subsequently, the immediate area was cordoned off as a team from SOCO swarmed in to take over the scene and the adjoining club premises. The ID of the two victims caused major concern from the outset, due to their personal effects having gone conveniently 'missing' overnight, although a wallet was found some distance away from the scene of the crime. As suspected, it had been completely vandalised, although it was certainly recognisable by the inscription DONNA emblazoned on one side. On further examination at a later date, forensics initially failed to grasp the significance as to why the larger of the two victims' fingerprints came to be plastered all over the wallet in question.

"Exclusive! Macabre! And bloody interesting," was the pathologist's reaction within five minutes of making himself known at the scene of the crime. The resident DCI in charge was eager to bypass any personal observations, instead pushing for a more professional opinion and hopefully some defining answers to "my biggest bloody nightmare!" as he surveyed the grizzly scene, seemingly baffled by the manner in which both victims had met their demise, especially in the case of the "poor bleeder with the presumably broken neck. One can only assume that he had a serious fallout with a centurion tank!"

Even death can reduce a person to spontaneous jesting. In this particular case, it was left to the pathologist to take up the mantle. He was old school, and still retained a keen sense of humour should the appropriate situation surface. "Find the tank responsible, Chief Inspector, and you've found yourself a murderer, dear boy!" he stated equivocally. Suffice to say, the inspector was far from impressed, and pursued him for an approximate time of death on both counts.

"Eh, let's see now." He checked his watch. "Uhm, I make it almost 5.30am, so we're probably looking at two or three hours ago, yes most definitely!" Clearly, the inspector wasn't convinced.

"How can you be that sure?" he enquired loftily.

"Namely the cold temperature of the night, linked to the progression of rigor mortis setting in. Anything else?" As facts go, his prognosis appeared to be the best on offer. A motive for the two killings could have been anybody's guess, and as for the murder weapon, "Timbuctoo would be the best place to start!" Meanwhile, an extensive search of the immediate area did uncover a fortuitous piece of evidence in the form of a bunch of keys, spotted by an eagle-eyed DC, that were secreted in the waste skip. One key in particular proved to be invaluable. It belonged to the club's safe, housed in the office of the late victim.

From amongst the effects that were later retrieved, a letter was found, addressed to a certain Mr Enrico Maniella, residing somewhere on offshore Jersey. The envelope also contained a bona fide cheque, made out for a substantial amount of money. Unfortunately, the actual wording in the letter itself gave no indication as to the purpose of the cheque. Moreover, the local plod failed to understand why it had never been posted, as the date on the letter heading was written nine days before the killings.

Because of reporting restrictions, any information affecting media interest was kept low key, while all other lines of enquiry were ongoing in pursuance of factual evidence. Twenty-four hours later, the local press, plus the bespoke tabloids, had a field day once reporting restrictions were finally lifted.

The *Stonewater Gazette* ran with:
BIZZARE KILLING IN CLUBLAND
TWO VICTIMS' BODIES RECOVERED

whereas the big boys, through influence alone, were more adventurous in their headlines:

GANGLAND GRUDGE MURDERS ROCK SEASIDE
TOWN!

It didn't take long for local traders and the tourist board alike to latch onto the many connotations deriving from the above headlines as a means of free advertising. On a more personal level, and contrary to popular belief, Ronnie Callaghan, without exception, held his own theories close to his chest as he viewed the drama unfolding on the regional television channel, having shared first-hand experience of a bloody week of virtual homicide those six distant years ago. He shook his head in a positive manner after summing up the whole rotten drama in two distinctive words, allowing poignant memories to come flooding back and haunt his awakening memory: "Docklands revisited," he spelt out. "Yeah, just about sums up the whole lousy issue!" Or did it?

The incident in itself, unbeknownst to him at this moment in time, could well hold certain repercussions from another source, should he wish to consider the facts. It was a lot of shit to take on board at one time as another threatening aspect closer to home emerged. He was yet to connect all of the events that had erupted in the last couple of months, as a mental picture of the poison pen letters he'd received now came into the equation. Ronnie was left in no doubt as to their origin by placing Rossetti in the frame from the outset as he recalled his initial concern when confiding in Siddie. "What other manic bastard, apart from Rossetti, would stoop to this shit?!"

Siddie was quick to concur, insisting on the need to be more vigilant. At worst, a renewed wake-up call had come out of it, but as of now, Ronnie felt convinced that Rossetti, for whatever reason open to him, had played a major role in the two killings. He would also confess to "being bleedin' worried, knowing that the nutter is still on the loose, while possibly carrying a shooter!" Sometimes it pays not to know, but that would defeat the logic based on Rossetti's game plan of softening up Callaghan for the inevitable bloody climax, or so he strongly believed, toppling the one remaining hurdle that stood between him and his infamous destiny.

To make matters clear, in the game of Mind Roulette the present score was now 30 Love. Consequently, the man to beat was none other than Rossetti himself, as he coolly delivered yet another ace slap into Callaghan's court. 'Good game to win' from an observer's point of view, the point now being, who would be man enough to break his serve?! With everything to play for, only time itself would release the answer to that enigma.

Fast forward forty-eight hours give or take a gulp. From the moment the Rinse's brains became a forensic statistic, Rossetti could still be found overdosing on an adrenaline boost suitably aided by a bottle of 'falling-over liquid' doubling up as a comfort zone, while all around were still reeling at the aftermath. He left off briefly, but only to draw breath. *God!* he convinced himself, *I'd almost forgotten just how bloody good it tastes!* Strange choice, when considering there were enough empties lying around to open up a glass factory!

Swallowing hard, he managed to force more Scotch down his throat. Stopping short, he lowered the bottle to half-mast as a reminder gatecrashed his coming-out party. Slowly and methodically he wiped his mouth with the back of his grimy hand, while at the same time ogling a sea of mixed bank notes that lay strewn on top of his bed. He allowed himself a delayed smile of sorts, albeit a way to prevent an unwanted housefly from settling on his cheek. The longer he looked, the more intense his body language grew. By now, the duvet of notes seemed to take on a mind of their own as they infiltrated his addled brain, seducing his senses in the process.

Almost immediately, he lurched forward as the notes appeared to give him the come-on. With hands outstretched, he began to stroke and fondle the ill-gotten money. Breaking off suddenly, he grabbed a fistful and tossed them high in the air. Like pregnant snowflakes, they fell down all around him. This time around, he managed to laugh but in a hideous manner, screaming as he did so. "Can yer see me now, Rinse? You still owe me big time! I can't see yer paying the tax on this poxy lot!" Once again, he held the bottle of Scotch aloft in a mock toast to the late Rinse. "Here's to you, Frankie boy. Thanks again for the bleedin' investment! Oh, by the way…" He paused to allow his massaged ego to get the better of him. "Better still," he snarled, "let's just call it dead money!" From the outside looking in, the Rinse, in a manner of speaking, could be gifted into thinking that he'd beaten Rossetti in one respect. The fact he was now dead would render him sober, as such, whereas pissed as he was by now, Rossetti would still find himself incapable the following day. A sobering thought indeed!

A constant obsession with materialism could be one thing, but even that could end abruptly when abused. His body language now spoke volumes; he firmly believed that the bonus surrounding his ill-gotten wedge solved everything. Blinded as he was by the power of ego, he felt a veil of insecurity had been lifted as an echo from the late demented Rinse came to mind. "Yer off the hook, period!" The validity of such a desperate statement would now come under close scrutiny in time to come, meanwhile leaving Rossetti to juggle with his own gutless conclusions.

Having said that, he was also well aware of the importance of future momentum if, and when, his vendetta alluding to Callaghan's demise was to remain a success. The time, he considered, was now ripe for him to move on. Within the next twenty-four hours, he could be found in the five-star sanctity of the AA, lording it up in the bar. "You sure he really went away?" one particular barman was heard to comment. At this, the manager's ears pricked up and he duly returned a dour look before replying, "Bloody hard to say! But, as from now, yer holiday break is over!" Thankfully, that endearing statement doesn't wash with everybody. Indeed, one charismatic figure in particular, residing in offshore Jersey, would readily beg to differ as he meticulously prepared to pack a smallish travel bag for a three-day stopover in mainland UK. Acting on a whim, he'd decided on 'trading places', or, as he likened it, quote, 'a working holiday minus the grief', the emphasis being on minus! Having finalised the necessary packing for his intended trip, he poured himself a welcome drink with a view to relaxing and then acquainting himself with a specific file he'd retrieved from a nearby roll-top bureau, the contents of which related to his spontaneous departure.

Glancing at his watch, he noted it was now 9.15am. An hour later, he placed a call to Jersey Airport control to submit a flight plan when applicable to take off at 11am with the intention of landing at Shoreham Airport, West Sussex, and in the meantime, would the ground crew prepare his privately owned Piper Cherokee monoplane? There appeared to be a slight moment of confusion, causing an unexpected delay in which the caller's pedigree came under scrutiny.

"I'm sorry, sir, what was that name again please?"

"Oh, M A N I E L L A. Enrico Maniella, that is." He took his time spelling it out.

"Ah yes, I have your credentials right here. There doesn't appear to be a problem. Thank you for calling in, sir. Your flight papers and long-range weather forecast will be available at your disposal. Good day, and have a good trip." Maniella smiled to himself in a discreet and professional manner as he replaced the handset.

"You can rest assured that is one aspect I can guarantee," he mused confidentially. Some fifteen minutes or so later, the boots of his Ferrari Spider were burning rubber as he roared along the A4 coast road heading for St Peter, and an eventful seventy-two hours. It was a much-relieved Enrico Maniella who finally touched down at Shoreham Airport well over schedule due to an unexpected cross wind mid-Channel. At least with officialdom negotiated, clearing customs would prove to be a mere formality.

The following step of his journey entailed taking possession of a hire vehicle, courtesy of Hertz. With the A27 trunk road a stone's throw away, he soon found himself facing the increasing frustration of life in the fast line due to the intense volume of traffic as he endeavoured to head for his destination, Stonewater, some thirty miles away. Installing himself in a two-star B&B doubling up as a base became a requirement he needed to readjust to, working, as he did, under the auspices of a cloak and dagger existence. "Patience," he would emphasise, should he ever come under cross-examination, "forms ninety per cent of my success rate!" Discounting the norm, he now found himself saddled with the self-assured and totally boring proprietor of the B&B, pushing the other ten per cent to the limit as he flagrantly pursued a one-man verbal assault whilst attempting to unravel Maniella's occupation in life, and seriously pissing the man off in the process.

"No, don't tell me… I'm pretty certain that I'm right when I say you're involved in the 'insurance business'!" He wouldn't let go, and continued his adamant stance. "I get guys like you booking in all the time, I've just got this feeling." Maniella's breeding held any reckless answer in check as he sat cloth-eared and silent, praying that the obnoxious little shit would fade away into obscurity. Left with nothing to contest, the proprietor now felt that he was on a roll. "So yeah, I reckon you sell life insurance to be precise!" he sniggered, and continued, "I'm right, aren't I?"

Maniella never wavered as he fixed the nauseating nuisance with a cold, calculating look that said everything, but gave nothing away in return. His eyes narrowed as he finally broke his educated and prolonged silence. "On the contrary, my friend, I like to think I'm a cut above selling! In fact, I persuade all my clients into cashing them all in!" We will never be party to how the proprietor interpreted the evidence to his claim as their conversation came to an abrupt end. Suffice to say, Maniella's breakfast plate the following morning strangely contained twice the food on offer to the other guests!

Upon leaving the B&B a little later on a full and contented stomach, he picked his hire car up and headed for the centre of town. Moments later, he parked up adjacent to a leading national bank. Carrying a small suitcase, he lost no time in seeking the manager with a view to gaining access to a personal safety deposit box housed in the bank's vault. Having satisfied the manager with the necessary criteria, he was ushered inside and given the procedure directive. "Your time is your own, sir, and likewise your privacy. I'm sealing the door now, so if you don't mind ringing the assistance bell at your convenience, somebody will be along to let you out."

In spite of his solitary confinement, Maniella still felt prompted to glance over his shoulder before approaching the aisle in which his security box was housed. *Old habits die hard*, he reminded himself. He then afforded himself a smile as a distant afterthought regarding the late Tito 'the Butcher' Santini resurfaced. *Unlike the vast majority of my clients*, he mused.

Reaching inside, he carefully withdrew a highly veneered shallow wooden case, which he reverently placed on a nearby comfort table. Releasing the catch, he delicately raised the lid, swallowing hard as he did so, full of expectancy as to the box's contents. The look of sheer satisfaction that crossed his face far outweighed the use of words as a .44 Magnum Blackhawk Beretta was exposed. It was resting in a red-velvet-lined designer pocket, ably supported by an additional in situ silencer, plus a full clip of ammunition. Placing the box in his case, he lost no time in summoning a security guard to let him out of the vault.

Clearly something was bothering him. Sitting outside in his car, he felt the urge to take stock before making a move in any one specific direction. He was well aware that any knowledge of interest in his intended victim could well prove to be obsolete within some six years. It was now left to chance to ascertain that the facts he held secret still remained kosher. Glancing up, he noted an inquisitive traffic warden approaching the car. Fortunately, he'd paid his dues; the warden afforded him a derisive look and went on his way.

Maniella's eyes once again came to rest on the case placed on the passenger seat. Staring long and hard he appeared to be deep in thought, then said in a low sympathetic manner, "What a crying shame you can't answer back, my trusted friend. There's so much you could divulge." He sighed deeply before continuing in the same vein. "Wishful thinking, eh! But I feel sure we can find a clue between us." Anyone would have thought he was addressing another person rather than a concealed .44 Magnum!

A pensive look suddenly clouded his face as he continued to meander. "Six years is a lifetime in our business, and you've been locked away far too long! A bit of luck wouldn't go amiss right now. I suggest we retrace our steps and go back to the beginning, don't you?" Turning the key in the ignition, he checked his mirror before pulling away from the bay. Grim-faced, he booted the accelerator and headed toward the Docklands area of Stonewater.

## CHAPTER 27

# FOR WHOM THE BELL TOLLS

'Cometh the hour, cometh the man.' Ronnie could have been excused for thinking that the sudden change in the weather was anything less than personal, on this particular occasion the emphasis being on inclement weather. Easing himself slowly out of bed, he crossed toward the nearest window, hesitating briefly before pulling the curtains to one side. Peering through the gap with sleep-lined eyes only confirmed the reason why he'd spent half the night tossing and turning. The incessant rain continued to lash down as he endeavoured to conjure up a ray of hope, solely with the intention of snatching a few quid at the market. Whatever the outcome, he was under orders to make himself available due to a stock delivery. "Typical bleedin' Monday morning. What poxy chance has a man got?!" he moaned as he prepared to get his breakfast underway.

A couple of hours later, soaked to the skin and his money pouch a monkey lighter, found him holed up in Toni's market café. Halfway through his first cappuccino, a soul-destroyed-looking Siddie made an impromptu appearance. Ronnie glanced up as he approached. "I was beginning to wonder how long it would be before yer made a show. Not even you would have a clue how to make money in this bloody weather." Siddie gave a disgruntled glare and sank down into an adjoining seat, just as Toni arrived holding a welcome cup of coffee.

"There you go, mya friend. For you, huh. I saw you

coming, now you enjoy." Almost immediately, Siddie's face creased with satisfaction.

"Nice one, Toni. I'm just about ready for that, mate," he said gratefully. In spite of the proverbial money climate, Siddie nevertheless felt eager to chat in general. "Well, I gotta say..."

"Yeah, what?" surmised Ronnie.

"Just that yer looking more like yerself, mate, know what I mean?" On reflection, he might have inadvertently implied, 'I didn't mean it to sound like that!' As it turned out, Ronnie was quick to respond.

"Yer having a laugh, mate, ain't yer? I'm not sure how to take that! It ain't exactly a bleedin' reference, especially with a face like mine!"

"What I really meant was that yer don't look so stressed out, in spite of what's been going down recently."

"Yeah, guess so, I can relate to that. Take those two recent killings for example, it's like they happened weeks ago. Then of course, there's the poison pen letters to consider. They seemed to have died a death too, thank gawd." Breaking off, Ronnie decided to check the contents of his cup; it appeared to be almost empty. "You gonna have another one, mate? You might as well, it's still pissing down outside."

"Why not? You're paying already," Siddie jested. A cracked silence briefly followed before they both laughed simultaneously.

"Yer a crafty git, yer getting bleedin' worse," Ronnie endorsed. Turning round to catch Toni's eye, he signalled for another two cups. Minutes later, Siddie glanced up from stirring his coffee.

"What's the SP on the gym these days? Is young Simmons still up for it?" he enquired. Momentarily, Ronnie appeared to be caught verbally flat-footed before responding.

"Funny you should mention that! Something just

reminded me…" He stalled before continuing. "Nah, it's not that important, it can wait." At this point, Siddie had no intention of settling for second best.

"Callaghan! Yer a putz, never kid a kidder. What's going down?"

"Well…" He shook his head. "Look, you ain't gonna believe this!"

"So try me."

"Okay, so bear with me. It all kicked off the other evening, shortly after locking the gym up." Leaving off briefly, he took a swig from his cup before continuing. "I had this weird feeling…"

"Yeah, I'm listening!"

"Well, I felt that I was being watched, know what I mean?" Siddie somehow stifled a laugh before continuing.

"Blimey, mate, sounds like yer got a stalker on yer case. You should be so lucky!" His suggestive tone left Ronnie feeling less than impressed.

"You can bleedin' laugh, but it ain't a one-off! And I don't do poxy coincidences either. To my knowledge, the same incident has occurred two or three times before."

"No offence, mate. Tell me, did yer actually spot anybody?"

"Nah, not as such, although on one occasion I happened to notice a strange figure lurking close by the gym. It sorta stuck in my mind, know what I mean?"

"Must have been something about him, yeah?"

"Exactly! From where I was standing at the time, he looked at me like he was half a raspberry. I got the distinct impression that the geezer had a gammy leg!"

"Face?! What about his face?" Siddie fired back.

"Nah, not a chance. Besides, it was too bleedin' dark at the time."

"Pity, although yer don't seem to be too over-worried

about it." Ronnie took his time to scoff before replying.

"What's the bloody point, mate? Yer only winding yerself up. To be honest with yer, I'm more bleedin' worried about unsold stock at the moment!" Under the circumstances, Siddie felt obliged to agree not to disagree, and diplomatically allowed the conversation to drop. On the flip side, any major concern he may have harboured appeared to be only lent. His current fears lay well beyond the horizon. Deep down, his sixth sense began telling him that there was far more to Ronnie's alleged stalker than met the eye. The fact that Rossetti was allegedly on the loose had now clearly motivated his reasoning. On the other hand, Ronnie had made the point that the mysterious figure he'd seen came across as being notably crippled. This, in turn, ruled him out of contention. Besides, the only affliction, to his knowledge, that Rossetti ever carried was a psychotic warped personality! In conclusion, his line of thought could now be found knocking at the door of fate which, for the time being at least, had remained in closed. That is, until circumstances well beyond his control could blast it open again.

"You alright, mate? Yer looking a bit lost." Ronnie's intervention swiftly brought him down to earth with a crash.

"Oh, yeah, blimey, I was miles away."

"In that case, yer picked a choice moment to come back then. It's actually stopped bleedin' raining. Get that coffee down yer throat, my son, and let's get out there amongst the punters."

Endeavouring to forestall any further grief, the following evening couldn't arrive quick enough for Ronnie. Full of expectation, he found himself basking in contentment, especially when overseeing the running of the gym. Like the vast majority of sessions, this particular night would be no exception to the rule, especially where productivity was concerned. The 'world of leather', as always, remained a hard act to follow, existing as it did on a distorted recipe of blood, sweat and tears, but which, in return, only brought the best out in each individual.

From the very first bell, the session had become 'satisfaction guaranteed', quoting Ronnie as he later reflected on the input of the stable as a whole. Pausing for thought, he noted that the time was now just after 11pm, and that young Simmons had been the last to leave some fifteen minutes earlier. As per normal, Ronnie had chosen to linger, mainly to ensure that nothing had been overlooked after clearing up. His actions had become a ritual he'd performed for as long as he cared to remember. He gazed tentatively around the four walls of the gym before finally focusing in the direction of the ring. Frowning, he found himself doing a double take; it soon became clear that something or other was bothering him.

Once again, he narrowed his eyes in an attempt to confirm his suspicions. "Damn!" he tutted. "How the hell did I manage to miss that! Bleedin' thing is still on." His problem primarily lay with the session timer mounted on the wall behind the ring which hadn't been turned off.

Placing his kit bag down, he approached the ring apron and casually slid between the bottom ropes. Crossing the canvas, he swiftly manipulated the sensor control timer. He shook his head as he did so and afforded himself a smile before rebuking himself out loud. "Yer silly old sod, yer losing the bloody plot. Still, nobody's ever gonna..." Momentarily, any self-induced feelings were put on hold by a sudden distraction. An anxious look creased his face as he sensed that something or somebody had invaded his private party. A strong feeling that he was no longer alone in the gym circulated in his brain, causing his heart to race and his body to stiffen. Acting on instinct, he swung round sharply as if in anticipation and in so doing proved that his initial gut instinct had been the right one.

The impact of the unrehearsed situation he now found himself in could only be equalled by the force contained in a full-blooded right-hander. A look of sheer disbelief sought refuge in every line on his face; his jaw sagged to an all-time low, leaving him utterly speechless. Totally mesmerised, he could only look on as the figure confronting him outside the ring slowly morphed into his life-long nemesis. None other than the elusive Paul Rossetti! He was also brandishing a handgun, Ronnie quickly noted.

Owing to the circumstances, the stage was now set for Rossetti to inject a degree of sanity as he forcibly lowered Ronnie down onto a more sinister plane. "Yeah, yer don't have to look no further than me, Callaghan!" he snarled. "It's yer old pal Rossi come back to haunt yer. And just for the record, yer got it right the first time, just like everybody else did, and not forgetting that asshole Terry Winters. You all figured me as being dead and buried six poxy years ago!" By now, he was almost choking on an adrenaline rush from a surge of power, while at the same time waving the shooter wildly to emphasise his point. "Yeah, I fucked the world that day when I managed to get out of that fire at Slatteries'. But it cost me big time. All down to you, Callaghan!" Breaking off, he used his free hand to motion downward at the gimpy leg that he'd sustained whilst escaping from the blazing inferno. He then continued ranting, "And while we're at it, this poxy face arrangement you left me with came by way of a bonus!" Leaving off briefly, he pointed at the prominent scar on his face, now distinctively reddened through temper.

He'd heard it all before. The verbal diarrhoea spewing out of Rossetti's mouth went clean over Ronnie's head. But the shooter his nemesis brandished was telling him something else. The sudden change in Ronnie's circumstances had left him floundering. Rossetti's untimely intervention had virtually stunned him into submission. His mind was now racing like a Wurlitzer as he desperately sought to make some sense out of a life-threatening situation. Any attempt to shut it out remained futile. *Fuck's sake! Wake me up somebody, this has to be my worst nightmare!* he convinced himself inwardly. His thoughts ran to nothing.The only respite on hand came by way of a sudden cold sweat rushing over his body like a tsunami.

Meanwhile, Rossetti's sick, leering face contrived to put the explosive scenario into perspective. *Shit! This is as real as it gets*, he convinced himself. Deep down, from somewhere embedded inside his fuddled brain, his survival instinct began to scream back at him, desperate to balance the situation. *I need to keep him talking*, appeared to be the best option. "Yeah, just as I thought, there ain't a back door invented that you haven't crawled out of at some time or other. Yer didn't really fool me for a minute. I figured it was you all along as far as the poison pen letters were concerned. Yer might just as well have signed 'em yerself, it was that bleedin' obvious! Oh, and one other thing comes to mind. That fiasco over at clubland six years ago now. I wouldn't mind betting you were involved in that too. It had yer name all over it. Two simultaneous backstreet murders, all in one night! Yeah, you really excelled yerself, and for what, I ask?!"

"You've got a big mouth, Callaghan! But yer right of course. Those two particular dummies decided to fuck with me. Big mistake! Yeah, they both caught a cold that night, and a fucking bad one at that! You have to admit; I've come a long way in the last six years. So from now on, it's about respect on my part. I'm Premiership league, top of the table, and I ain't going away until I finish what I started. Know what I mean?" His over-massaged ego now looked primed and ready to explode at any given moment. Ronnie, for his part, remained uneasy as a sense of déjà vu stared him directly in the face, the only difference being that this time around, Rossetti, given the opportunity he craved, wouldn't have missed even if he'd been wearing a blindfold!

Quickly and deliberately his nemesis minimised any possible alternative conclusions by releasing the safety catch on the shooter. Trance-like, he approached the ring.

"You think yer so damn smart, Callaghan. But yeah, the day I managed to escape from that inferno at Slatteries' I fucked the world! Okay, so it cost me big time and no thanks to you!" Breaking off, he once again highlighted the injuries he'd sustained and not before he continued to rave in the same vein. "You fucking owe me, Callaghan, big time! You bastard! But it all ends 'ere, d'ye understand?" Desperation on his part now began to run at a premium, leaving Ronnie to swiftly up the ante by playing the ego card and praying that Rossetti would bite. *It might just buy me some thinking time*, he reasoned.

His nemesis, meanwhile, had other ideas. Content with milking his victim's preconceived demise, he began to taunt him. "Shall we end it all 'ere, Callaghan, or better still, inside the ring! Think about it. It makes sense to me, you always were a fucking loser in my book as a fighter. Now back off from the apron and get in there." Once inside the ring, Ronnie instinctively backed away, cringing as his back met the ropes, bringing him to a virtual standstill. Rossetti let out a maniacal laugh as his victim was forced to do his bidding. "Nothing fucking changes!" He was almost screaming by now. "Yer know yer place, you've had yer back on the ropes all yer poxy life!" Stepping up into the ring, he took his time before finally levelling the shooter directly toward his intended victim.

Instinctively, Ronnie lowered his eyes in a last ditch attempt to shut out the image of a crazed Rossetti, firmly convinced that any form of redemption on his part was obsolete. Like a lamb to the slaughter, he braced himself for the inevitable explosion signalling the end of his trauma. When it eventually came, it didn't sound like any normal firearm being activated but rather more of a subdued noise that reverberated around the gym. Almost immediately, he felt a prickly sensation from countless droplets of what appeared to be blood showering his face. Strangely enough, he didn't feel any pain and decided that hell wasn't such a bad place after all. In sheer contrast, a terrifying scream from somebody close by in perpetual agony brought him back into the real world as he forced his sticky eyes to focus.

Almost immediately, he was able to ascertain that Rossetti was no longer in front of him. Instead, he could be seen grovelling on his knees and whimpering like a maltreated dog. What was once his trigger hand now resembled a grotesque stub of diffused flesh and splintered bone. The handgun, Ronnie noted, now lay on the opposite side of the ring. He opened his mouth in a vain attempt to speak. But nothing of any consequence came out, although it didn't stop him from making a dire attempt to retrieve the shooter. In the event, he never even came under orders, as an alien voice halted him dead in his tracks. The statement came across as a suggestion as opposed to a direct order. It was concise on delivery and moreover, like its owner, stank of high breeding.

"I really wouldn't bother if I was you, Mr Callaghan. I presume that is who you are? That being the case, trust me when I say that the gun you were intending to pursue is of no useful consequence to you whatsoever! As such, I don't intend apologising for my spontaneous interruption. Moreover, I am strictly a businessman you understand. Furthermore, I have no quarrel with you personally, you understand. Under the circumstances, saving your life was a vital necessity. As for this wanton garbage…" stopping short, he averted his interest toward a blubbering Rossetti, "… he won't be going anywhere!" and emphasised his point by flourishing his hand-held Beretta.

Once again, Ronnie found himself at odds with what now transpired. Seconds ago, he'd been facing almost certain death, courtesy of Rossetti. And now, he'd been seemingly granted an audacious reprieve due to third-party involvement. Given the surrealist scenario and state of mind he was in, Ronnie's simplistic reply appeared crass in anybody's language: "Thanks, mate, I owe yer one!" Suffice to say, his benefactor remained unmoved by his off-the-cuff comment, brushing his understated words to one side. His cold-looking, emotionless face remained passive and businesslike as he once again focused his attention on Rossetti still grovelling on the blood-soaked canvas.

"And you, of course, must be Mr Rossetti!" He leaned forward, squinting slightly as he did so. "Yes! There's no doubt of that! Although I have to say that you're a lot uglier than the mugshot I have to hand. Not that it changes anything, of course, I hasten to add." He pondered before continuing. "What a pathetic little bastard you are. It seems hardly worth the contract that I…"

At this, Rossetti was beside himself while hallucinating on a recipe of sheer terror and undulating fear as he cut their pro-active conversation short.

"Contract! Contract!" he whined, "God! Yer not…" Staking his claim abruptly, the stranger made his presence official.

"I do apologise; I forget to introduce myself. My name is Enrico Maniella, although I trade under the name of Manilla, Buffy Manilla, international hitman, that is."

"Manilla! Yer can't be!" screamed Rossetti. "The Rinse

reneged on the original contract, surely yer know that?! Don't yer see, I'm off the hook, so help me." Completely ignoring his pleading outburst, Manilla turned towards Ronnie who appeared to be totally fazed by what was going down. When he finally spoke, his plea came across as more aligned toward a sympathy vote.

"I apologise,your witness to the utter crap I'm forced to put up with, Mr Callaghan," he sighed. "But then you're always going to get one psychotic nuisance, wouldn't you say?", which just about summed up Rossetti's forthcoming epitaph. Meanwhile, Ronnie went through the motions, nodding trance-like as Manilla veered back toward Rossetti. "Yes, you're right, of course, by stating that the Rinse didn't pursue any contract on your head personally. But I'm here to represent another client, who unfortunately is no longer with us. Having said that, he did pay out on one particular contract in full shortly before his regrettable demise, in this particular case, the said victim being you, Mr Rossetti, and I'm duty bound to honour his wishes!"

"Who the fucking hell are we talking about 'ere?" he remonstrated. "This has to be some sort of a sick poxy joke!"

"Joke!" responded Manilla. "The joke, as you so strongly put it, is on you, I'm afraid. The client who instigated this particular contract on you went under the name of Winters. Or, should I say, Mr Terry Winters to be precise, late of Stonewater?" The implication that a link to the fire destroying Slatteries' gym six years ago had now decided to surface rendered Rossetti momentarily speechless. The look of horror carpeting his face was in itself priceless. And, more to the point, unphotographable!

"That… that was six poxy years ago! You can't… you can't do this to me!" he whined. By this time, Manilla had heard and seen enough. Business was business, and his patience was fully overstretched.

"Six years, you say! In that case, I suggest that you've had a bonus in life. And, in answer to your question, I can, and I will!" Without hesitation, and subsidised by a matter-of-fact attitude, Manilla pointed the Beretta directly down at the cowering figure of Rossetti. Blandly, he pulled the trigger twice. Two distinctive 'phut' sounds carried on the air as the silencer automatically kicked in. Immediately, Rossetti's now defunct torso lifted spasmodically from the canvas as two lethal rounds of death ripped into his chest. In doing so, the bottom rope of the ring became wedged in the small of his back, leaving the bedraggled mound of useless flesh and bone lying arched over backward at a crazy angle.

Grimacing, Ronnie could only look on helplessly in utter disbelief at what he was witnessing. Slowly, one arm slid downward and collided with a supposedly defunct brass signal bell situated on the ring apron, causing it to ring; a measured silence then followed. Finally, Manilla glanced across to catch Ronnie's eye, smiling confidently before remarking drily, "I get this feeling, Mr Callaghan, that this piece of shit won't be coming out for the next round! Is there anything you'd like to add to that?"

*A million and one questions would do for a start*, Ronnie thought to himself, but went instead for the obvious. "Why here? And more to the point, how the hell did you find Rossetti in the first place?" Manilla offered a rare smile before replying.

"It was never going to be an easy task; you understand? Suffice to say, in my line of business one needs to be ahead of their game. It's important that I have my own means of detection. In Rossetti's case he made his present whereabouts that much easier for me. His enforced absence away from Stonewater following the Terry Winters murder did little to persuade him that Docklands would become a good move back. His arrogance in finishing what he'd set out to do those six years ago has now proved to be his downfall… and…"

"His intention being to silence me full stop!" echoed Ronnie.

"Precisely! Fortunately for me, his ignorance enabled me to terminate this particular outstanding contract as well. I, for one, always finish what I've started. Time is meaningless in my business. Opportunities in my chosen profession are rare, Mr Callaghan. For the last six years, Rossetti has got away with murder, so to speak."

"Yeah, in more ways than one!" agreed Ronnie decisively. "That aside, you still haven't told me how you managed to track him down."

"Let's call it personality deduction or basic intuition, Mr Callaghan. People like Rossetti are habitual and, at the same time, predictable. They also need to be in their own comfort zone. With that in mind, he made the grave mistake of returning to the public house, the AA, formerly the Rat and Trap. Armed with that knowledge, I was able to keep him under surveillance. So, in answer to your question, he inadvertently led me directly to you! Moving on, were you aware at any time that he'd been stalking you over the last couple of days?"

Inwardly, Ronnie could only concur as recent facts now resurfaced, and in doing so slotted into place. Nodding glibly, Ronnie, still in a semi-comatose state, glanced across at the bedraggled blood-soaked figure of his former nemesis. "Strange, in a way, I almost feel sorry for the poor bastard."

"Sentiment, in his case, is cheap, Mr Callaghan. I don't need to remind you of the fact that he fully intended to eliminate you!"

"And me! Where do I fit into your game plan?" Lowering his handgun, Manilla took a step backward before answering, at the same time dispelling any personal recrimination he may have held.

"You have nothing to fear from me personally, Mr Callaghan. On the contrary, your present wellbeing has been my priority. I wish you no harm, except to say…" he paused momentarily before finishing, "… a favour, if you will." Ronnie wasn't about to argue his case, and nodded eagerly while sighing with utter relief. Slowly, and using his free hand, Manilla extracted a buff brown envelope from his inner coat pocket.

Reverently, he handed it over to a startled-looking Ronnie before speaking.

"Can you ensure that the police get this please?" Still somewhat mesmerised at this point, Ronnie mumbled an acknowledgment. "I class this as my calling card, you understand?" And went on, "I like to keep my actions in an orderly fashion. The police will, of course, understand my motives, okay?" Ronnie looked completely fogged at this and nodded for the sake of it. "Oh, before I forget," Manilla prompted, "could you give me the grace of fifteen or so minutes before informing the police as to my act of retribution? I would appreciate it, and while we're at it, there is one other important factor that had occurred to me." A brief strained silence ensued, leaving Ronnie to fidget nervously as Manilla slowly and meaningfully tapped the barrel of his handgun before continuing. "I feel sure that any statement given on your behalf to the police regarding my description as such will bear little or no resemblance to me whatsoever!" He broke off once more to give Ronnie a reassuring look, effectively leaving him stranded in a verbal wilderness.

With diplomatic ease, Manilla bailed him out by emphasising the point in question. "Thank you once again for your cooperation, Mr Callaghan. I sensed it wouldn't have been a problem, but I needed to ask all the same!" He then smiled as only winners smile, adding, "I felt sure that you would understand my viewpoint!" The point was made, and who the hell was Ronnie Callaghan to disagree? Besides, he had the rest of his natural life to consider as an added bonus. And it didn't include perpetual grief! Without further ado, Manilla pocketed the Beretta before turning on his heel and heading for the door.

At the last moment, he turned round in a casual manner before exiting and shouted out, "Have a good life, Mr Callaghan, I wish you well!" In return, Ronnie gave him a token wave and not before turning his renewed attention back to the lifeless form that was once Paul Rossetti. He continued to stare at the torso for some time in an attempt to exorcise every shred of malignant hate he'd ever felt for the man. Eventually, he glanced upward. For the first time in months he felt a sudden rush of freedom and wellbeing consuming his body. Clenching both fists tightly, he spoke through gritted teeth in Manilla's direction.

"You, and me both, mate!" he echoed. "You can take it from me that my life started from the minute you pulled that trigger, end of story!" Five minutes later, he reached inside his tracksuit and retrieved his Blackberry mobile. The end… maybe!

**The Fingerless Gloves**
**Down, But Not Out!**

# EPILOGUE

The well-oiled expression 'Dead men tell no tales' didn't figure in Ronnie Callaghan's present troubled persona. Given all the facts, he now found himself locked into an unescapable bubble of inconvenience following Rossetti's sudden and fortuitous murder. None more so than by Ronnie himself. Two weeks on, and all things considered, Rossetti's death by default should have been a distant memory. As yet, nobody had come forward to claim the victim's body. This in turn, had only prolonged Ronnie's desire to move on. Right now, an image of Rossetti's coffin holding up six foot of earth would have given him a welcome escape.

Finally, a breakthrough to hopefully ease his stymied person came by way of a police notification of the final details of Rossetti's funeral. Suffice to say, Ronnie, in spite of an overall reprieve, found he still had certain issues with the content. Primarily, there was no clear-cut confirmation regarding ownership of Rossetti's remains. Secondly, a diplomatic suggestion from the police advising him not to attend Rossetti's funeral only fuelled his frustration as to their reasons. It would appear that even after death, Rossetti's lingering influence seemed to be dictating the terms and conditions!

If at any time, Ronnie had felt the urge to open up and express his thoughts, he would have started and ended with the same conclusion. "Why do I have this monumental feeling that in spite of everything, this vendetta isn't over yet!" Time itself is a great healer, so we're led to believe, in the meantime leaving Ronnie Callaghan to languish in his own self-inflicted beliefs.

# GLOSSARY

| | |
|---|---|
| Ante | Money |
| Banged up | Taken into custody |
| BBBC | British Boxing Board of Control |
| Bent | False/Illegal |
| Big fellow | Heaviest punch bag |
| Blown away | Murdered/Killed |
| Bottle | Bravado |
| Brief | Solicitor/Lawyer |
| Brown bread | Dead (slang) |
| Bubble | Bubble and squeak/Greek (slang) |
| Bubullah | Sweetheart/Darling (Yiddish) |
| Bung | Backhander |
| Bungarian | Duel Hungarian/Bulgarian |
| Bust | Police raid |
| Charlie | Cocaine/Heroin |
| Chutzpah | Spirited (Yiddish) |
| Contract | Murder by arrangement |
| Crack | As above |
| Craic | Having a joke |
| Decked | Floored |
| Dive | Drinking club |
| Face | Villain |
| Fingered | Exposed/Named |
| Firm | Gang/Team |
| Folding | Paper money |
| Funk | Chance/Hope |

| | |
|---|---|
| Gaff | Building |
| Giving it large | Mouthing off |
| Gorilla | Minder/Bouncer |
| Grand | £1,000 |
| Grief | Unwanted aggro |
| Heist | Bank raid |
| Hitman | Paid assassin |
| Karzy | Toilet |
| Klutz | Dreamer/Naïve person (Yiddish) |
| Kosher | True/Legal (Yiddish) |
| Kvetch | Scold/Complain (Yiddish) |
| Manor | Locale/District |
| Meet | A specific date |
| Meshugenah | Blaspheme (Yiddish) |
| Moody | Unreal/Plastic |
| Mouthpiece | Boxer's gumshield |
| Mullered | Murdered/Killed |
| Nifty | £50 |
| Nobbins | Money thrown into ring following fight |
| Old Bill | Police force |
| Plastic gangster | Acting the part |
| Putz | Despicable person (Yiddish) |
| Rackets | Organised crime |
| Raspberry ripple | Cripple (slang) |
| Safe house | Hideout |
| Scam | Complete rip off |
| Schmaltz | Old world charm (Yiddish) |
| Schmuck | Nasty person (Yiddish) |
| Schtum | Maintain silence (Yiddish) |
| Shickered | Get drunk (Yiddish) |
| Schnorrer | Cheapskate |
| Shooter | Handgun/Firearm |
| Smackhead | Druggie |

| | |
|---|---|
| Snout | Police informer |
| SP | Ready information |
| Spot | A job of work |
| Stable | Boxers allied to one gym |
| Suss | Work out/Deduce from |
| The dogs | Best there is |
| The Smoke | London |
| Tuccus | Backside (Yiddish) |
| Wedge | Folding money |
| Weighed in | Settled up |
| Wino | Alcoholic |

# ACKNOWLEDGMENTS

I would like to thank my wife, Sheila, for all her support and tolerance throughout my writing career. I would also like to mention James Watson once again for his superior computer back-up assistance when required and his creative involvement in designing the book cover graphics, and to my mother who introduced me to the 'bleeding business' in the first place as a young kid. Not forgetting anybody I have ever met, inside or outside of the ring, whilst I participated in the 'leather business' over the years. To one and all, you have my greatest respect and admiration… keep punching! Last but not least, my grateful thanks to my publisher, Troubador Publishing Ltd, for services rendered.